MW01104441

True Colours

Lucinda Chester

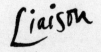

First published in 1997 by
HEADLINE BOOK PUBLISHING

A HEADLINE LIAISON paperback

10 9 8 7 6 5 4 3 2 1

ISBN 0 7472 5629 2

Typeset by Avon Dataset Ltd, Bidford-on-Avon, Warks

Printed and bound in Great Britain by
Cox & Wyman Ltd, Reading, Berks

HEADLINE BOOK PUBLISHING
A division of Hodder Headline PLC
338 Euston Road
London NW1 3BH

For Nancy and Sarah

One

Tony tried to concentrate on the phone call. Martyn Sellars spent literally thousands at the gallery. Anthony Pearson, as the manager of Russell Street Gallery, should be bending over backwards to please his best client, not drifting off into a daydream. The very least he should be doing was listening to the man, hearing what he had to say.

The problem was, in a word, Isobel.

Isobel Moran, the freelance journalist Tony had met at a party, three weeks before, and with whom he was conducting a very intense affair. Since the moment that Isobel's mouth had met his, and he'd felt her hand feathering over his thigh, he hadn't been able to think straight. He'd been operating from one organ only – and it wasn't his brain.

Concentrate, he told himself fiercely. Don't think of Isobel. Don't think about what happened last night. Don't think about the way her mouth felt round your cock . . .

But it was too late. He was already in fantasy-land, remembering what had happened, the previous night. How Isobel had stripped him very slowly, very surely, her dark eyes full of a mixture of passion and pleasure at her power over him. How she'd knelt in front of him, her glossy dark hair brushing his torso; and how she'd looked up at him, her smile knowing and sending a shiver of lust down his spine, before she lowered her mouth over his cock . . .

He swallowed hard. Christ. He had to concentrate. For all he knew, he could just have agreed to find Sellars a couple of unknown Picassos to add to his collection. 'Perhaps we should discuss this over lunch. I'll ask my secretary to book something.' He named an expensive restaurant in Mayfair, the sort that would placate Sellars if he realised that Tony hadn't been listening to him. 'How about Friday, at quarter to one?'

He breathed a sigh of relief as his client agreed, and hung up. Swiftly, he cleared the line, and dialled his secretary's extension.

'Tony, you sound flustered,' she said, a hint of amusement in her voice.

'Yes, well. I'm just having one of those days,' Tony acknowledged wryly. He'd worked with Monica Redding for too long to lie to her. 'I'm taking Martyn Sellars to lunch. Could you book me a table for two for Friday, please – say at about quarter to one?'

Monica whistled as he named the restaurant. 'You'll be lucky.'

'I am – I've got you. You're a born charmer, and you always manage to persuade even booked-up restaurants to let me have something,' Tony informed her with a grin.

'Flattery will get you nowhere,' came the tart and teasing response. 'I'll bring you a coffee. You sound like you could do with it.'

'I could. Thanks.' Tony replaced the receiver and raked a hand through his short dark hair. He needed something to keep him awake. It was okay for Isobel; as a freelance, she could work the hours she chose. She wasn't tied to office hours. If she wanted to make love all night, steep until lunchtime, and then work until dinner, she could.

And that was exactly what she had done, since she'd met him.

He rubbed a hand over his face. Maybe he should take a few days off, to get this mad passionate phase with Isobel out of his system. Then, maybe, their relationship would settle into something normal. The only thing was, he was afraid that it never would. Every day, Isobel managed to surprise him, show him some new sexual trick that kept him on the edge of ecstasy...

He shivered at the thought, his pupils enlarging until his green eyes were almost black. Christ, he had to stop thinking about her. He had to concentrate on his business – at least, while he was at the gallery. And even though he would have loved to take a week or so off and spend it in bed with her, he couldn't afford the time.

Not now that he had the Alex Waters retro to sort out. Sighing, he pulled the file from his in-tray, and began to read through it.

A few minutes later, his office door opened.

'Thanks, Monica,' he said, not looking up from his papers.

The cup of coffee he'd been expecting wasn't forthcoming. Frowning, he looked up to ask his secretary if something was the matter – and looked straight into Isobel's face.

'Hello, loverboy,' she said, her voice husky. She placed her hands on the edge of his desk, and leaned forward to kiss him lightly on the lips. Although she was wearing a smart red suit, the skirt was short enough to show her shapely thighs to their best advantage, and – he registered, with shock, as his eyes drifted to her cleavage – she was wearing nothing beneath the sharp tailored jacket, not even a bra. Which meant that she was probably wearing nothing under her skirt than a pair of silk lace-topped hold-up stockings . . .

'What are you doing here?' he asked, shocked.

Her dark eyes glittered slightly. 'Aren't you pleased to see me, Tony?'

'Well – yes, of course I am – but . . .' He sighed. 'Sorry. I was expecting Monica, with some much-needed caffeine, so I could go through this bloody file. Let's start again. Hello, Isobel.' He stood up, and walked round the edge of his desk; Isobel slid her arms round his neck, and he bent his head, his mouth opening over hers.

When he broke the kiss, he was flushed and shaking. He ran a hand through his hair. 'God, Isobel. I can't think straight, when I'm with you.'

She stroked his face. 'I know you're busy, and I know you're working, but . . . I just wanted to see you.' She disentangled herself from his arms, and went to lock his office door. Tony watched her, his eyes narrowing.

'What are you doing?'

'Tut, tut. I can't believe that you became the manager of this gallery by asking such obvious questions,' was the teasing response. She stood, leaning against the door, and slowly unbuttoned her jacket.

Tony stood up, glancing at the window, and she shook her head, anticipating his move to pull down the blinds. 'Leave it. I like to see what I'm doing.'

'But—'

'We're on the fourth floor, Tony. No-one's going to see any-thing. And if they do, from the other side of the street with a pair of binoculars, they'll just be in for a little treat – won't they?' She tossed the jacket onto a chair, and shook her head back. The movement made her generous breasts shimmy; Tony licked his lips as he noticed how dark her areolae were, and how her nipples had puckered and hardened. He walked round to the front of his desk, and leaned against it, watching her.

'Oh, Tony, Tony, Tony.' She laughed, and reached behind her, undoing the zip of her skirt and pushing the garment over her hips.

As he'd half suspected, Isobel wasn't wearing any knickers: just a pair of black lace-topped hold-up stockings. His cock hardened at the thought that she'd maybe sat on the Tube, teasing some businessman or other with that come-hither smile and a deft re-crossing of her legs which made the infamous Sharon Stone movie look tame.

She let the skirt fall to the floor, and kicked it aside. She was wearing a pair of very high-heeled black patent leather stilettos which made her hips sway when she walked. Tony let his gaze travel down her body, and gave a sharp intake of breath at the sight. Her figure was perfect, her breasts high and generous, her waist narrow, and her hips curvy. Her pale skin was in sharp contrast with the dark glossy hair on her head and the curly thatch of her delta. Her skin was almost alabaster – despite the fact that women with her dark eyes and hair usually had an olive tinge to their skin – and the only blemish was a mole in the crook of her arm. She could have been, Tony thought dreamily, a living sculpture, one of the beautiful nudes he'd occasionally exhibited at the gallery . . .

She caught his gaze, and smiled indulgently at him. She raised her hands to her hair, lifting up the glossy tresses, and pouted at him. He grinned as he recognised the pose she'd adopted – the pose from *The Siren*, a work by one of the minor Pre-Raphaelites which he'd always loved and a framed print of which hung in his bedroom so that he could see it when he woke up in the morning. Had Isobel lived a hundred years or so before, she would have been perfect as an artist's model, he thought. She had that same wide generous mouth as Jane Morris and Lizzy Siddall, that same dark and mysterious look about her. Rossetti would have loved her. Rossetti would have been unable to resist taking her to his bed – just as Tony couldn't resist her.

She licked her lower lip, then dropped her hands again, and sashayed across the room to him, the height of her heels exaggerating the sway of her hips. 'Tony.' Her voice was like a caress.

'I'm supposed to be working.' It was a feeble protest, and both of them knew it.

She smiled again. It was a warm day, so he was working with his jacket off. It was a moment's work for her to undo his patterned silk tie, and then unbutton his crisp white cotton shirt, running her hands over his chest.

He shivered at the feel of her fingertips against his skin. Although Isobel was vampish in most things, she kept her nails short, saying that she couldn't type properly with long nails. Besides, talons wouldn't have suited her. They would have made her look too hard, too calculating. Whereas she was simply the most sensual woman he'd ever known, with a huge appetite for sex, combined with a sharp mind.

He held his breath as she undid the buckle of his black leather belt, then undid the button of his trousers and slid the zipper downwards, easing the dark worsted over his hips. She pushed him back against the desk, and slid her hand into his boxer shorts, freeing his cock. He closed his eyes in bliss: then, suddenly, an alarm bell rang in his brain. He opened his eyes again. 'Isobel – I've got an important meeting, later today. I can't go to it wearing a crumpled suit.'

She grinned. 'What's the matter? Scared that they'll all guess what you've been doing, and think you're a bad boy, making love in office hours?'

'No.' He sighed. 'More like I have deals to conduct, and I can't afford to lose them by looking as though I couldn't give a toss about my business.'

'You could always go out and buy yourself a new suit.' She fingered the pure cotton of his shirt. 'And if I did crumple this . . . Well, you could always buy another.'

He closed his eyes. 'Isobel. There are days when you want to play games, and there are days—'

She cut him off by the effective movement of drawing his face down to hers and kissing him deeply, the pressure of her mouth against his making him open his lips.

When she broke the kiss, he swallowed hard. 'Oh, Christ, Isobel.'

'It was just a whim,' she said. 'I wanted to take you across your desk, while you were still wearing your prissy office suit. But – ' she shrugged ' – no matter.'

'Some other time,' he promised her. 'Friday?' Then he remembered: lunch with Sellars. 'No, not Friday.'

She grinned. 'Maybe I should just ask Monica for a copy of your diary, so I can work out when I can come in and ravish you.'

'Something like that.'

Her hands slid down to curl round his cock. 'It's a pity to waste this, though.'

'So what are you going to do about it?'

'This.' She closed the file on his desk, placing it back in his in-tray. Then she removed his cufflinks, placing them carefully on top of the file, before sliding the soft cotton from his shoulders. Tony stifled a grin as she shook out the creases and hung the shirt neatly over the back of his chair.

She bent to unlace his shoes; he helped her, lifting one foot and then the other so that she could remove them and his socks. His trousers followed; again, she folded them neatly, making sure that the creases were perfect, before laying them over the back of his visitor's chair.

'I think you can indulge me, now,' she said softly, sliding his boxer shorts down but leaving them to hobble his ankles.

She slid her arms back round his neck, and he bent his head to kiss her, nibbling her lower lip so that she opened her mouth, letting him kiss her more deeply. He slid his hands down her sides, moulding her curves and then squeezing her buttocks; she pulled her mouth from his.

'What?' He frowned, his eyes darkening in surprise.

'I thought *I* was supposed to be the one taking *you*,' she said. He coughed. 'Sorry.'

Her eyes glittered. 'There's a way round it.' Licking her bottom lip again – the way she did when she had a particularly exciting idea, he'd begun to realise – she turned her back on him, bending over so that he had a good view of her quim. Then she stepped out of her shoes, and rolled down her stockings.

Tony watched her, waiting. He wasn't sure what she had in mind, but he liked the view enough to keep quiet and indulge her. She put her shoes back on again, then stood posing for him for a moment. His cock twitched in anticipation: she looked very, very good. And what was going to happen next would be something even better, he knew.

She smiled, then, and walked back over to him. 'Tony.' She rubbed her body against his: she was so soft, so beautiful, he thought. Then, taking him by surprise, she pushed him back against his desk. Before he had a chance to realise what she was doing, she'd secured his left wrist to the leg of his desk with one of her stockings.

'Iso—' he began, but she cut him off again, kissing him fiercely while she tied his other hand.

'This,' she said. 'This is what I want.' She slid her hand over his body, feeling the way that his muscles stretched and relishing the sense of power. This big, powerful man was tied to his desk, for her delectation, and she was going to enjoy every second of it.

She let her hand drift down to stroke his cock; he gasped as she made a ring of her thumb and forefinger, and slowly masturbated him. She kept the movements slow, teasing; when he was groaning and a bead of clear moisture appeared in the eye of his cock, she climbed up onto the desk, straddling him and letting her quim rest lightly against his cock so that he could feel how ready she was for him, how hot and moist her sex-flesh was. She was half-tempted to make him use his mouth on her – but then again, maybe that would be better, later. Right at that moment, she wanted to feel him inside her.

The only bad thing about having Tony tied up like that, she thought, was that he couldn't stroke her breasts. Still, she could do that for herself. She smiled, then, eased one hand between their bodies, lifting herself and fitting the tip of his cock against her entrance. She gave a small sigh of pleasure, and lowered herself gently onto his cock.

'Christ, Isobel, you feel so good,' Tony murmured huskily.

She leaned forward to kiss him, and her nipples rubbed against the hair on his chest, creating a gentle friction that made her want more. She sat up straight again, and slid her hands up her body, cupping her breasts and rolling her nipples between her forefingers and thumbs.

Tony groaned. 'Isobel. I want to touch you – but I can't.' He tugged at his bonds. 'Release me.'

'Not a chance.' She pouted at him. 'I'm in charge, now.'

'What am I supposed to say – "Yes, Mistress,"?' he teased.

She grinned back. 'That's not quite what I had in mind.'

'Then what?'

'Tell me what you'd do to me – if you could. And I'll do it.'

He laughed. 'And if I told you that I wanted to lick your clitoris? You'd have to be a contortionist!'

'But there's nothing to stop me doing the next best thing,' she said. 'Touching it.' She continued stroking her breasts with one hand, and let the other slide down between their bodies again. She began to move over him, lifting her body and flexing her internal muscles as she pushed back down again; at the same time, using the same rhythm, she rubbed her clitoris, teasing the sensitive nub of flesh with a light and yet accurate touch. Which brought her close to the edge of orgasm within seconds

'Oh, yes,' he breathed, feeling what she was doing to herself and remembering what it was like when he did it himself.

Remembering how responsive she was, the little noises of pleasure she made when he slid his finger deep inside her, then let it skate over her clitoris, anointing the hard bud with her musky juices. The lighter his touch, the more she liked it; he made a mental note to buy a peacock's feather from one of the little junk-shops in the street behind the gallery. He had a feeling that Isobel would appreciate being made to come with it.

Seeing the faraway look in his eyes, Isobel wondered what her lover was thinking about. Was he thinking about her? Was he remembering past love-making sessions – and there had been plenty of those, in the short time they'd known each other – or was he thinking about something for the future, introducing her to some new sensual delight?

She smiled, and stopped rubbing herself; she lifted her hand to his face, then slid her finger along his lower lip so that it was coated with her musky juices. He licked his lip clean, then drew her finger into his mouth, sucking hard. He could smell her arousal, vanilla and honey and musk, and it drove him wild. He tilted his pelvis, pushing up as much as he could, and Isobel continued to move over him, rocking back and forth so that her swollen clitoris rubbed against the base of his penis.

He groaned again, and she lifted up so that his penis was almost out of her, moving very gently so that only the tip of his cock slid in and out of her. He tugged against his bonds but, although she hadn't tied him tightly enough to hurt, the knots were strong enough to hold him. He couldn't pull her closer, squeeze his body as deeply as he could into hers. He was completely under her control.

'Christ, Isobel,' he said, his voice husky with a mixture of annoyance and pleasure, and she bent to kiss him again, tasting herself on his mouth. She moved her upper body so that her nipples rubbed his chest, and flexed her internal muscles round him, so that her quim seemed almost to ripple against his flesh.

He could tell how excited she was; her face was flushed, her lips were reddened and swollen, and there was a tell-tale rosy mottling spreading over her breasts. Her quim felt like liquid fire, slippery and hot; the way she was using her muscles round him, he was close to the edge himself. He cried out, tipping his head back; he almost saw stars as he came, his body pouring into hers. And then she was coming, too, her internal muscles contracting sharply round him; she slumped against him, burying her face in his neck, and he turned his head so that he could kiss her hair.

They lay together for a few moments; then Isobel kissed the tip of his nose, lifted herself from him, and untied his wrists, dropping her ruined stockings into his waste-basket. He sat up, pulling her into his arms, and kissed her hard. 'Isobel. God, you drive me wild,' he informed her, his voice low and rough with passion.

'Good.' She disentangled herself, urging him to his feet, and knelt down in front of him, licking every scrap of juice from his cock; when he was clean again, she pulled his boxer shorts back up. 'Do you have a tissue?' she asked as she climbed to her feet again.

He shook his head. 'Sorry. You could ask Monica.'

She grinned. 'I think not.'

His gaze slid down to her thighs. They were glistening with his juices; he tipped his head on one side. 'I could always return the favour.'

'You could,' she agreed, her voice low and slightly husky.

'The only thing is, once I start . . . I'm not sure if I can stop,' he warned her, dropping to his knees. She was still wearing the black stilettos; he was shocked at how much it turned him on, seeing her wearing nothing but a pair of shiny high-heeled shoes.

'I think I can cope with that,' she told him, sliding her hands into his hair.

He grazed his mouth along her thighs; when he was in his teens, he would have been slightly repulsed at the idea of licking his own semen from a woman, but he'd gained a lot of experience between then and his thirty-fifth birthday. And, since he'd met Isobel . . . anything was possible.

He licked her clean; the smell of her arousal was still strong, and he couldn't resist drawing his tongue along her quim. She still felt soft and puffy; it was too much for him, and he began to lap in earnest, alternately sucking her clitoris and pushing his tongue as deeply as he could into her vagina. She moaned, the pads of her fingers digging into his scalp and urging him on; he continued to lick her, until he felt her body tense, and then flutter under his mouth. He waited until the aftershocks of her orgasm had died away, then stood up again and held her close, stroking her hair.

'I can't believe that you've been walking around London with no underwear,' he said softly.

She chuckled, curling her fingers round his erect cock. 'But the thought excites you.'

'Yeah,' he admitted, flushing.

'What time's your meeting?'

'Twelve.'

'Better get you tidied up, then.'

'Isobel . . .' His brow creased as she began to dress him, slowly restoring him back to the pristine businessman he'd been before she'd walked into his office. 'You were dead to the world when I left, this morning. I thought you'd be spending the whole morning asleep.'

She smiled. 'I don't need quite as much sleep as you do, Anthony darling.'

'No.' He stroked her face. 'So do you have an interview, or something?'

'Yes, and no. Would you believe me if I said that I woke up, thought of you, and felt horny?'

Tony shook his head. 'Not when you come in wearing a suit like that.' He nodded to her suit, which lay crumpled on the floor of his office.

'It was part of the reason.'

'And the other part?'

'That involves you, too.' She paused. 'Or it *could*, if you were interested.'

His eyes flickered briefly. The way she was talking, it sounded

11

like business. 'Interested in what, exactly?'

'I have a commission to write a series of articles about modern artists.' She smiled. 'Since my meeting at ten, with the editor of a certain rather high-profile arts magazine.'

Tony frowned. 'And you went to your meeting dressed like that?'

She laughed. 'Not quite. It's my favourite interview suit. I admit, I wasn't wearing a bra – I can't, with the cut of that jacket, unless I wear a prissy shirt and ruin the effect – but I was wearing knickers.'

Tony's frown deepened. 'What happened to them?'

'I didn't fuck my way to the commission, if that's what you're implying.' Her voice was suddenly hard with anger. 'I got it on the merit of my work.'

'From what I've read of your stuff, I know.' He winced, knowing that he'd upset her. 'Sorry. I didn't mean that at all – I know you're good, Isobel. It's just the idea of you walking round London with no knickers . . .' He shivered.

'Mm, I thought you might appreciate that. So, *after* my meeting, I went to the ladies' and removed my knickers. They're in my handbag.' She shrugged. 'I thought I'd come to vamp you, to celebrate my commission, and see if you fancied having lunch with me.'

'If I didn't have a meeting, I'd take you out to celebrate,' Tony said. 'Somewhere very nice.'

'But you can't.'

'So let's make it dinner, instead. With champagne.'

She nodded. 'It's a deal. But that isn't the only reason that I came to see you.' Isobel took a deep breath. 'I want to interview some of your artists. It does us both a favour. Your artists are showcased, which attracts people to the gallery; and it makes my articles topical, because I'm writing about people who are being exhibited right now, not three months ago.'

Tony's brain kicked back into business gear. 'You're right,' he said.

'So.' She smiled. 'Do you have a schedule?'

'Of course.' He took a file from his desk, and pulled out a sheet of paper. 'These are the shows planned for the rest of the year.'

Isobel scanned the paper swiftly. She recognised a few of the names on there; three of the first four artists were becoming very popular. Her eyes widened as she saw the fifth name on the list. 'Alex Waters? Isn't he . . . well, dead?'

Tony shook his head. 'I thought he was, too; but apparently not. He was in an accident, about ten years ago, and hasn't painted since – which is a shame, because he was very promising. I've always liked his work, and I negotiated with his agent to do a retro exhibition.' He shrugged. 'It's taken months to get him to agree to it, but I think it's worth all the hassle. His work's fantastic.'

'Right.' Isobel was thoughtful. 'Do you have any photographs, or anything?'

'Yes. I asked his agent to give me shots of all his work – it'll help me decide what to put where. Normally, I let one of the others handle the exhibitions, but I want to do this one, myself.'

'It sounds special,' Isobel said.

'It is.' Tony opened the file. 'Take a look at this.'

Isobel leafed through the A5-sized photographs in silence. The paintings were very raw, and very erotic; even the line-drawings, a style of art she didn't particularly like, made a pulse thrum into life between her legs. 'These are seriously good, Tony,' she said, her voice filled with a mixture of admiration and lust.

'I know.'

'I want to interview him.'

Tony shook his head. 'He doesn't do interviews.'

'He didn't do exhibitions, either, but you managed to change his mind,' she pointed out.

'It took months of negotiation even to get him to agree to show work that's a few years old. No way will he talk to you, Isobel. Just believe me, on this one – you're wasting your time.'

'No.' Her jaw was set. 'I want to talk to him. He'll be the highlight of the series.'

'If you piss him off,' Tony said, 'so he has a tantrum and pulls the exhibition . . .'

Isobel put her hand on his. 'I won't do that. I'm a professional. You know that.'

'I know, but we're talking about a man who doesn't paint any more. He won't do interviews.'

'Maybe, but I need to try. Please, Tony.' She bit her lip. 'This commission's an important one. If I do it, and I do it well, it'll make my career. I'll be able to name my price for articles, instead of scrabbling around and being nice to editors I don't personally like, just for the sake of a lousy commission. I worked hard for this break, Tony. I need to make the most of it.'

He sighed. 'Okay. I'll give you his agent's number. But he's a tough negotiator, I warn you.'

'Leave that to me.' Isobel had ways of dealing with tough negotiators. The suit she was wearing was one of them: if her opponent was a man, he was usually too busy trying to catch a glimpse of her breasts to pay attention to the meeting, and if it was a woman, Isobel always went for the 'girls being outrageous together' line. It worked, every time.

Tony turned to his contacts book, while Isobel dressed, and wrote down the name, phone number and address of Alex Waters' agent.

'JJ Wrenn,' she read, taking the paper from him.

'Short for James John, but everyone calls him JJ,' Tony told her.

'Right.' She smiled at him, and glanced at her watch. 'You have a meeting in precisely fifteen minutes. Better get going.'

'Yes.'

She tipped her head on one side. 'I'm going back to my place – but, before I do, can I make a phone call?'

He rolled his eyes. 'To JJ, I presume?'

'To JJ,' she confirmed.

He nodded, and leaned over to kiss her. 'Well, good luck. I'll pick you up, later – about eight okay with you?'

'Fine.' She smiled at him. 'Have a good meeting.'

'Yeah.' He sighed. 'And good luck with JJ.'

She smiled back. She believed that you made your own luck – and Isobel worked hard enough to make herself very lucky indeed.

Two

'Hello?'

Isobel didn't like the sound of the woman on the phone. She had a prissy voice, which was just a little too precise. The educated luvvie type, Isobel decided, and forced herself to smile at the receiver. It was an old trick, but it always worked – if you smiled, you didn't sound haughty or miserable when you spoke. You sounded friendly, approachable, and nice to do business with. 'Could I speak to Mr Wrenn, please?'

'I'll see if he's free.' Meaning, he's here, but I don't necessarily want to let you talk to him, Isobel thought crossly. 'May I ask who's calling?'

'Isobel Moran.'

'And what shall I say it's about?'

That's none of your bloody business, Isobel thought; she forced herself to smile again. 'I'm interested in the work of one of his clients.' Which was true – as far as it went. If the Educated Luvvie decided that it was a potential sale, so much the better. It would mean that she'd let Isobel speak to JJ Wrenn, and Isobel would get the chance to persuade JJ to let her interview Alex Waters.

'I'll put you on hold for a moment.'

Cow, Isobel thought. Just stop messing around, and put me through to him. Still, at least it was a silent switchboard, she realised with relief, not one of those machines that played synthetic versions of Mozart, or repeated the first three bars of Vivaldi's *Spring*, ad nauseam.

She leaned back in Tony's chair, drumming the fingers of one hand on the desk, and flicking through the photographs again with her other hand. Alex Waters was incredibly talented. Sensuality oozed out of every line, every piece of shading. She would have liked to buy one or two pieces for the house she shared with Sophie, but she knew that the price would be well out of her range – even if Tony were nice enough to forego his commission.

Just when she was about to give up, slam down the receiver and take a taxi to Wrenn's office instead, there was a soft click. 'I'll just put you through.'

'Thank you.' There was no point in being rude to the Educated Luvvie, Isobel decided. She might need her, later, if JJ Wrenn wasn't as tractable as she hoped.

There was a pause, then a soft West Country voice came on the line. 'Ms Moran?'

Very politically correct, Isobel thought, applauding mentally. 'Mr Wrenn.'

'Call me JJ,' he said. 'Phoebe tells me that you're interested in one of my clients' work.'

Phoebe being the Educated Luvvie, Isobel presumed. 'Yes.' She paused. 'JJ. I don't like doing business on the phone. Would you be free for lunch, so we could discuss things, then?'

'When?'

She decided to gamble. 'How about today?'

There was a rich chuckle. 'My, Ms Moran, you are keen.'

'Isobel.'

'Isobel. Yes, all right, then. Where, and what time?'

'In an hour's time?' She named a small Italian restaurant in Leadenhall. It was a place where one of her City journalist friends lunched, and as Annabel was very fussy about where she ate, it would be good. It also wasn't too expensive, so Ralph, the editor of *Vivendi*, wouldn't mind footing the bill – particularly if it meant that he'd have an exclusive on Alex Waters.

'All right. I'll see you then.'

Isobel cleared the line, then flicked through her filofax to find the number, and quickly rang the restaurant, ordering a table for two in her name. She explained that she was meeting JJ Wrenn. 'If I'm delayed, can you look after him and put the drinks on my bill, please?'

The waiter was politely efficient. 'Of course, Ms Moran.'

She glanced at her watch. She was four stops from Liverpool Street on the Central line; from there, it was a ten-minute walk to the restaurant. She looked ruefully at her skirt. It was crumpled, but there was no way she could iron it before she met JJ. She was too far from the house in Pimlico. And she didn't have time to nip to Oxford Street for a replacement, either. All she could do was buy a new pair of stockings at the station concourse when she got to Liverpool Street.

She sniffed. She still smelled of sex, despite the fact that Tony had cleaned her so well with his mouth. She'd have to go to the perfume counter when she bought her stockings, and spray herself liberally with Opium, to mask it. Pleased that her strategy was sorted, she took her knickers from her handbag, dressed swiftly, raked a hand through her hair, checked her reflection in the glass of one of the paintings on Tony's wall, and left his office. She smiled at Monica as she closed the door behind her. 'See you later, Monica.'

Monica smiled back at her. Although part of her disapproved of the pushy young journalist, she couldn't deny that Isobel was good for Tony. Since he'd met her, he'd lost that workaholic and slightly desperate look. He still looked tired, but at least it was for a decent reason – not because he was spending fifteen hours a day at the gallery and taking work home with him. And although Monica suspected that Isobel was a bit of a man-eater, Isobel had a certain indefinable appeal. Maybe it was because she was brave enough to do things that other women didn't dare to do. 'See you later,' she echoed.

There were no delays on the Tube; Isobel found herself at Liverpool Street even more quickly than she'd hoped, with enough time to buy the stockings and spray herself with perfume, as she'd planned. She went into the toilets to put on the stockings and comb her hair properly; then she retouched her lipstick and mascara, and looked critically at her reflection. She decided that yes, she'd do: she looked professional and, although her skirt was still crumpled, JJ wouldn't notice it under the tablecloth.

When she reached the restaurant, JJ wasn't there, to her relief.

She sat down, ordered a glass of mineral water, and contented herself with watching the City types standing outside in the arcade with their glasses of trendy real ale, braying with laughter. Thank God she wasn't part of that world, she thought; she wasn't sure how Annabel could stand it. The architects had made a good job of Leadenhall, though; the arcade was pretty, very Victorian, and full of delightful knick-knack shops and bars and restaurants.

What would JJ be like? she wondered. She'd liked his voice, but it was ageless. He could have been anything between thirty, her own age, and sixty. She was lost in her thoughts when the waiter coughed politely beside her.

'Ms Moran? Mr Wrenn is here.'

'Thank you.' She stood up, and looked straight into a pair of very blue and very shrewd eyes. She smiled, extending her hand. 'Isobel Moran.'

'JJ Wrenn.' He took her hand and shook it warmly.

Despite her affair with Tony, and the fact that she shared a house with a lecturer who had several artist friends, Isobel had no preconceived ideas about what an artist's agent would look like. Even so, JJ wasn't what she expected. He reminded her very much of John Thaw in his role as Inspector Morse. His hair was thick and white, and his eyes, behind the small round wire-rimmed glasses, were a very deep cornflower blue. There were deep laughter-lines etched around his eyes, and he had a sensual mouth. He was also very well-dressed; she recognised the cut and cloth as designer rather than chain-store, and his shoes were obviously hand-made, highly polished Italian leather.

Isobel judged him to be somewhere around his late forties or early fifties. When he was twenty, she thought, he must have broken a few hearts. Those stunning eyes, combined with that soft burr in his voice, was enough to charm any woman into bed. Sophie would like him, Isobel thought, and she wondered briefly whether she could engineer a meeting between JJ and her house-mate. Sophie could do with meeting a decent man, rather than the wimp she'd been going out with for nearly a year. And if that

20

decent man was an artist's agent, so much the better.

Sophie painted very good still-lives, but she never exhibited or sold her own work, which Isobel found strange. Sophie had little confidence in her talent, and preferred to stick to a safe occupation: teaching history of art. She'd refused to show even Tony her work; so there was little chance of her showing her work to JJ. Besides, Isobel reminded herself, she was there for a different purpose – to talk to JJ about Alex Waters. She could try to help Sophie another time.

The waiter brought a menu. JJ refused a starter, patting his stomach and saying that he was trying to cut down on his calorie intake, but his eyes were twinkling as he said it. In the end, they both settled on gnocchi with a tomato and wild mushroom sauce, and a mixed salad, teamed with a bottle of pinot noir rosé.

'So,' JJ said, when the waiter had gone. 'Do you want to talk business now, or after lunch?'

Isobel spread her hands, and gave him what she knew was a disarming smile. 'That's up to you.'

'Let's get it over with, so we can enjoy lunch,' he said. 'So you're interested in the work of one of my clients?'

'Yes. Alex Waters.'

'Right.' He nodded slowly. 'We're staging a retro-exhibition of his work in a few weeks, in Russell Street Gallery.'

'I know,' Isobel said with a smile. 'Tony's a friend of mine.'

JJ smiled back. 'And that's why you're here – to persuade me to sell you something before the exhibition opens?'

She shook her head. 'I like what I've seen of his work but, to be honest, I think it'd be out of my price range.'

JJ's eyes narrowed. 'So what precisely *is* your interest in my client, Ms Moran?'

'Isobel,' she corrected.

'Isobel.' His voice still had that soft West Country burr, but also held a hint of steel.

Isobel decided that this was a man who preferred the direct approach. 'What I want,' she said, 'is to interview him.'

To her surprise, he tipped back his head and laughed.

'What's so funny?' she demanded.

'Alex doesn't do interviews.'

'Why?'

JJ's face was impassive. 'He just doesn't.'

'Look, I'm not going to muck-rake, or anything like that. I just want to know more about him. I have a commission for *Vivendi* magazine, to write a series of articles on young artists – good artists, I should add – and I want to talk about their work, their influences, and why they paint what they do.'

'Well, you're on a losing wicket there. Alex doesn't paint any more, and he doesn't give interviews.'

Isobel nodded. 'Fair enough. I've been honest with you, and you've been honest with me.' She shrugged. 'Let's just enjoy lunch, shall we?'

The gnocchi was as good as Isobel had hoped, and the wine, being summery, complemented it perfectly. They chatted lightly, avoiding the subject of Alex Waters, and discovered that they liked each other, sharing similar tastes and having a similar sense of humour.

They both chose tiramisu for pudding. 'It's my weakness,' JJ admitted as he finished the sweet confection. 'I can't resist home-made puddings.'

She grinned. 'I'd make you puddings every day of the week, if you could get me an interview with Alex. Spotted dick, lemon meringue pie, jam roly poly, rhubarb tart with almond pastry . . .' She licked her lips, slowly and deliberately. 'I'm a good cook, JJ. Just name it, and I'll make it for you.'

'If your cooking tastes anywhere near as good as it sounds, I could be tempted.' He laughed. 'It's a nice try, Isobel, but I'm afraid that it's wasted. As I told you, Alex doesn't do interviews.'

Isobel didn't usually drink at lunchtime; the combination of the wine and the liqueur in the pudding was enough to make her reckless. Knowing that what she was about to do could blow everything sky high, yet unable to stop herself, she slipped her right foot from her shoe, and began stroking JJ's ankle with her toes.

She'd bought silk stockings, and the material felt sleek and smooth as she caressed his ankle; JJ raised one eyebrow, but he didn't push her away. Instead, he began to talk to her about art, and how he became an agent. Isobel listened, smiling at him, and let her foot drift upwards, towards his groin.

The damask tablecloths were large, and hid what she was doing from the waiters and the other diners. JJ had obviously experienced something of the kind before, or he was a damn good actor, because he didn't seem in the least put off by the way she was caressing him. Even when she began to stroke her foot over the growing bulge in his trousers, he continued to talk to her as though they were having a perfectly ordinary conversation.

Isobel smiled, nodded politely, and concentrated on what she was doing. The bulge at his groin was gratifyingly large: JJ Wrenn was a man, she thought, that she'd like to go to bed with, at some point. She had a feeling that he could teach her a lot, and that he was virtually unshockable – a combination she liked, in a man. Tony was a sweetheart, but she couldn't let herself go completely with him: she had to take it slowly, not scare him away. Whereas JJ was a man who could probably introduce her to so far undreamed-of pleasures . . .

She massaged the shaft of his cock with her big toe, rubbing gently; JJ shifted slightly in his seat, easing his erection, and she smiled at him. 'JJ.' She licked her lower lip slowly, deliberately, and he chuckled.

'I haven't met a woman like you for years.'

'Well.' Her lips twitched. 'I thought about dropping my napkin, and retrieving it rather slowly – but then I decided that it wouldn't be too subtle.'

'No.' His eyes glittered, the only outward sign that he was beginning to lose control. Isobel was impressed.

'Tony said that you're a tough negotiator.'

JJ spread his hands, acknowledging the compliment. 'And Tony's your friend?'

'Lover,' Isobel confirmed.

'Long-term?'

'Potentially.' She grinned. 'But I'm not easily satisfied. And neither, I think, are you.'

'Indeed.'

She continued massaging his cock with her foot, varying the speed and pressure of her strokes; he tensed slightly, for a fraction, and she smiled, gently removing her foot and sliding her shoe back on. She'd brought him just to the point of orgasm. Too far, and she'd have lost her chance. Leaving him on the edge was a sure-fire way of letting him know that she meant business. 'JJ.' Her voice was low, husky and sensual. 'All I want to do is talk to him.'

He was silent for a moment; then he nodded. 'Okay, Isobel, I'll see what I can do – but I can't promise anything.' He sighed. 'I should tell you why Alex doesn't do interviews.'

'A bad experience with a journalist, or a critic?' she guessed.

JJ shook his head. 'There was an accident. He let a friend of his drive him home from a party. It was a powerful car; the driver couldn't really handle it, took a corner too fast, and there was a crash. The driver died.'

Isobel winced. 'I'm sorry.'

'Yeah. Well, Alex was thrown onto the road, head first. He was concussed for a while, and had a broken arm and ankle.' JJ shrugged. 'When he came to, the doctors discovered that the impact had damaged some of the nerves in his ears. He was profoundly deaf. He hasn't painted since, and he doesn't talk to people. If I want to see him, I have to drive down to the Fens on the offchance that he'll see me – and if he doesn't want to talk to me, he won't.'

'So his speech was affected, too?' Isobel was shocked. She knew that impact damage could cause deafness – one of her childhood friends had been left partially deaf after a horse-riding accident – but she hadn't realised that it could affect speech, as well.

'He can speak well enough, when he chooses to. Most of the time, he hides behind sign language. It's his way of getting rid of people.'

24

Sign language. A light flicked on in Isobel's brain. Sophie was learning sign language. She smiled. 'I think,' she said, 'that I might have a way round the problem. Please arrange a meeting for me, JJ. I don't care where it is, or what time – I'll travel anywhere, any time, to talk to him. Just make it soon.'

'You're determined,' JJ said, 'so I won't bother trying to dissuade you. But don't say that I didn't warn you . . .'

Isobel was almost hugging herself with glee when she left the restaurant. Despite JJ's doom-and-gloom predictions, she had a feeling that he would set up the interview. He was too shrewd a businessman not to realise what an interview in a magazine like *Vivendi* could do for his client – and his percentage. So all she had to do now was to persuade Sophie to help her; she knew that that would be easy. Sophie was so nice, she didn't refuse to help anybody. Most of the time, Isobel tried to persuade her friend to be more assertive, telling her that it was perfectly acceptable to say no to people; but this time, she had every intention of taking advantage of her friend's good nature.

She took the tube back to Pimlico, and headed for the local deli. Sophie was probably home, by now, and working in the attic room that she used as a studio. If Isobel made some good coffee, and served it with the tiny Italian almond biscuits that Sophie loved, she had more chance of persuading her friend to agree to help.

'Isobel Moran, you're a conniving bitch,' she told herself, but her tone was one of resignation, even wry amusement, rather than self-loathing.

Ten minutes later, she poured boiling water into the cafétière, added two mugs to the tray, arranged the plate of biscuits, then headed up the stairs. As she'd half expected, Sophie was in her studio, sketching; she knocked on the door. 'It's me. I thought you might like a coffee,' she called through the door.

'You're a mind-reader, Isobel! Thanks. Come in.'

Isobel balanced the tray on one knee, and opened the door. Sophie was working on a still-life of some irises and gypsophilia;

Isobel, knowing how shy her friend was about her work, made no comment, although she appraised it with a swift glance. It was good – very good. So why didn't Sophie have the confidence to do something about it?

Isobel was sure that it had something to do with Sophie's old art tutor. Sophie had decided not to go to art school, at eighteen, and had gone to university instead, to study history of art, though she was always evasive if anyone asked her why, or just muttered something about not being good enough. Isobel had seen enough of Sophie's work to know that it wasn't true. There was definitely something there . . . But even twelve years of friendship hadn't unlocked Sophie's reticence about the reasons behind her decision.

Isobel and Sophie had been allocated adjoining rooms on the downstairs corridor of their block, and although they were complete opposites – physically, as well as temperamentally, because Sophie was tall and vague and fair-haired and wore glasses – they'd become firm friends, and had ended up sharing a house after university. Isobel regarded Sophie as her best friend and mainstay; Sophie, in turn, trusted Isobel more than she trusted anyone else, was grateful for her more fiery friend's habit of protecting her, and was indulgent of Isobel's wild streak.

'Good day?' Isobel asked.

'Not too bad.' Sophie wiped a hand over her face, not noticing that she'd wiped a streak of green paint over her forehead.

Isobel smiled, retrieved a tissue from the box in the corner of the room, and dabbed her friend's face. 'Messy pup,' she said affectionately.

Sophie flushed. 'God. Anyone would think I was twelve, not thirty!'

'Well. Have some coffee.' Isobel nodded at the plate. 'And I thought you might like some of these.'

Sophie looked at the biscuits, and then at her friend. She grinned. 'Spit it out, then.'

Isobel made her eyes look wide and innocent. 'What?'

'You only ever buy biscuits like this when you want me to do something,' Sophie said.

'No, I don't.'

'Yes, you do. What is it, this time? Making up a foursome for dinner?'

No, of course not. Anyway, you're going out with Gary. I wouldn't do that to you,' Isobel said. Though that wasn't strictly true. Isobel didn't think that Gary was good enough for Sophie; her friend needed someone with a little more life in him. But it wasn't the time to discuss that – not when she wanted Sophie to agree to help with Alex Waters.

'Then what is it?'

Isobel grinned. 'Oh, dear. Am I that obvious?'

'Yes – and you know damn well you are. So, what is it, this time?'

'If you know me so well,' Isobel teased, 'then you can guess, can't you?'

'Right. You want to move out and live with Tony, but one of his friends needs a place to stay, and you thought it might be nice if he moved in here and you moved in with Tony?'

Isobel's face registered horror. 'No way! I'm keeping my independence, thank you very much! Anyway, this place is just right for two. Three would be a crowd. I don't want anyone else moving into our house.'

Sophie chuckled. 'In that case, I give up.'

'Soph. I need a favour. A big favour.' Isobel tipped her head on one side, looking as appealing as she could. 'Can you teach me sign language – like, in half a day?'

'Sign language? Why?'

'It's a commission I'm working on.'

'Some commission.' Sophie regarded her friend's attire. Although Isobel had a generous figure, she had the type of curves which meant that she could wear the most outrageous outfits. Like her red suit – worn without a bra, and low-cut enough to make most men look three times, let alone twice. Isobel always wore it when she had a business meeting with a man, because they were always so busy looking at her cleavage, they would agree to almost anything. This time, there was a subtle difference; Isobel was usually immaculately groomed, but her skirt looked decidedly crumpled.

Isobel flushed as she caught Sophie's gaze. 'I had the meeting at *Vivendi* before my skirt got like this.'

'Tony's fault?'

'Who else's would it be?' Isobel asked crossly. 'I'm not that much of a man-eater.'

'No, of course not.' The look on Sophie's face didn't match her words.

'Soph, I'm *not!*'

Sophie grinned. 'That gets you back for the biscuits.'

'Considering you've already eaten three . . . Seriously, Soph, I need to learn sign language, and fast.'

Sophie shook her head. 'I know that you pick up things incredibly quickly, Isobel, but even *you* can't learn it in half a day.'

Isobel sighed. 'In that case . . . Could you do me a different favour, then?'

'What?'

'Help me.'

Sophie frowned. 'Help you to do what?'

'I'm setting up an interview with someone who's profoundly deaf,' Isobel said. 'I need someone who can help me with the interview.'

Sophie shook her head. 'Sorry. My signing isn't up to it.'

'You're the best person for the job.'

'No. God, I'm only on stage one – that's the equivalent of GCSE. Getting me to interpret would be like – oh, I dunno, leaving a twelve-year-old in a tiny village in the middle of France, where they didn't speak English, and expecting her to make her way home.'

It was unusual for Sophie to be so assertive; obviously, she'd had a bad day, Isobel thought. But Sophie was also very curious. If Isobel held out long enough, Sophie would ask for more information. Silence was a very powerful weapon. She smiled to herself, and sipped her coffee.

Ten minutes later, Sophie cracked. 'All right, I give in. Who are you interviewing?'

Isobel wrinkled her nose. 'You probably wouldn't be interested.'

'Tell me.'

'No. It's not important.'

'Isobel – do you want me to do this favour for you, or not?'

'Okay,' Isobel took another sip of coffee, enjoying the suspense. 'If you really want to know, it's a guy called Alex Waters.'

'*Alex Waters?* As in the painter?'

Isobel nodded.

'But – ' Sophie frowned ' – he hasn't painted in years.'

'I know.'

Sophie flushed. She'd had a major crush on Alex Waters, when she'd been a teenager. He was only five years older than herself, but he'd had so much talent. He'd crashed into the news with his erotic sketches, and Sophie had fallen in love with him: for the way he painted, as well as his dark good looks. She'd even fantasised about going to study with him – before she'd realised that she'd never make it as an artist, and would be better off teaching history of art, instead. And now, she had the chance to meet the man himself . . . 'No. I can't do it.'

'Sophie, he's one of the greatest living artists.' Isobel was careful not to mention Sophie's crush on Alex. She could remember Sophie telling her about it, years before, after too much cheap cider; it was a confidence which Isobel hadn't repeated. A confidence which Isobel had almost forgotten, until Sophie had said his name in that way, just now, and flushed so deeply.

'Even so.'

'*Vivendi* commissioned me to do a series on modern artists. I want to do Alex Waters.'

Sophie shook her head. 'He hasn't even exhibited his work, let alone painted, for about ten years. No way will he agree to an interview.'

'Is that so?' Isobel took another biscuit. 'I have two pieces of information for you, Ms Know-it-all Hayward. Firstly, he's exhibiting – at Tony's place, in three months' time. It's a retro.'

'You're kidding.' Sophie was shocked.

'Seriously. Tony's arranging it himself, he showed me some photographs of the pictures, and they're good. Bloody good.'

'What's the second bit of information?'

'I had lunch with JJ Wrenn, his agent, today.'

'How did you manage that?'

'Easy. I rang him up and asked him to meet me.'

Sophie rolled her eyes. 'Only you would have the nerve to do that.'

'If you don't ask, you don't get.'

'And that's the other reason why your skirt's crumpled?'

It was Isobel's turn to roll her eyes. 'No. I didn't sleep with him.'

'You did something with him, though. You look guilty.'

Isobel laughed. 'Better not to ask, Soph, you wouldn't approve.' Sophie was far from being a prude, but she wasn't quite as liberal as Isobel. 'Anyway, JJ says he can probably fix up an interview; but, like I said, I need someone to help me. Someone who knows sign language.'

'Isobel, I'd help you in any way I can, you know I would – but my signing just isn't up to it.'

'You don't need to do every word,' Isobel coaxed. 'Just do enough to get me some answers.'

Sophie sighed. 'I need to think about it.'

'Sure.' Isobel smiled, knowing that by the end of the evening, Sophie would agree. She'd think about it, and realise that she couldn't possibly turn down a chance like this. She stretched. 'Anyway, I need a shower.'

'Are you going out with Tony, tonight?'

'Yes. He's picking me up, at eight.'

Sophie smiled. Tony was steadier than most of the men in Isobel's past, and she had a feeling that Tony might even be the one to tame her friend. 'Right.'

'What about you? Seeing Gary?'

Sophie shook her head. 'It's his evening class, tonight. So I'm doing some work, then having a very long bath, and an early night.'

'Right.' Isobel smiled at her friend. 'Well, I'd better get myself ready. See you later.'

'Have a good time.'

'I will.' Isobel nodded at the biscuits. 'Don't worry about saving me any of those.'

Sophie chuckled. 'I won't!' She smiled again, as Isobel left the room, and turned back to her still life.

Three

When the light had faded, Sophie eased her shoulders, then cleaned her brushes and left the studio, closing the door behind her. Her stomach rumbled vaguely, but she couldn't be bothered to go to the kitchen and cook something. She rarely did bother, if she was there on her own; cooking was a chore, rather than a pleasure, and it was something she often traded with Isobel in return for hoovering or ironing, which her house-mate detested as much as Sophie detested cooking. Besides, she'd eaten the biscuits that Isobel had left her, and she'd had a good lunch at the university. She didn't need another meal.

Isobel.

Her brow creased into a frown. Isobel had had some mad schemes, in the past, but this was her maddest, yet. Interviewing Alex Waters. Sophie rolled her eyes. Everyone knew that the man didn't give interviews. He didn't even paint any more. He'd just completely dropped out of circulation. And yet . . . There was a small knot of excitement in her stomach. If Isobel did pull this off – and if anyone could, Isobel was the one to do it – she would need someone to help her with the sign language. Which meant that this was Sophie's one chance to meet the man she'd idolised, years before.

On impulse, she headed downstairs to the living room. One wall was crammed with bookshelves; Isobel's very large and somewhat dog-eared paperback collection sat on the top shelves, and the large coffee-table art books Sophie had collected over the years were stacked neatly on the lower shelves, for balance. All were in alphabetical order; Isobel had teased Sophie about it, saying that she should have been a librarian rather than an art historian, but Sophie had been cheerfully impervious to the comment. It made sense to have the books like that, so you could find what you wanted, more quickly.

She skimmed the shelves, and picked out her dictionary of modern painters. It was old and well-thumbed. She'd bought it when she'd been fifteen – Alex had been twenty, at the time, and she'd been at the peak of her crush on him – and she'd bought that particular edition for the photograph of him in it. She opened the book, and the pages fell open automatically under *Waters, Alex*.

She stared at the photograph, smoothing the glossy page thoughtfully with her thumb. Alex was fifteen years older, now; she wondered if he'd changed much. The face that stared out from the book was filled with youthful arrogance; and yet, he was so very, very sensual. The way his mouth curved, the lower lip full and inviting; she caught herself tracing the high cheekbones, the smooth skin, and flushed.

Christ, what was she doing? Going back to her old adolescent crush? Yes, Alex Waters was a very good-looking man. According to the biographical note, he was a little over six foot tall; and she knew from other photos that he was broad-shouldered and narrow-hipped, his body well-toned. His dark hair was a little longer than fashion had dictated at the time, curling slightly at the collar, and looking tousled, as though he'd either just got out of bed, or had just been running on a beach with the wind in his hair. His eyes were dark, and very intense; his skin was very pale. He looked almost Russian: haughty and – well, *regal*, she thought. Yet, at the same time, his eyes were blatantly inviting the woman looking at him to come to his bed, let him use his mouth and his cock and his hands to drive her to a frenzy of pleasure.

Sophie swallowed, and shut the book. It was ridiculous, wondering if Alex Waters would still be the same. Of course he wouldn't be. He was fifteen years older. For all she knew, his hair could be shot through with grey, rather than being lush and dark, and it could be long and thin and straggly, brushed forward to hide a thinning crown. His physique, too, could have run to fat, and those alabaster cheeks could be jowly now and broken with veins, from drinking too much red wine on his own, for too many nights. Those come-to-bed eyes could be bloodshot and puffy, and that beautiful sensual mouth twisted with cynicism . . .

No, she should just forget the idea. Even if her signing were good enough to help Isobel, she didn't want to have her old dreams shattered. Idols were best kept that way, she thought – in your mind, and at a distance, where they would have the personality you dreamed for them. At a distance, they couldn't disappoint you. In her mind, Alex Waters would always be young, attractive, and very talented; she wanted him to stay that way. If she met him and discovered that he was old and ugly, his brilliance gone to waste . . . No. It was too horrible to think about.

Cross with herself, she pushed the book back into its place on the shelf. And yet she couldn't help lingering, letting her fingers drift over the spine of another book. A much thinner book, this time, but one that was equally well-thumbed. A book of Alex's paintings.

They were all very different, from the sensual line-drawings of nudes to the more detailed oil portraits. But all of them had that incredible energy. Alex had specialised in portraits, and they'd been very, very good. He'd captured all of his subjects perfectly, coaxing their inner personalities to the surface; his paintings of Deborah Harry and Jessica Lange were justly famous, as were his portraits of Marie Helvin and Jerry Hall. He'd brought out their sensuality, and the paintings had been popular enough to be made into prints and sold in all the postcard-and-poster shops in the mid-Eighties.

His erotic drawings had been something else: and Sophie had had her first solo orgasm while browsing through a book of them. Something about them had made her want to touch herself; she'd ended up masturbating with abandon, fantasising that Alex was there, urging her on so that he could paint her touching herself, pulling at her nipples and sliding her middle finger deep inside her. She'd rubbed her clitoris until the energy fizzing through her body had suddenly exploded, and she'd virtually seen stars, she'd climaxed so hard . . .

She flushed at the memory. Really annoyed with herself, this time, she shoved the book into the shelves, and stomped upstairs.

She might as well get the idea out of her head, right now. It was completely stupid – completely ridiculous – and she was cross with Isobel for suggesting it, and with herself for even considering it. 'How stupid can you get, Hayward?' she berated herself loudly. 'And even if he did meet you, he wouldn't be interested. He's the sort who'd like pretty, petite and immaculate women, not tall and well-built women who don't wear make-up and definitely don't wear designer clothes.'

She stalked into the bathroom and ran herself a deep bath, adding liberal quantities of the expensive aromatherapy oil with seaweed extracts that Isobel had bought, the previous week. She knew that her friend wouldn't begrudge it; they shared most things. Her mouth curved wryly – most things except men, that was. Isobel's tastes and hers didn't coincide there; though even if they had, she wouldn't have wanted to share a man with Isobel. Isobel, she knew, had done something like that in the past – and more. Sophie wasn't exactly virginal, but Isobel's sex-life made her own sexual experiences look tame. On balance, Sophie thought that she preferred it that way.

She wrinkled her nose and stripped, putting her discarded clothes neatly into the wicker laundry basket. Where Isobel was untidy, scattering her possessions around and generally leaving stockings trailed across the bathroom carpet and the lids off pots of cleanser and moisturiser, Sophie was neat – almost fanatically so. Isobel ribbed her for it, but Sophie always knew where everything was: unlike Isobel, who lived by the 'volcano principle' – that important things would always drift to the surface of clutter – but who was usually forced to have a manic tidying session once a fortnight when her theory failed and the missing item remained buried.

Testing the water with the tips of her fingers, Sophie winced at the scalding temperature, and added some cold water. Then she piled her hair on top of her head, secured it with a pin, and stepped into the bath. She leaned back against the rim of the bath, and closed her eyes; the water lapped gently round her, the scent soothing and relaxing her. She began to breathe more deeply, using a relaxation technique she'd learned when Isobel had dragged her off to yoga classes; she'd stayed the course rather longer than Isobel, not having such a low boredom threshold, and she still practised the odd movement and breathing exercise when she felt particularly tense.

She let her mind go blank, and tried to focus on her boyfriend, Gary. But instead, to her intense annoyance, she saw Alex Waters' face. Alex as he'd been when he was twenty, haughty and handsome. The sort of man who looked like he was in control, and was an irresistible challenge. The thought of making him so aroused that he forgot himself, and cried out in abandon as he came ... 'Oh, what the hell,' Sophie said, and let herself drift into the day-dream.

She was lying in the bath, and Alex was kneeling beside her. He was wearing a pair of very old, faded denims, the material incredibly soft to the touch, and a dark green cotton shirt with a grandad collar. The sleeves were rolled up to the elbows; he wasn't wearing a watch, and he was holding a bar of soap, and smiling at her.

His usual haughtiness wasn't visible; instead, his eyes were laughing and there was a teasing smile playing about his lips. He looked lively, full of mischief, and incredibly sexy. When he looked at her like that, she wanted him to touch her, to stroke her skin and arouse her. She smiled back at him and leaned back in the bath, arching her body slightly in offering to him. He soaped his hands, putting the soap casually onto the edge of the bath, and began to lather her skin, working first on her shoulders and then drifting down to her breasts.

He paid meticulous attention to each one, lifting and stroking it, squeezing it slightly as he soaped her skin. As her nipples hardened, he traced the aureolae with the tip of his finger, making her shiver. Her eyes were closed so that she could concentrate on the pleasure he gave her; she couldn't see his face, but she knew that he was smiling. Alex was a man who believed in pleasure, and enjoyed giving it as much as receiving it.

He rested his palm very lightly against her nipple, so that his hand was only just making contact with her body, and began to rotate his palm, very slowly, in tiny erotic circles. It made her arch her back and push against him; he chuckled, and repeated the action with her other breast, stroking the soft underside and teasing her nipples until they were so hard that they hurt.

He rinsed the soap from her skin before it dried, then worked up a lather between his hands again, working over her ribcage and her midriff. The way his fingers glided over her skin felt incredibly erotic, and she opened her mouth in an 'o' of pleasure. He let his hands drift lower, stroking her abdomen, and she tensed as the tips of his fingers traced the curve between her abdomen and her pubic bone. He grinned, and let his hand rest on her delta for a moment.

Just as she thought that he was going to let his fingers drift along her quim, parting her labia and touching her more intimately, his hands moved again, and he lifted one of her feet, soaping it and stroking it, concentrating on the arch of her foot and the hollows of her ankles. His touch was gentle, yet sure, and surprisingly unticklish. Sophie tipped her head back, relaxing and enjoying the way he touched her.

He continued to massage her foot, his hand moving slowly up over her ankles, up to her calves, and finally to the sensitive spot behind her knee, making her shiver. His fingers feathered over her inner thigh; again, he stopped short of her quim, and repeated the action with her other leg. By the time his fingers reached up to her thighs, Sophie was trembling, and her sex felt warm and puffy.

Alex smiled at her. 'So, what do you want, Sophie?'

She flushed. 'I want you to . . . to touch me.'

His smile broadened. 'Anywhere in particular?'

Her flush deepened. 'You know where.'

'I want you to tell me, Sophie. Tell me what you want.'

She swallowed hard. He knew how difficult she found this. She wasn't a prude; she just wasn't used to talking like this. *I want.* It seemed too pushy. And as for describing in precise detail what she wanted . . . She had the vocabulary, but it made her uneasy. One set of words marked her down as a boffin, a teacher who wasn't close enough to life to use more earthy words; the other made her feel like a whore, a demanding foul-mouthed bitch. 'I want . . . I want you to – to touch me. I want you to touch my – my quim.' She forced the words out. 'I want you to make me come with your fingers, and then – then, with your cock.'

'It wasn't so hard, sweetheart, was it?' He stroked her face affectionately; then he let one hand drift over her thighs, so very slowly; then, at last, she felt him touch her with the intimacy she craved. She felt him slide one finger between her labia, parting them. She shivered as the heel of his palm pressed against her delta; she felt him stroking her, teasing her clitoris into a hard swollen bud.

She gripped the sides of the bath and tipped her head back as he continued to touch her, bringing her arousal to a peak. He slid one finger into her, pushing back and forth gently at first, then speeding up the rhythm and adding another finger, and another. The soles of her feet became warm and tingly; the sensations moved up through her calves, through her thighs, then rushed like a whirlpool into her gut, spinning round and exploding.

Her internal muscles flexed hard round his fingers; he smiled, waiting until the aftershocks of her orgasm had died down, then drew his hand up to his mouth, licking the musky juices from his fingers. Then he smiled and stood up, stripping swiftly and letting his clothes drop to the floor.

Sophie licked her lips. Now that she'd reached the first plateau with him, she wanted more. She wanted to feel him inside her, filling her and stretching her with his beautiful cock. She knelt up to help him, her fingers struggling with the button of his jeans; he helped her, and she slid his jeans and boxer shorts down together. When the material reached his ankles, he kicked them away, and stood there, watching her, his head tipped slightly to one side.

The gesture appealed to her; but the clean lines of his body appealed to her even more. Alex, as usual in the house, was barefoot; and, naked, he was magnificent. Every muscle was sharply defined, and he would have been an inspiration to the most jaded life class. Sophie wasn't sure whether she wanted to paint him, to sculpt him, or to make love with him most.

His cock was already hard; Sophie shivered in pleasure as she looked at him. He was so perfect. She had sketched him again and again, in her mind's eye, but the reality was oh, so much better. Unable to help herself, she reached out to touch him, her fingers curling round his cock.

His breath hissed. 'Sophie.'

She nuzzled the end of his cock with the tip of her nose, and he closed his eyes, sliding his fingers into her hair. 'Oh, Sophie,' he muttered, his voice husky.

She thrilled to the sound. He was aroused – Alex Waters, dynamo, *enfant terrible* of the art world, the most gut-wrenchingly attractive man she'd ever met, was aroused. By her.

'Please,' he added.

It was her turn to tease. She cupped his balls with her other hand. 'Please what?' Her breath fanned his cock, making him shudder.

'You know.'

'Tell me what you want.'

He grinned wryly. 'Touché.'

She grinned back. 'Tell me, Alex.'

'You know what I want.'

'Tell me.'

'I want you to wrap your delectable mouth round my cock. I want you to lick me. I want you to suck me.'

She paused, as if considering it, then grinned. 'Why not?'

His eyes crinkled at the corner. 'Ah, Soph. One minute, you're a witch; the next minute, you're a tumbled innocent, looking up at me with those big blue eyes; then, you're a tease; then, you're this goddess who's ever so slightly out of reach. I never really know where I am, with you.'

'Really?' She rubbed her cheek against his abdomen.

He stroked her hair. 'All I know,' he said softly, 'is that I need you. I need you like I've never needed anyone else.'

It was a heady experience: the haughty Alex Waters admitting that he needed anybody – and particularly, he needed her . . . She bent her head, and slowly opened her mouth over the tip of his cock. His sharp intake of breath made her smile against his skin; it amused her and touched her in equal measures that such a small act could affect him so profoundly. Then she began to work him with her mouth, sliding her lips up and down his shaft, using her tongue deftly round his frenulum; he groaned, and she let the hand cupping his balls drift further back, stroking his perineum and pressing lightly against the sensitive spots.

She felt his body grow taut, and his balls lift and tighten; then, at last, his orgasm flowed through him, and he came, filling her mouth with warm salty liquid. She swallowed every last drop; then Alex knelt down, cupping her face in his hands.

'Oh, God, Soph,' he muttered hoarsely. 'I needed that so much.' He kissed her hard, not caring that he could taste himself on her mouth.

Her loins kicked again as the kiss deepened, his tongue caressing her palate. Alex was so incredibly sexual. The way he kissed was almost enough to make her come. The next thing she knew, Alex was kissing his way down her body, nipping at the sensitive spot at the side of her neck and licking the hollows of her collarbone. His mouth tracked downwards, and then he was sucking fiercely on one nipple, then the other. She arched against him, and he began to use his teeth, grazing the sensitive tissues just enough to give her pleasure, but staying on the right side of pain.

She moaned, sliding her hands into his hair and digging her fingers into his scalp to urge him on, and he lifted her to her feet. He sank to his knees again, kissing her belly and slowly, oh, so slowly, moving southwards. Just as he'd teased her earlier, with his fingers, he teased her with his mouth, covering her skin with kisses and licking her in places which she usually found ticklish, but which were suddenly major erogenous zones, under his mouth.

And then, at long long last, she felt his breath fanning her quim. She widened her stance, not worried about slipping, because Alex was supporting her with his hands; she moaned as, with one deft movement, Alex licked from the top to the bottom of her slit. He repeated the action again and again, speeding up the rhythm until she was quivering. He brought her to another orgasm, but he didn't stop there; he climbed into the bath beside her, lifting her. Her legs automatically lifted round his waist, for balance, and he slid one hand under her buttocks, stroking them, before fitting the tip of his cock against her sex.

As he pushed into her, he dropped to his knees; she gripped the side of the bath as he began to move inside her, pushing gently at first. The water lapped round them, and her quim fluttered round his cock; he felt so good, so very good. She leaned back, resting her neck on the edge of the bath, and he began to thrust harder, pushing deeply into her and bringing her to a higher plateau.

Sophie had lost enough of her inhibitions, by that time, to rub her own breasts, squeezing the nipples and rolling them between finger and thumb. Alex continued driving into her, pulling her deeper into the swirling vortex. She cried out his name, feeling her muscles contracting sharply round his cock; as she heard his answering cry, she felt his cock throb deep inside her as he, too, came . . .

Sophie pushed her feet against the bath, her hand working rapidly between her thighs; then she felt the tension in her muscles peak, and ebb away in a delicious release. She groaned and sat up, dragging her other hand across her face. Christ, what was she doing? She'd been going out with Gary for long enough for them to be thinking about getting engaged – and here she was, masturbating in the bath over another man. A man she'd never met, a man she wasn't likely to meet – unless Isobel's crazy scheme came off – and a man who wouldn't be interested in her, in the first place.

Furious with herself, she washed herself, hauled herself out of the bath, and scrubbed herself dry. If it had been anyone, she should have seen Gary, not Alex. This was getting much too far out of hand. But then, Alex would refuse to do the interview anyway, so it didn't really matter – did it?

Four

'JJ.' Isobel purred down the phone. 'Sweetie, how are you?'

'Fine.' There was a hint of amusement in his voice, as though he knew that she was playing up to him – and that he enjoyed the game as much as she did. 'I have some news for you, my dear.'

'Good news, I hope.'

'Yes. Alex has agreed to the interview.'

'You sound surprised.'

'I am. He's usually an awkward bastard, refusing to see anyone unless he really has to. Or maybe he's realised that if he plays ball over this retrospective, and lets me publicise it properly, he'll make enough of a pile to let him continue his Howard Hughes act.' JJ's harsh words were tempered with genuine affection for his client. 'Anyway, he's agreed to do it, one day next week. So when do you want to do it?'

Isobel thought about it. There was one day when Sophie didn't have lectures; it was the best day for it. Although Sophie hadn't actually agreed to do it, yet, Isobel was sure that her friend's misgivings were mainly because the interview wasn't definite. Now that it was . . . Well, Sophie would agree to do it. 'How about Wednesday?'

'Wednesday, it is. Shall we say eleven o'clock?'

'Fine.'

'Don't be late – he has a thing about lateness. God knows why, because he never even wears a watch. I suppose he has the equivalent thing, time-wise, of perfect pitch. He just *knows*.'

Isobel chuckled. 'Do you always slag him off like this?'

'Usually to his face,' JJ admitted cheerfully. 'Over a bottle or two of red wine. Though it's pretty difficult to pick a fight with him. If he's not in the mood to bite, you have to resort to writing

43

down insults, or relying on the odd sign or two. And he's a lot better at signing than anyone else; so, eventually, you just have to give up.' He paused. 'So is your friend going to act as interpreter, in case he gets sniffy with you?'

'Yes.'

'Good.' There was a pause. 'Give me a ring, and let me know how you got on with him. I will, of course, need to approve copy before you submit it to your editor.'

Isobel chuckled. 'Your mind's never off business, is it?'

'No.'

'All right. Where am I doing the interview?'

'At his cottage. It's in the middle of nowhere, so I'll get Phoebe to do you a map and some directions.'

'Thanks.' Isobel paused. 'Maybe we can have dinner, after the interview.'

'Sounds good to me. Ring me when you get back, and we'll sort something out.'

Something, Isobel thought wickedly, meaning more than just dinner. Something more like continuing what they'd started in the restaurant, but where they couldn't be disturbed. She knew that it wasn't fair to Tony; but then again, she reasoned, Tony would just have to accept her for what she was. A woman who liked good sex, with men who liked a little variety . . .

'I've already told you, I can't do it,' Sophie said.

Isobel topped up her house-mate's glass. 'Please, Soph.'

'No. I *knew* there was something behind you offering to cook dinner, tonight.'

Isobel rolled her eyes. 'You make me sound like a mercenary bitch.'

'Mercenary, yes; bitch, only sometimes,' Sophie said.

Isobel stuck out her tongue. 'Just because you're my best pal, it doesn't mean you can be quite so honest with me! Look, Soph, I thought you were against the idea because it was so much in the air. It's a fact, now. I'm seeing Alex on Wednesday, at his place.' She sighed. 'Still, if you don't want to do it, I'll find someone else. I don't suppose you'd let me have your sign-language teacher's phone number, would you?'

Sophie bit her lip. 'Isobel – can't you just leave him alone?'

'Why? All I want to do is to interview him about his work. No muck-raking, nothing about his private life: just his work, who's influenced him, and why. You can see the questions, if you like – I've done a standard format for all the artists I'm going to interview.' Isobel spread her hands. 'I can't say fairer than that.'

'Hm.' Sophie didn't answer; she merely ate another forkful of pasta.

Isobel decided to play it cool, and switched the topic to something less controversial. She chatted lightly over dinner, talking about films and theatre; in the end, Sophie sighed, and took a swig of red wine. 'All right, all right. You're so bloody relentless. I'll do it.'

'You're wonderful.' Isobel pushed her chair back, and came round to Sophie's side of the table, hugging her. 'Thanks. It's really important to me.'

I know.' Sophie bit her lip. 'It's just that – well, Alex was a big hero of mine, when I was a kid. I'd hate to find out that he has feet of clay.'

'From what JJ says, he's an awkward bastard, who'll only talk to you when he feels like it. It sounds like he enjoys playing the temperamental artist.' Isobel shrugged. 'But you probably knew that, anyway.'

'Mm.' Sophie finished her garlic bread. 'I've made one mistake, though.'

'What's that?'

'Saying yes, right now. If I'd held out until Monday, you'd have cooked every night for the next fortnight.'

Isobel chuckled. 'It can always be arranged.'

Sophie grinned back. 'I'll hold you to that.'

The following Wednesday saw Isobel and Sophie heading down the M11 towards Cambridge.

'It'll only take about an hour to interview him,' Isobel said.

45

'Let's go to Cambridge, afterwards. We can have lunch, and do some shopping – the shops are great, and I know this lovely little pub by the river. It looks like the inside of an old ship, inside, with wooden walls and ceilings and floors.' She smiled. 'We can have a nice girly day out.'

Sophie did not respond.

Isobel glanced sideways at her friend. 'You're quiet, Soph. Second thoughts?'

'I just don't know if I'm good enough, Isobel. I mean, I'm only at stage one.'

'I hope,' Isobel said, 'that the fact that you're there, and that you know some sign language, will make Alex Waters relax enough to talk to me. He's not dumb; JJ says that he's a bit moody, and prefers not to talk, sometimes. But if having someone who can sign – even if it is only a little bit – makes him loosen up enough to talk to me, I can write my questions to him, and he can . . . Oh, I dunno, write the answers, if he likes.'

'So, really, you don't need me at all.'

'Yes, I do. And I do appreciate that you've given your day up for me – helping me, instead of painting or going off somewhere with Gary.'

'Gary has lectures, all morning.'

'Well. I appreciate your company, anyway.' Isobel took her left hand off the steering wheel, and squeezed her friend's hand momentarily. 'Look, Soph, this is important to me. I really want it to work.'

'What if he won't talk to you?'

'That's defeatist talk. Anyway, it isn't an option. JJ said that he agreed to this. He wouldn't have agreed, if he didn't want to do it.'

'I suppose not.'

Isobel grinned. 'Trust me, will you?'

'Last time you told me to trust you,' Sophie said, half cross and half laughing, 'we were on holiday in Turkey. You said that I ought to leave my hair uncovered, because Turkish men like fair hair, and they'd give us a better deal.'

'True.'

'And I was groped by every bloke in the bazaar! One of them even offered you a hundred camels to take me off somewhere.'

Isobel chuckled. 'But we got the cheapest and best souvenirs, did we not?'

'I suppose so.' Sophie lapsed back into silence, staring out of the window. The more she thought about it, the more she wanted to ask Isobel to turn the car round and take her back to London. But she knew that Isobel wouldn't do it: this was too important to her.

The thought that she was going to meet Alex Waters, after all these years . . . It turned her stomach to water. What could she say to him? It was just too awkward. She flushed deeply as she remembered her long bath, dreaming about Alex and masturbating over her fantasy. Christ. What made it worse was that she'd felt so guilty about it, that when she'd seen Gary, the following night, they'd ended up having a huge row over something trivial; and then she'd gone to bed in a huff, and masturbated over Alex again.

God, what was wrong with her, that she kept needing to touch herself? And, even worse, fantasising about a man she'd never met, and who probably wouldn't like her in the first place?

She glanced at Isobel again. At least Isobel wasn't intending to vamp the artist, Sophie was relieved to see. Isobel was dressed in a pair of taupe tailored trousers, a smart black shirt, and a pair of flat black leather court shoes. She'd added a black Alice band, to keep her hair off her face, and was wearing small round wire-rimmed glasses which made her look extremely intellectual – a professional and serious journalist. Sophie smiled to herself. Alex wasn't to know that the glass in the Armani frames was plain, rather than prescription.

Sophie was dressed simply, in a summery cotton print skirt and a loose white cotton shirt, a straw hat and flat navy leather court shoes – an outfit which Isobel had immediately dubbed as 'Laura Ashley country wear'. Sophie wondered whether she, too, should have worn trousers, a smart office-like outfit; but then again, it really wasn't her. As a lecturer, she was more comfortable wearing leggings and a baggy sweater, or a loose shirt and a longer-length skirt. She wasn't the tailored sort; besides, she had a horror of emphasising her generous bust, preferring more camouflaging outfits. And her glasses were less modish than Isobel's: the large frames suited her face more than Isobel's fashionable ones would have done.

Sophie began to fidget, twisting her hands together. 'Isobel . . .' she began.

Isobel shot her a sideways look. 'Just relax, will you? Soph, he won't bite you.' Sophie flushed, and Isobel grimaced. 'Sorry. I didn't mean to snap at you; I suppose I'm just as nervous as you are. I want this to go well.'

Strangely enough, it was Isobel's admission of nerves which calmed Sophie. Isobel, the cool and calm professional, who never let anything faze her, was nervous?

As they reached Cambridgeshire, Isobel turned to Sophie. 'There's a map in my briefcase; I think we might need it. JJ gave me written directions, as well.'

'Does he live that far off the beaten track, then?'

'Apparently so. It's called Fen Cottage, so you can guess what sort of place it is. A tiny little one-up one-down place, full of spiders, and with no neighbours for fifty miles.'

The exaggeration made Sophie smile; she leaned over to the back seat of the car, and retrieved Isobel's soft leather briefcase. She opened it, and her eyes widened. Although Isobel was always messy at home, she was immaculate, at work. The brief-case contained a conference folder, with an A4 narrow-ruled pad on one side, and a pocket containing JJ's direction, a map and a neatly-typed list of questions on the other. There was a pen in the spine; a blue roller-ball, because Isobel detested ballpoints, but always ended up covered in ink if she used a fountain pen.

There was also a camera; Sophie frowned. 'I didn't realise that you were planning to take any photographs.'

'I can hardly use stock shots of him – they're ten years out of date. I need an up-to-date photograph, to accompany the article.

If he doesn't want to be photographed by a professional, maybe he'll let me do it.'

'You've got a nerve, I'll give you that much,' Sophie said. She took the map and the directions from the folder, and replaced the folder in the briefcase. She glanced at the map, finding her bearings, and then nodded. 'Okay. You take the next turning on the left. We have to go through the village, and then through the fens towards his cottage.'

Having something to do took Sophie's mind off her nervousness at meeting Alex Waters. Isobel smiled to herself as she heard her friend's confident voice directing her. She'd actually memorised the directions, the night before, but she knew that if Sophie's mind was unoccupied, she'd be fretting about meeting Alex, and her nerves would be worn to a frazzle before they reached Fen Cottage – which would make the interview very difficult indeed.

Eventually, they drove down a very narrow road, which had grass growing down the middle of it, and a small flint-and-brick cottage came into view at the very end. There had been no other houses for the past three miles; the place was in the middle of nowhere.

'This must be Fen Cottage,' Sophie said.

Isobel pulled to a halt on the gravel in front of the cottage. There was no garden; the patch of ground surrounding the cottage was a jungle, full of huge thistles and a nettle patch. The place looked as though the owner really couldn't be bothered to do anything with it. Sophie was surprised; the friends of hers who were artists were usually proud of their gardens, and had stunning colour-schemes – like her own blue and white scheme in terracotta pots, in the courtyard of their Pimlico house.

Sophie glanced round as she closed the car door. 'I can see why he picked this place.'

'The endless East Anglian skies, you mean?' Isobel asked.

'The whole quality of the light out here is different. It's perfect for a studio.'

Isobel smiled affectionately at her friend. 'Soph, you're wasting this on me. As far as I'm concerned, a picture's just a picture.'

Sophie scoffed. 'Oh, come on! You share a house with me – a lecturer in history of art – and you're having an affair with the manager of an art gallery. You know at least half a dozen artists. You write articles about the art world. You appreciate art a hell of a lot more than the average person, and you know it.'

'I suppose so.' Isobel inclined her head towards the door. 'Shall we?'

Sophie nodded, and followed her friend down the cracked paved path to the front door. There were weeds growing out of the cracks, and the whole place had an air of desolation about it, as though no-one had lived there for years. It was eerily quiet; there was no traffic, which was only to be expected, but there was also no birdsong.

Sophie frowned. 'Are you sure that this is the place, Isobel?'

'You were in charge of the map. You tell me.'

'Well . . .' Sophie shrugged. 'Are you sure that he's expecting us, today, then?'

'Yes.' Isobel marched up to the front door, and stopped. 'Oh, shit.'

'What?'

'He's deaf, so how can we get his attention? He won't hear us if we knock, or if we ring the doorbell.'

'A lot of deaf people have the doorbell wired so that a light flashes when it's been pressed; they do the same sort of thing with their phones.'

'Right.' Isobel sighed. 'Well, here goes.'

She pressed the doorbell, and waited. Nothing happened. Isobel glanced at her watch. 'I'll give him another two minutes to answer, then I'll ring again.' They waited in silence; the seconds seemed to drag by. The longer they waited, the more nervous Sophie suddenly felt: it was as though they were intruders, not wanted. The whole place was menacingly quiet, as if time and sound had stopped.

Isobel gave a big sigh, and leaned on the doorbell.

Sophie winced. 'For God's sake, Isobel, you're going to wear the bell out!'

There was still no answer; Isobel shrugged. 'Maybe his bell isn't working properly. But he is expecting us.'

'Isobel, you can't—'

But it was already too late. Isobel had tried the front door, discovered that it was unlocked, and opened it. Feeling awkward, Sophie followed her inside. The hall was dark and dingy; the place was clean, but it looked as though it hadn't been decorated for years. The walls had once been white, but the paint had yellowed with age; the skirting boards and doors were equally discoloured. There were no paintings hung on the walls, no rugs on the bare floorboards – nothing to make the place look as though it was someone's home. This, Sophie thought, was just a place to live. Nothing more than that.

There was an open door at the end of the hallway; Isobel walked towards it, and pushed it open. 'We've found the kitchen,' she said.

The room contained a fridge, an ancient cooker, a battered pine dresser, and an equally battered scrubbed pine table, flanked by two benches. The floor was red flagstone, and the walls were again that aged creamy colour. It was tidy, but again, the room had the air of being merely functional. It wasn't a place where people would sit and chat over coffee or a bottle of red wine; and it certainly wasn't a place where someone like Isobel would cook happily, humming snatches from popular arias and throwing herbs around and filling the air with fragrant smells. It was the sort of place where people would make themselves a cheese sandwich – if they could be bothered. The only sign that someone had used it was a glass containing the dregs of red wine, and a plate covered in crumbs, both placed neatly next to the sink.

'Hello?' Isobel called.

'It's a waste of time. He won't hear you,' Sophie reminded her quietly.

Isobel winced. 'I didn't think.'

'Look, Isobel, I really don't think we should—' Sophie began, but Isobel had already marched out of the kitchen, and across the narrow hall to the living room.

It was furnished equally spartanly. There was no television, no phone, no hi-fi. There were no pictures on the walls, no knick-knacks adorning the mantelpiece – not even a clock. There was a sofa, which looked old but not particularly worn, a bookcase, and a low coffee table. There was also a portfolio flung carelessly on the table; Isobel picked it up.

'Isobel, we can't—' Sophie began.

'Can't what? The man isn't here. He's obviously gone for a walk, or nipped out to the village, and forgotten the time. JJ probably asked him to sort out a portfolio of work to show me, as part of the interview.' Isobel shrugged. 'So, I reckon he meant us to see these.'

Sophie wasn't so sure, but Isobel was unstoppable. She turned over the first sketch, and drew a sharp intake of breath. 'Christ. Soph, this is *good*. It looks recent, too; the paper feels new.'

Sophie glanced over her friend's shoulder, and flushed. The sketch was of a woman reclining on a sheepskin rug. She was propped up on one elbow, and her mouth was open, her lower lip shiny. Her breasts were full, and her nipples were very hard, almost painfully so; Sophie felt her own nipples tingle in sympathy. The look on her face was that of a woman who'd just been very deeply satisfied. Sophie, remembering her day-dream in the bath, could imagine just what Alex Waters had done to his model to put that sort of look on her face.

The second picture was a similar pose to one of Sophie's favourite paintings, Degas' *Woman drying herself*. The model – the same woman as in the first sketch, Sophie assumed – was sitting with her back to the artist, a towel draped loosely round her so that the divide of her buttocks was just visible. There was a small, subtle difference, though, in the lines of the painting. The model's legs in this picture were spread more widely apart, and her hand – although you couldn't see it – was obviously working between her legs.

Isobel turned over the third painting, her hand shaking slightly. It was a different model, this time, but one who had an equally lush body. She was lying on her side, tilting slightly backwards, in front of a mirror. Her lower leg was stretched out, the toes pointed and the leg tensed. The foot of her upper leg was flat against her knee, with her knee pointed towards the ceiling. Her head was tipped back, and her eyes were closed. One hand was placed on her midriff, fingers pointing downwards towards her shaven delta, as though she were about to pleasure herself

'My God,' Isobel said softly. 'I'm not sure if this makes me want to touch myself, more, or to touch *her*. It's a hell of a horny picture.'

She turned to the next drawing. It was a close-up from what looked like the same modelling session. The focus was entirely on the woman's torso, from her navel to her knees. Again, she was lying on her side, in the same position as the previous sketch; but this time, in the mirror, you could distinctly see the heel of her hand pressed against her mons veneris, rubbing her pubis, and her middle finger was inserted in her quim, up to the second joint.

The next sketch in the series was again concentrated from the woman's knees to her navel; this time, though, there was a man crouching between her legs. His palms were placed flat against her thighs, widening her stance, and the tip of his tongue was made into a hard point, pressing against the tip of her clitoris.

Sophie's colour deepened as she recognised the face. Alex Waters. He looked older than the photograph in her book, but it was still very recognisably him. His hair was still down to his collar, curling, and his face was still smooth, with those high and haughty cheekbones. He looked exactly as she'd imagined him, in her fantasy, and the knowledge made a pulse beat hard between her legs.

'What wouldn't you give to change places with the model?' Isobel murmured huskily. 'Christ, I can almost feel him doing that to me.'

Sophie didn't answer; she was too busy trying to push her feelings back under control.

'He's gorgeous,' Isobel breathed.

'Don't vamp him, Isobel,' Sophie warned, her voice faintly unsteady.

'I'm not going to. I'm here to do a job. But . . .' Isobel swallowed. 'God, I think he'd turn any woman on. It makes me wet just thinking about it.'

'Isobel!' Sophie said, scandalised.

'Come on, don't say he doesn't affect you that way, too. If he's as gorgeous in the flesh as he is in the last photo I saw of him, I think any woman would be wet within seconds, wanting him.' Isobel moved her thumb over the sketch, careful not to touch the paper, but unable to stop the movement of stroking his face.

Suddenly, without warning, a hand descended on both their shoulders. The women jumped, and Isobel let the portfolio fall back onto the table with a shriek. They both turned to face Alex Waters, who was looking extremely angry.

Isobel recovered her composure first, holding out her hand. 'Isobel Moran.' As Sophie had advised her to do, she spoke very slowly and deliberately, facing him, so that he could read her lips easily. She smiled willingly at him, but Alex was impervious to her charm. He simply pointed to the door.

Isobel looked at Sophie. 'Remind him about JJ, and the appointment,' she hissed urgently.

Sophie, desperately trying to remember the sign for 'agent', and failing, fell back onto signing out the letters. She drew a J on her left palm with her index finger, curving down from the tip of her middle finger to her thumb, and repeated the action.

Alex frowned, as if to say, 'What the hell does he have to do with you?'; both Isobel and Sophie were surprised at just how expressive his face was.

'Tell him,' Isobel hissed again.

Sophie couldn't remember the sign for 'arrange', but 'meeting' was easier. Both index fingers held up, the rest of the fingers bunched into a fist, hands moving together. Then she pointed to Alex, and to Isobel, and signed 'JJ' again.

Alex looked at her, his eyes narrowing; then shook his head, and pointed to the door. Looking at Sophie, he curved one arm in front of his body, keeping his palm flat, and dropped his hand sharply.

Sophie nodded. 'Isobel, he wants us to go. *Now.*'

'What about my interview?'

'Isobel, I think we'd better go. You can sort this out with JJ, later.' Sophie looked apologetic, tipping her head to one side. She drew her right hand across the middle of her ribcage, keeping her palm flat, and made a small circular clockwise movement: *sorry.* She mouthed the word, too, adding, *for disturbing you.*

Alex said nothing, but stood there with his arms folded, and jerked his head towards the door.

'Come on, we've got to go,' Sophie said. She took Isobel's arm, and hustled her out of the door.

'Christ, I don't believe this.' Isobel was furious as she walked back to the car. 'Who the hell does he think he is? Agreeing to an interview, then chucking me out and refusing even to speak to me?'

'Isobel.' Sophie laid a hand on her friend's arm. 'We were in the wrong. We should have waited until he invited us in.'

'Balls. He had no intention of letting us in. I leaned on the doorbell, long enough.'

'Even so. It's his home, Isobel.'

'You call that hovel a *home?* It's just somewhere to live.' Isobel shook her head. 'Christ, the man's insane. He's lived on his own for too long; he can't cope with the outside world. It's obvious. I bet he has his groceries delivered, too – left outside the back door, and he leaves a cheque in an envelope under a brick, or something.'

'Now you're being ridiculous.' Sophie felt drawn to defend Alex. There had been something so vulnerable and lonely in his eyes, for just a moment, when she'd signed to him; then, the shutters had come down. 'Anyway, you said yourself that the sketches looked recent. Someone must have modelled for them.'

'That, or he did them from memory.' Isobel wasn't mollified. 'Bloody JJ. I'm going to ring him, and tell him to come down here to sort this out.' She took her mobile phone from her handbag, and switched it on. It beeped twice, and went off. Isobel, enraged, snarled at it. 'Oh, *fuck!*'

Apart from using the word 'bloody', Isobel wasn't usually given to swearing; Sophie raised an eyebrow. Her friend was really upset by all this. 'What's up?' she asked softly.

'It looks like the battery's flat. I could have sworn that I charged it up, yesterday morning – unless I accidentally left it switched on in my briefcase.' She rolled her eyes. 'Christ. Well, we'll drive to the village. There's bound to be a phonebox – or at least a phone we can use, in the local pub. *If* it's open.'

Sophie was surprised. Isobel was usually infuriatingly positive about things. 'It probably will be.'

'Come on, then.' Isobel unlocked the car door, and slid into the driver's seat. She put the keys in the ignition, and turned them; nothing happened. She frowned, and tried it again. Still, nothing happened. 'Christ, I don't *believe* this!' she said.

'What's up?'

'I don't know.' Isobel made a dismissive wave of her hand. 'I leave all that sort of thing to the garage. I'm hopeless with engines. All I know is, it won't start.'

Sophie winced. 'Sorry, I can't help you there, either.'

'Well, *he* must know. He's a bloke – and blokes know about cars, don't they?'

'Not necessarily.' Sophie coughed. 'And he's furious with us for barging into his house and snooping in his portfolio, so why should he help us?'

Isobel grimaced. 'You're probably right. So what now, Dr Watson? Dare you brave the lion's den, and ask if we can borrow his phone?'

'There wasn't one downstairs.'

'Well, JJ must get in touch with him, somehow. It must be somewhere else in the house.' Isobel rubbed her jaw. 'There's nothing else for it – apart from walking to the village, and I don't fancy doing that.' She spread her hands. 'What do you think?'

'We could ask – but just let me do it, will you?'

'I'm entirely in your hands.'

'Okay.' Sophie climbed out of the car again; Isobel followed her to the front door. Sophie pressed the bell, and waited; eventually,

Alex opened the door. He stood there with his arms folded.

Sophie looked straight at him. 'Hello. Can you help us, please?' She signed quickly: 'help', a flat hand trying to lift a heavy palm, and then 'please', lifting her hand to her mouth, touching her fingers to her lips and bringing them away in a curve.

Alex's face was still impassive, but there was a flicker in his eyes: whether it was amusement at her awkward signing, or whether he was impressed at her persistence, she wasn't sure.

She tried again. 'The car won't start.' She made as if she was steering a car, then shrugged and looked bewildered.

Alex spread his hands, as if to say, 'And what do you want me to do about it?'

'Can I use your phone, please?' 'Phone' was easy: thumb and little finger stretched out, middle fingers curled together, and the hand lifted to the face as though she were speaking into a receiver.

He shook his head.

'Please?' Sophie asked, signing as she spoke.

He shook his head again.

'Right.' She bit her lip, and took her diary from her handbag, and a pen. She flicked quickly to the blank pages at the back, and began to write in it. *Sorry, my signing isn't very good. Please can we borrow your phone to ring a garage?* She handed the diary to him; he read it, and took the pen from her.

'I don't have a phone. Walk to the village,' was the answer.

Isobel, who was reading over Sophie's shoulder, glowered. 'Tell him he's an arrogant, awkward bastard.'

A flicker of amusement passed across Alex's face; he signed quickly.

'What's that?' Isobel asked.

'Not sure.' Sophie put her right index finger across her arm, sliding it downwards, and brought her hands to her lips again in a curve, her fingers touching her lower lip. 'That's "slow down, please",' she told Isobel, who was frowning in bewilderment.

'Right.'

Alex repeated the signs again, this time more slowly. *My parents were married.*

Sophie suddenly realised what he meant, and couldn't help laughing. 'He said his parents were married.'

Isobel glowered. 'Bloody hell. He's being deliberately awkward.'

Alex nodded.

'I hate you,' she said.

He gave her the thumbs-up. *Good.*

Isobel folded her arms, and turned her back on him. 'Bloody, bloody bastard! I wish I'd never thought about doing this.'

'Isobel, you're being rude. Don't turn your back on him,' Sophie said softly.

'Why not? He's turned his back on us.'

'Put it this way, if you want to get your interview... Turn to face him. It's one of the quickest ways to upset a deaf person, turning your back so they can't see your face. That, or talking with your hand over your face so they can't lip-read.'

'Okay. What's the sign for "sorry"?'

'Hold your palm in front of you, just under your ribcage, and move it up and down, in a clockwise circle.'

'What does it mean if I do it anti-clockwise?' Isobel asked.

'Probably the opposite.'

'Right.' Isobel turned back to face Alex. 'Sorry.' She repeated the gesture Sophie had described. Then she took the pen and diary from Sophie. *We'll walk to the village. May we have some water first, please?*

Alex read it, and was silent for a moment; then, finally, he nodded, and moved aside, ushering them inside.

Five

Sophie and Isobel followed him into the kitchen; he filled two glasses from the tap, and handed one to each of them. His fingers touched Sophie's as he handed her the glass, and she shivered: it felt as though an electric shock had just run through her body. Alex, too, was aware of it; his dark eyes watched her keenly, but he said nothing.

Sophie flushed, and concentrated on drinking the water. 'What's "thank you"?' Isobel asked, *sotto voce*.

'Same as "please", but two hands.'

'Right.' Isobel gave Alex her best smile, and signed 'thank you'.

He shrugged, but didn't reply.

Isobel mimed sketching, pointed out of the door, and gave Alex the thumbs-up sign.

He curled his lip, and lifted one palm, making a pushing movement.

'What's that?' Isobel asked.

'Either he's telling you that you're pushy, or he's telling you to back off. Probably both.'

'Hm.' Isobel had brought her briefcase with her; she opened it, and brought out her conference folder. She wrote quickly on the pad. *Mr Waters, I arranged with your agent, JJ, to talk with you today. Would you prefer me to come back another day?* She pushed the note towards him; he read it swiftly, and shook his head.

Isobel smiled. *May I talk to you now?* she wrote.

Again, he read it, and shook his head. He mimed draining the glass, then pointed at the door.

Isobel sighed. 'Sophie – you try. Talk to him in sign.'

Sophie shook her head. 'I don't think that this is such a good idea.'

'I need that interview, Soph. Please.'

Sophie coughed. 'It won't work.'

'But will you try? Please?'

'Okay. But on condition that if he asks us to leave, we leave right away.' Sophie turned to Alex and smiled at him. He tipped his head on one side, waiting. She brought her hands together in front of her body, keeping her hands flat and her palms towards her, and locked them together between the thumbs and fingers.

To her embarrassment, Alex laughed, and walked over to her, bending down so that his mouth was next to her ear. 'Yes, I'd like that very much,' he whispered huskily.

Sophie frowned, not understanding; he stroked her face, pushing a tendril of hair behind her ear, and brought his mouth close to her ear again, his breath fanning against her neck and making her shiver. 'You just asked me if I'd like to have sex with you.'

Her face flamed. 'I didn't!' she exclaimed, shaking her head emphatically.

He lifted one eyebrow, and grinned.

'What's going on?' Isobel demanded.

'I . . .' Sophie was too embarrassed to admit to her friend that she'd mixed up the sign for 'friend' with the one for 'sexual intercourse'. She pointed to Isobel; Alex grinned, and mimicked her earlier sign, followed by a swift sign of pushing, and pulled a face. Sophie got the gist straight away. Alex didn't want to have sex with Miss Pushy, thanks very much.

Sophie resorted to paper, scribbling the words down and pushing the pad across to him. *What I was trying to say* – she underscored 'trying', heavily – *is that my friend would like to interview you.*

Alex took her hands, and put them into a very similar position to the one she'd used; the subtle difference was that her right index finger rested along the top of her left palm. Then he whispered in her ear. 'That's "friend".'

Her eyes widened. 'Sorry.'

'I'm not.' He grinned. 'I meant it, about your other sign. I'd like to make love with you – very much so.' His voice was low and husky; it sent a thrill through Sophie. He was being incredibly rude, whispering to her and ignoring Isobel; she knew that she ought to disapprove, but what he was saying to her . . . A shiver ran along her spine. The famous Alex Waters was chatting her up!

Watch it, Hayward, she told herself sharply. Number one, you're virtually engaged to Gary; number two, you're supposed to be helping Isobel get her interview; and number three, you don't sleep around. Not in this day and age. With Alex Waters, it would be just sex – no more, no less. Pure, uninhibited sex. No strings, no ties, no excuses.

A picture of his sketch flashed into her mind, and her skin coloured again. Sex. Finding out at first-hand what Alex had done to his model, to put that look on her face . . .

'What's your name?' he asked, still whispering to her.

He was near enough for her to smell his clean masculine tang; and his lips were almost brushing her ear. Sophie was shocked to find that she was aroused, her nipples hardening and her sex growing moist. No man had ever had that effect on her, before – even Gary.

She picked up the pen. *Sophie*, she wrote.

'Sophie. Wisdom.' His breath fanned her ear. 'Are you wise, I wonder, as well as beautiful?'

He was playing with her, and she knew it. And yet she couldn't resist him. *You're being rude to Isobel*, she wrote swiftly.

He grinned. 'So?' he whispered.

Isobel watched him, her eyes narrowed. She had no idea what he was saying to her friend, but, from the look on Sophie's face, Isobel could make a pretty good guess. He was trying to charm her into bed. If that happened, she thought, Sophie would be living out one of her teenage fantasies. And maybe, just maybe, Sophie could also get the answers to the questions for her. She stood up. 'Look, it's obvious that he isn't going to talk to me.'

'I'm sorry.' Sophie bit her lip, feeling guilty. She'd been virtually encouraging Alex in his rudeness.

'But he might talk to you. Why don't you stay here, while I go and find a mechanic?'

'I – look, Isobel, you can't go into the village on your own. It's miles away.'

'I'll be perfectly all right.'

'But you said that you didn't want to walk into the village. That's why we asked him if we could use his phone.'

Isobel rolled her eyes. 'Look, this is your one chance to talk to him about art. I suppose it's like me meeting a famous and reclusive writer I really admire – it's a one-off, so I'd make the most of it, in your shoes.'

'Right.'

'Besides, I need that interview.' She shrugged. 'He won't talk to me; but it looks as though he likes you.'

Sophie flushed. 'Isobel . . .'

'See you later. The questions are in my folder. Just do what you can for me, please?' Isobel winked at her, and left the kitchen.

'Miss Pushy's leaving me alone with you? That's very, very dangerous,' Alex told Sophie, taking her hand and drawing it up to his mouth. He kissed the tips of her fingers, in turn, and gently sucked her middle finger.

Sophie's eyes widened. God, the man knew how to seduce a woman. He'd obviously done it a lot, to be that skilled. She snatched her hand away, embarrassed and cross. She didn't want to be just another notch on his bed-post. And yet – she could so easily imagine herself making love with him.

'Talk to me, Sophie.' He took her hand, leading her over to the kitchen table, and sat down, patting the seat next to him. Sophie sat down, leaning against the table. 'What are you doing with Little Miss Pushy? Apart from the fact that she's your friend. I don't imagine that you have sex with her.' His lips twitched. 'Though *she* might like to have sex with you.'

Why do you keep talking about sex? Sophie wrote fiercely.

'You started it.' He took her hand, running his thumb and

forefinger up and down her fingers in turn.

She snatched her hand back again. *Isobel wanted to interview you. You agreed to do it.*

'Maybe I changed my mind.'

This was surreal, she thought. He was talking to her – but she could only sign to him, and badly, at that. Not trusting herself to make another mistake, she'd resorted to writing her words on paper. And it was difficult to argue with someone when you weren't communicating on equal terms.

'Want a coffee?' he asked, surprising her.

She nodded. 'Please.' That, at least, was one sign she knew was right.

'It'll be black, only. I don't use sugar, and I don't have any milk. Not fresh milk, anyway.'

She smiled. 'Thank you.'

He filled the kettle, switched it on, spooned instant coffee into two mugs – good coffee, she noticed – and came back to sit next to her. 'So how do you know Little Miss Pushy?'

'Don't keep calling her that. Her name's Isobel.'

He grinned, and stroked her face. 'Don't be so uptight. You know she's pushy. And she *is* little – about a foot shorter than me.'

Sophie smiled ruefully, and began to write, explaining that Isobel was her best friend, and they'd shared a house in London since university.

'You're very different.' He tipped his head on one side. 'Why did you come with her, today?'

'Because I'm learning sign language. She thought it might be helpful to have someone who could sign – but she wasn't trying to patronise you,' Sophie added hastily.

'I see. And why exactly are you learning sign?'

'It's complicated. I teach; one of my students is partially deaf, and I don't like it that she misses so much at lectures.' Sophie shrugged. 'I want to learn sign, so I can teach others who can't hear my lectures.'

'What do you teach?'

'History of art.'

'I'm history; I used to be an artist.' He paused. 'Do you teach about me?'

She shook her head. 'But I've always liked your work.'

'Indeed.' He stood up, abruptly, and made the coffee, returning with two mugs.

'Mr Waters . . .'

'Call me Alex.'

She smiled. This really was surreal. One of her long-term heroes, telling her to call him by his first name? 'Alex.' She rolled his name on her tongue, and flushed as she realised that she'd like to use her tongue on parts of him, not just his name. Christ. She had to keep control of herself. She was supposed to be helping Isobel. 'Would you let Isobel interview you?'

He shook his head.

'Then would you let me interview you, for Isobel?'

'Why?'

'Because she's my friend, and I want to help her.'

He sighed. 'Bloody JJ. I don't know why I let him talk me even into having people here – let alone agreeing to be interviewed.'

'Please?'

He paused; then, finally, nodded. 'All right. I'll do it. But it's not for Little Miss Pushy. It's for you.'

She handed him the list of questions; he took the pen from her, and began to write swift, terse and accurate answers. His inspiration was Burne-Jones, who painted angels. He'd always known that he wanted to paint. And yes, he still painted – but he painted only for himself, now, not for show.

Sophie watched him, and itched to sketch him: though she knew that she wouldn't do him justice. She'd always found anatomy difficult, and Alex was a man who exuded energy and movement. She couldn't translate that onto paper.

Her gaze drifted to his hands; he had beautiful hands, she thought. Slender yet strong, artistic, and very, very graceful. She could imagine those hands working on her body, and it made her shiver. Forcing herself not to think about that, she watched his face. The past ten years had been kinder to him than she'd expected. There were none of the deeply etched lines, broken veins or greying and thinning hair that she'd told herself he'd have. His hair was still dark, and still curling into his collar, as though he normally wore it short, but hadn't had it cut for a while. He hadn't run to fat, either; his body was firm, his muscles toned.

He was still as beautiful as in the photograph she'd fallen in love with, all those years before. He still had those incredible cheekbones, and a mouth which made her itch to trace her finger along it. His dark eyes were very intense; she'd seen them change from anger to amusement to pleasure, in the space of a few minutes. Alex was a volatile man; and he was incredibly, intensely, attractive.

She swallowed, trying to force herself to think of Gary, but it wasn't working. She could imagine Alex kissing her, all too easily. Then he'd unbutton her shirt, so very slowly, and caress each inch of skin as he uncovered it. And then . . .

She became aware that he was clicking his fingers by her ear. 'I've finished your questions. Wake up,' he said.

She smiled back. 'Sorry.'

'Penny for them?'

She shook her head. No way would she tell him what she'd been thinking!

'Sophie.' His voice grew husky, and he lapsed back into sign. He held his right hand up to his face, bunching the tips of his fingers and thumbs together as if he were finger-spelling the letter B, and then spread his fingers in a graceful sweep.

She shook her head, not understanding.

'You're beautiful,' he said softly.

She flushed.

'I want to paint you.'

She couldn't help the question. 'Like your other paintings?' The ones she'd seen in the living room, with Isobel.

He nodded. 'I want to paint you for me, not for show.' He clenched his hand into a fist, and drew it down his sternum.

Sophie frowned. 'I don't understand.'

'Desire,' he enlightened her. 'I desire you, Sophie. Very much.'

65

'I . . .'

'Oh, what the hell.' He bent his head, and kissed her.

It was better than her fantasy in the bath. His mouth was soft and sure, very gentle and yet very demanding, all at the same time. He took tiny bites at her lower lip, and she was lost, opening her mouth under his and letting him slide his tongue against hers. She closed her eyes; she could hardly believe that this was happening. Alex Waters was kissing her – and not just kissing her, but kissing her extremely thoroughly, and extremely well.

He broke the kiss. 'Sophie.'

Her eyes glittered. 'Yes?'

He cupped her face in his hands, making sure that she could see his lips. 'I want to make love with you.'

With you, not *to* you; the tiny change in emphasis made all the difference in the world. She couldn't turn him down. 'I . . .' She swallowed, knowing that she was about to do something incredibly stupid, but not being able to help herself. 'Yes.'

He smiled, and stood up, drawing her to her feet. 'Come with me.'

'Where?'

'To my bed.' He bent to kiss the tip of her nose; although Sophie was five feet eight, she was still a good five inches shorter than he was. 'Apart from the fact that it's a damn sight more comfortable than making love on my kitchen table, I'd rather have a closed door between us and the outside world, in case Miss Pushy comes back early.'

Isobel. Sophie closed her eyes. 'Alex. We shouldn't be doing this.'

'Why? Don't you want to?' He lifted one hand, brushing it over her erect nipples, which were clearly visible through her shirt. 'These tell me that you do.'

She swallowed. 'But . . . we're strangers.'

She spoke slowly, with exaggerated lip movements, so he followed her words effortlessly. 'Does that matter? Sophie, I want you – and you want me. What's wrong with that?'

Gary, for a start; but she couldn't tell him about her

almost-fiancé. She sighed. 'Alex. Don't make it hard for me.'

He grinned. 'I bet you'd blush if I told you that I already am hard for you.' His grin broadened, and he stroked her face. 'I was right. Sorry. I don't mean to be crude, to embarrass you. I suppose I'm not used to company.'

'Why do you live here, alone?'

'Is this on the record?'

She shook her head. 'I'm not a journalist, like Isobel. I'm asking because I want to know.'

He shrugged. 'It's easier, on my own. There's no-one to bother me. But, sometimes . . .' He bent his head, kissing her lightly on the mouth. 'Oh, Sophie.'

Her eyes glittered with unshed tears. 'You're being unfair.'

'I know, but I can't help it.' He tipped his head on one side. 'I want to paint you, and I want to make love with you. I want to kiss you all over, taste you and touch you and look at you. I want to feel your body moving against mine. I want to hear you with my hands.'

'Alex . . .'

'I wish I could hear you properly. I bet your voice is soft and low. Gentle and sweet, and surprisingly sexy, because you look like a pure English rose.'

She flinched. 'Now you're using emotional blackmail to get me into bed.'

He shook his head. 'I'm being honest. You had nothing to do with this.' He touched his ears, and shrugged. 'If you don't want to, I won't force you.'

She closed her eyes. The worst thing was, she did want to. From the moment his fingers had touched hers, so casually, she'd felt a surge of desire for him – greater than she'd ever felt for any man before. It wasn't just because he was her old hero. There was something about him – some kind of chemistry that sent her body haywire and her senses reeling

'Sophie. May I kiss you?'

She evaded the question. 'Why wouldn't you talk to Isobel?'

He grinned. 'Because, as she put it so succinctly, I'm an awkward bastard.'

'Yeah, and don't I know it.'

He chuckled. 'Sophie. Stop kidding yourself. You can feel it, too.'

'Feel what?'

'This.' He took her hand, placing it on his heart; she was surprised at how hard and fast his heart was beating. 'It's the same for you, too.' He transferred their linked hands to her breasts; her heart thudded against their fingers. 'See?'

'Alex – don't do this.'

'I want you, Sophie,' he persisted. 'Come to bed with me.' He kissed her, very lightly, and led her out of the kitchen.

I shouldn't be doing this, she thought. No way. I'm going to make a fool of myself, I'm being unfaithful to Gary, and – and Alex Waters is the most gorgeous man I've ever met. I can't help myself. I want him.

'Stop worrying,' he said gently, stroking her face as they reached the top of the stairs.

Worrying? He hadn't been facing her, so even if she had spoken aloud, he wouldn't have known what she had said.

'It shows on your face.' He smiled at her, his eyes sensuous and warm. 'There's nothing to worry about, Sophie. It's the most natural thing in the world, making love with someone you find attractive.'

'But I don't sleep around.'

'I'm not asking you to.' He bent down to rub his nose against hers. 'This is just between you and me; and I don't have sleeping in mind.' He smiled at her. 'Sophie.' Again, he drew her hand up to his mouth, taking her middle finger between his lips and sucking gently. She shivered. 'Like I said, you feel it as much as I do,' he said, smoothing one hand down her back and pulling her against him.

She could feel the unmistakable bulge of his erection pressing against her. She couldn't quite believe that Alex Waters was turned on by her but, at the same time, it was like her old adolescent fantasy coming true. He wanted to make love with her. He wanted her. Eventually, she nodded. 'All right, Alex.'

He shook his head. 'No. I don't want this to happen just because *I* want this to happen. I want it to be because you want it, too.'

She swallowed. 'Alex . . . You should know. I'm involved with someone, in London.'

'I guessed as much,' he said unexpectedly. He picked up her left hand, running his thumb and forefinger along her ring finger. 'You're not married or engaged – just committed, hm?'

'Gary's not my fiancé,' she said quickly.

'But you'd like him to be?'

She closed her eyes. At that precise moment, she didn't know. Until she'd met Alex face to face, she'd thought that she could be happy with Gary, settle with him. Now . . . What?

'Just be true to yourself,' Alex said quietly. 'It's your choice, Sophie. If you want to, we'll go back downstairs, drink coffee, and exchange life stories.'

'And if I say I want the alternative?' Sophie was surprised at herself. She hadn't been intending to say that, but the words had somehow bypassed her brain, coming straight from her gut.

'If you want the alternative, just walk this way.' He dropped her hand, and walked through the door at the side of the hall. She followed him, and he closed the door behind them.

The room was as spartanly furnished as the rest of the house, containing a large old-fashioned wardrobe, a chest of drawers which didn't match, and a large double bed with a wrought-iron frame, a king-size duvet, and several large thick pillows. There wasn't a lamp or a table beside his bed; whatever else Alex did in his bedroom, reading wasn't part of it, she thought. Those pillows weren't there to prop up his head while he had his nose in a book: they were there for other reasons. Reasons which, she thought with a thrill, involved making love.

His eyes glittered. 'This is the last time I'll ask you, Sophie. Are you sure about this?'

She nodded. 'Yes, I'm sure.'

He removed her glasses, placing them on the table next to his bed. Then he began to unbutton her white shirt; as he uncovered each inch of skin, he caressed it with his fingertips, sensitising it, until Sophie wanted to push his hands away and rip her shirt off, regardless of the buttons. His eyes glittered, as if he knew what she was thinking, but he said nothing – just continued that slow, thorough exploration of her body.

At last, he undid the final button, and slid the garment from her shoulders. To her surprise, he didn't just let it crumple onto the floor, but hung it neatly over the doorknob. 'I hate ironing,' he said with a grin, 'and I don't think that you'd like Miss Pushy to see you all crumpled.'

'She's not that pushy,' Sophie protested, knowing that she was lying. Isobel was one of those women with boundless confidence, who knew what she was doing and always went for it.

'I don't want to talk about her. This is about you and me.' Alex laid his finger gently over her lips; she smiled, and drew his finger into her mouth, sucking gently on it.

He smiled at her, then, his lips curving with sensual promise, and unzipped her skirt. It fell to the floor in a rustle; she stepped to one side, and Alex retrieved the garment, hanging it on top of her skirt.

'Mm.' He walked back over to her, brushed the swell of her breasts with the backs of his fingers. 'So beautiful.' Again, he pulled his clenched fist down over his sternum; Sophie felt an answering kick of desire in the pit of her stomach.

He smiled at her widened eyes, and slid his fingers under the lace cup of her bra, pushing the material down to reveal her breast. He did the same with the other one; then he tipped his head on one side, scrutinising her. Sophie felt a slow flush spread over her face. Christ, what was she doing, letting him make her look so lewd, while he was still fully dressed?

As if he knew what she was thinking – and wanted to make her stop – he dropped to his knees in front of her, nuzzling his face against her bare midriff. She could imagine him kissing his way down her body, and the thought made her gasp, widening the gap between her legs and sliding her hands into his hair.

God, he felt so good; she nearly laughed as she remembered

her picture of the bloated, greasy-haired sot. Alex Waters was nothing of the kind. If anything, he'd grown even more attractive over the years, the faint lines on his face adding character rather than making him ugly. And the fact that this difficult man, who only spoke when he chose, was communicating with *her* . . . She shivered, and increased the pressure of her fingertips against his scalp.

Alex made a small murmur of pleasure, and hooked his fingers into the sides of her knickers. Sophie made no protest as he drew the wispy garment downwards; she leaned against him for balance, lifting first one foot and then the other, so that he could remove her knickers completely. She tensed as she felt his breath against her inner thigh; then relaxed again as she felt his tongue stroke over her skin.

She closed her eyes, willing him to kiss her more intimately, to put that beautiful haughty mouth against her quim and take her to the edge of pleasure; she was half-shocked at the raw current of desire flowing through her, but she was powerless to resist. Isobel, Gary, her job – everything was forgotten in the urgent need to feel Alex's tongue stroke the length of her quim. He teased her a little longer, blowing on the patch of skin he'd licked; she gave a groan of impatience and, at last, he slid his hands round to cup her buttocks, and began to lick her clitoris, letting his tongue move in a slow broad sweep across it, again and again and again. She gasped, and pushed her pubis against him; he laughed, and made his tongue into a sharp point, moving it rapidly over her clitoris in a figure-of-eight movement until she was moving against him in an agony of pleasure.

It seemed to go on forever, until she was balancing on the brink of her orgasm; the strength of it caught her unawares, and she cried out, shuddering against his mouth. Alex held her close, supporting her suddenly shaky legs, waiting until the aftershocks of her climax subsided; then he picked her up, and laid her on the bed. He stripped swiftly, unabashed by her gaze; God, he was gorgeous, she thought. Seeing him naked made her itch to touch him, to touch him and sculpt him and paint him.

His cock was impressive: beautifully shaped, and it made her want to caress him with her mouth and her hands. She licked her lips, and sat up; she put her hands behind, as if to take off her bra, but he shook his head. 'I like it. It makes you look wanton.'

She flushed. 'I—'

'You're not used to being wanton?' He grinned. 'You should do this more often, Sophie.' His eyes travelled her body. 'You're lovely. I still want to paint you.'

She shook her head. 'I'm not the type.'

'A private painting. Something for me – not for show. Just for you and me.' He sat on the bed, and drew his hand down her body, smoothing the curve of her abdomen.

She tipped her head back among the pillows, and he smiled. 'Sophie. Lovely, lovely Sophie.' He bent his head again, and caressed her swollen nipple with the tip of his nose.

She gasped, and he shifted, kneeling between her legs. 'Sophie.'

She opened her eyes, and looked at him.

'Tell me what you want.'

It was so close to her fantasy that her eyes widened in shock.

'Tell me, Sophie,' he murmured, drawing his finger along her lower lip.

'I want you to . . .' She swallowed, and looked away from his gaze, suddenly shy.

He smiled at her. 'Sophie.'

She looked back at him, and he put his hands together in the sign she'd used mistakenly in his kitchen.

'You and me. Is that what you want?' he asked softly.

God, but he had a gorgeous voice, she thought. The sort of voice that you could imagine whispering all sorts of insidious suggestions. The sort of voice that could make you beg and demand and . . . She nodded. 'Yes.'

'Tell me. Tell me what you want.'

The thing with Alex was that she didn't have to say it. All she had to do was mouth it. 'I want you to . . .'

'Tell me, Sophie.'

'I want you to make love with me.'

He grinned, as if he knew that she'd wanted to use an earthier phrase, but couldn't quite bring herself to say it. 'My pleasure.' He drew one hand between her thighs, gently caressing them apart, and knelt in front of her; he slid one hand between them, fitting the tip of his cock to her moist and puffy sex. Then, at long last, she felt him push against her; she pushed back, and he slid easily into her.

All the times she'd made love with Gary, with one or two other boyfriends – nothing compared to *this*, Sophie thought, feeling him fill her. She arched up, and he laughed, bending down to rub his nose against hers. 'Good?'

She nodded, not trusting herself to speak – knowing that he couldn't hear if her voice wobbled, but embarrassed all the same.

'You feel good, too,' he told her. 'Warm and wet – and beautifully tight. I love the feel of your cunt wrapped round my cock.'

She flushed at the coarseness of his words; then, as he began to thrust, she forgot her embarrassment and lifted her legs, wrapping them round his waist and pulling him deeper inside her.

'Lovely Sophie,' he whispered against her ear, easing his hand between them so that he could caress her breasts, rolling each nipple in turn between his finger and thumb. Sophie arched against him, and began to match his movements, pushing up as he drove into her, and flexing her quim as he withdrew.

She felt the ripples of her orgasm begin again, a warm rolling sensation on the soles of her feet, moving up over her calves; as it reached her solar plexus, she cried out, gripping her legs tight round Alex's waist. He gave an answering cry as the rippling of her sex round his cock pushed him into his own orgasm, and buried his head in her neck, breathing in her scent and holding her close.

After what seemed like hours – though Sophie knew that it could only have been minutes – she felt him soften and withdraw; he rolled over onto his side, pulling her round so that her head rested on his shoulder. She slid her arm round his waist, and lay against him, in perfect peace.

'Sophie.' He stroked her hair. 'Little Miss Pushy will be back from the village, soon.'

She sat up, then. 'We'd better dress.'

He smiled. 'I'd like to shower with you – but the water's probably cold, and I'd only end up making love with you again. The idea of you and water together is a bit too much for my self-control.' He licked his lower lip. 'You're as lovely as I imagined, downstairs.'

She flushed, embarrassed. 'We'd better—'

'Dress. I know,' he finished. He sat up, and kissed her forehead. 'Lovely Sophie.' He sighed. 'You're right.'

She stood up and dressed swiftly, raking her hand through her hair and hoping that Isobel wouldn't guess what had gone on between them; Alex took his time, watching her. Then, finally, he took her hand and squeezed it. 'Coffee, I think.'

'Coffee,' she agreed shakily. His eyes were sending her a completely different message – a much more sensual suggestion, and one she wanted to agree with. But then, there was Isobel to consider; and she couldn't bear the idea of Isobel condoning what she'd just done.

'Come on.' He handed her glasses back to her, smiled at her, and led her downstairs.

Six

He made them another cup of coffee; they sat at the kitchen table in easy silence, not needing to talk. Sophie was still half in a dream, replaying what had just happened, and trying to believe that it was really true; she didn't want to speak, in case she broke the spell. Alex merely watched her, saying nothing and photographing her mentally, for later. He was looking forward to painting her, in the privacy of his studio, sketching the remembered lines of her body, the way her head tipped back and her mouth opened with pleasure as orgasm poured through her. The way her eyes turned almost navy blue, when she was aroused, and her lower lip grew full and deep vermilion.

Some time later, there was the bang of the door; Isobel hadn't bothered with the bell, this time. She simply marched into the kitchen, her face betraying her bad mood.

'What's up?' Sophie asked.

'It's early-closing day in the village.' She glowered at Alex. 'And he bloody well knew it, when he let me walk there. It took me over an hour!'

Alex gave her a grin of pure wickedness, then winked at Sophie.

Sophie didn't rise to the bait. 'So we can't get the car fixed?'

'There wasn't anywhere open with a phone – not even the village pub. There wasn't a phone box outside the post-office, either. He doesn't have a phone – ' she jerked her thumb at Alex ' – and I don't have a charger on me, so my mobile's useless. So it looks like we can't do anything until tomorrow.'

'Right.' Sophie sighed. 'Unless we can maybe walk to the next house, use a phone there?'

'I tried a few houses in the village. The place is a dormitory

75

village for Cambridge, and the few people who were in didn't have a phone. I can't believe how backward the Fens are. I thought it was just a stereotype – but it really is a time warp, around here. I'm surprised they're not still using quill pens and candles.' Isobel rolled her eyes. 'It looks like we're stuck in this bloody place, for the rest of today.'

Alex was still watching her with amusement; he turned to Sophie, making his hands into what looked like claws, holding them towards himself, hunching his shoulders, and moving his hands up in small jerky movements.

'What's that?' Isobel demanded. 'A grizzly bear impression?'

Sophie's lips twitched. 'He's saying that you're angry. So yes, I suppose you could put it that way.'

Isobel glowered at Alex. 'I know you can speak. So why don't you?'

He gave her a mocking grin, and folded his arms.

Isobel paced the kitchen. 'I don't bloody believe this. This is England, for God's sake, not some banana republic! There must be some way to get in contact with London.'

'I'm afraid not. You're stuck here, until tomorrow.'

Isobel's eyes widened in surprise. It was the first time that she'd heard Alex speak; although she knew that his deafness was caused by an accident, so his voice wouldn't be affected – he wouldn't have the nasal intonation of someone who'd been born profoundly deaf, or lost his hearing at an early age – she still hadn't expected him to have such a rich, melodious voice. A voice which she could easily imagine whispering much more wicked and voluptuous things; a voice which made her stomach kick. He was incredibly attractive, she realised with shock. Once that scowl had gone and that hooded wary look in his eyes had vanished . . . Alex Waters was gorgeous.

He looked at her, holding his hand up as if holding a mug, and tipping it towards him. 'Coffee?' he asked, holding his head on one side and giving her a warm smile.

'Thank you.' She nodded, her surprise deepening. What had caused his sudden change of mood? Why had he suddenly decided to speak to her? JJ had said that Alex could be an awkward bastard; what he hadn't said was that Alex could be incredibly disarming, when he chose. One to you, JJ, she thought wryly. I wasn't expecting this.

As he turned to the kettle, she looked at Sophie, mouthing, 'What the hell did you do to him, Soph?'

Sophie flushed. 'Nothing.' She hated lying; but she knew that she couldn't tell Isobel the truth. It made her feel too much like a tart, a groupie who couldn't wait to get her knickers off for her idol, and she couldn't handle the feelings of shame that washed through her at the thought.

'Did you get my interview?'

Sophie nodded, and pointed to the sheet of paper on the side.

'Thanks, Soph. You're an angel.' Isobel smiled at her, and sat down at the kitchen table.

Alex returned with a cup of black coffee. 'There's no milk or sugar.'

'That's okay. I like my coffee like that, anyway. Thanks.' She nodded at her interview sheet. 'And thank you for doing that. I appreciate it.'

He said nothing, merely inclining his head.

A sudden thought struck Isobel, and she grabbed her pad, scribbling frantically, and pushed it towards Alex. He scanned it swiftly, grinned, and shook his head.

'Damn,' Isobel said softly.

'What's up?' Sophie asked.

'I just wondered if he knew anything about cars. Maybe he could fix it.' Isobel glowered. 'That's it. I swear, when I get back to London, I'm selling that bloody rust-bucket and buying a new one.'

Sophie chuckled. 'You've been saying that for nearly two years.'

'Yeah.' Isobel sighed. 'I never thought that it would die on me in the middle of nowhere, though. Christ.' She sighed. 'Well, we can't get the car fixed until tomorrow. The pub isn't open – and even if it had been, there was no mention of accommodation on the board outside. I shouldn't think it does bed and breakfast.' She bit her lip. 'That leaves us two choices. Either we have to sleep in the car, or he'll have to put us up.'

'Isobel, you can't ask Alex to let us stay here!' Sophie said.

'Well, I don't fancy sleeping in the car. Got any better ideas?'

Sophie's stomach turned to water. The longer that Alex and Isobel spent together, the more likely it was that Isobel would guess what had happened between them – and that was the last thing that Sophie wanted. Her time with Alex was – well, private, a kind of dream, and she wanted to keep it that way. 'You can't,' she said again.

Isobel merely smiled, and wrote swiftly on her pad again, passing the sheet of paper to Alex. He read it, and shook his head.

Please? Look, there's nowhere else for us to stay. We can't sleep in the car overnight.

Alex merely folded his arms again, and stared at her.

Isobel rolled her eyes. 'Oh, Christ. Soph, you ask him.'

Sophie shook her head. 'We can't impose.'

'It's his bloody fault in the first place. If he had a phone . . .'

'Isobel, it's pointless having a phone if you're deaf, and you know it.' Sophie's temper snapped. 'Can't you be reasonable about this? It won't kill us to sleep in the car.'

'Yeah.' Isobel grabbed the pad again, and wrote something else.

Alex read it, and his eyes narrowed. Yes, she had a point. Little Miss Pushy was a lot shorter than Sophie; she could sleep in the car without ending up with a crick in her neck, whereas Sophie would be far less comfortable.

The thought of Sophie spending the night in his house made him harden again. He could imagine creeping into her room in the middle of the night, waking her in the nicest possible way, with his hands and his mouth. The way that she'd make tiny noises which he couldn't hear, but which he could feel with his hands – small moans of pleasure as he stroked her to arousal . . . His eyes met hers, and she flushed deeply. He smiled to himself. She felt it as much as he did, but she was shy about it; he found her reticence enchanting. He'd never met anyone like her before, and he was shocked to realise just how badly he wanted to know her more.

Isobel caught the look which passed between them, and her eyes widened. Something had obviously happened while she'd been on her abortive trip to the village. She wasn't sure whether Alex had tried to chat up Sophie and she'd rebuffed him, or whether something more intimate had happened between them. Whatever: Alex was fascinated by Sophie. She folded her arms. This was a waiting game, she thought. And as Alex Waters so obviously lusted after Sophie . . . Well, he'd crack before she did. He'd let them stay.

Alex took the pad, and wrote swiftly. *I don't have any visitor's rooms.*

'That's okay. I'll sleep on the sofa,' Isobel retorted, not bothering to write, this time.

Alex looked at her, seeing the glitter in her eyes, and stood up. 'You can do what the hell you like. I'm going to paint.'

He stomped upstairs; there was the distinctive sound of a door slamming, followed by the click of a lock.

'Well.' Isobel spread her hand. 'That's that, then. Mr Volatile says that we can stay.'

'Isobel, I'm not sure if—'

'For God's sake, Soph, stop being so wet!' Isobel cut in. 'You know damn well we can't sleep in the car. I can sleep on the sofa; he's probably going to sulk in his studio until tomorrow morning, so you might as well have his bed.'

Sophie's flush deepened. Alex's bed – the bed where she'd shared so much pleasure with him, such a short time before.

'And before you start arguing,' Isobel added, 'you're too tall to sleep on the sofa. You'll get a crick in your neck, and you'll be in pain all day at work.'

Work. Sophie winced. 'God, I forgot about work.'

'There's no way of getting through to the university – unless you can find a friendly homing pigeon, or whatever it is they use around here. You'll have to wait until tomorrow,' Isobel said. 'If we go into the village early, somewhere will be open. You can ring them then, and tell them that you're going to be late. I'm sure someone in the department can cover for you. I mean, you've helped out other people often enough. They can help you, for a change.'

' I suppose so.'

'Exactly.' Isobel stood up, and went over to the kettle, filling it again. 'More coffee?'

'Mm.'

Sophie was silent as Isobel made them both another coffee; she cupped her hand round her mug, feeling miserable. All she wanted to do was to go home – to leave, before things got really difficult. She could imagine Alex and Isobel having a huge row, if they were in the same house for much longer, and the last thing she wanted to do was to be an interpreter between them.

'Well, we're stuck here, so we might as well go and sit in the garden – get some fresh air, and enjoy the English countryside,' Isobel said. Her tone was light, but there was a slight edge to it. Sophie knew why, too; Isobel had lived in a small country village until she was eighteen, and had been desperate to go to university in London. She loved the hustle and bustle of the big city. Silence and stillness irritated her, made her want to move around and do something – anything – to break the monotony.

Sophie followed her friend outside.

'I wonder why he's cut himself off like this?' Isobel mused.

'Don't start on him, Isobel. You've got your interview; and you promised not to muck-rake.'

'I know, I know. But a man as talented as this . . . Why throw it all away, Soph? It's such a waste. I know there was an accident, and I know he feels to blame – not because I asked JJ, but because I did some research, and looked up a few cuttings,' she said, seeing Sophie's eyes glitter protectively. 'The model who was driving was his girlfriend. Maybe he was supposed to drive, or something, but had had too much to drink – and so had she.' Isobel shrugged. 'I dunno. There's no point in speculating; and no, before you say it, I'm not going to be crass enough to ask him.' Her lips twitched. 'From the look of his portfolio, though, he hasn't lived the life of a monk.'

Sophie could have testified to that, but wisely kept silent.

'I suppose I'd be the same, if Tony had been driving and I knew that he wasn't in a fit state, and he'd been killed.' She shrugged. 'It must be difficult, living with that kind of guilt. Combine that with an artistic temperament, and it's no wonder he's so volatile. Nice for about one second, and an awkward bastard for the next hour.' She was thoughtful. 'And not being able to communicate . . . It must be awful. It was bad enough when he refused to speak to me, and I had to resort to paper.'

'Yes. If you're deaf, you miss a lot of conversation,' Sophie agreed. 'I know that from Adèle, my student. It's very frustrating.'

Isobel stared at the garden. 'This place is a complete mess.'

'Maybe he doesn't like gardening.'

'He could pay someone to do it. I dunno, make himself a place like Giverny.' Isobel and Sophie had gone to France for a month in the summer, three years previously, and Sophie had dragged Isobel to Monet's gardens. Isobel hadn't wanted to go, not liking Impressionist art, but had fallen in love with the place when they arrived there.

'He does portraits, not landscapes.'

'Even so.' Isobel stared at Alex's incredibly untidy back garden. 'You can't even call this a wild flower meadow. I bet it hasn't seen a scythe in three years. It's just – wild.'

'Maybe there are some rare plants in there.'

'Maybe.' Isobel was thoughtful. 'It's the sort of place you could do a garden makeover on. It'd make a great feature – maybe not for *Vivendi*, but for one of the homes and garden mags. Maybe I could have a word with one of the editors . . .'

Sophie rolled her eyes. 'Oh, for God's sake, Isobel. You've been lucky in getting an interview; no way will he let you dig up his garden, as well.'

'I suppose not,' Isobel said grudgingly. 'This is the sort of place people use as retreats. I couldn't handle it, though.'

'The idea of you having to spend a day without a phone or a radio is quite something,' Sophie teased.

Isobel rolled her eyes. 'Well, I'm just not the quiet and

meditative type.' She glanced up at the sky. 'I have to admit, though, this is impressive. Acres and acres of blue. Is this the sort of thing you'd paint, Soph?'

Sophie wrinkled her nose. 'I wouldn't describe my daubs as painting.'

'Come on, Soph. I like your still lives. That one you were doing the other day, of the irises – it's really lovely.'

Sophie shook her head. 'I just don't have the gift. Compare my stuff with Alex's – it's dull and lifeless. You can see the difference immediately.'

'Yeah. He paints people, you paint flowers.' Isobel saw the irritation on her friend's face, and put her hand on Sophie's arm. 'Sorry, Soph. I didn't mean that to sound so flippant. Seriously, I think your stuff is good. I wish you'd show it to Tony.'

Sophie laughed wryly. 'My work's hardly the stuff you'd see in a London gallery, and you know it.'

'How about JJ, then? He's a sweetie, Soph – you'd really like him.'

Sophie shook her head. 'Isobel, I paint for pleasure – nothing more. I paint for me.'

'That's something else you have in common with Alex,' Isobel said quietly.

She stamped down a patch of grass, checking it for nettles, and sat down; Sophie followed suit. They lapsed into a companionable silence, drinking their coffee; eventually, Isobel sighed. 'I'm sorry about all this, Soph. The whole thing was only meant to take an hour.' She smiled ruefully. 'And so much for our girly lunch and shopping spree in Cambridge.'

'Yes.' Sophie was suddenly aware that she was hungry.

Isobel wrinkled her nose. 'I wonder if our temperamental artist would mind if I fixed us something to eat?'

'We can't possibly—'

Isobel cut her off with a wave of her hand. 'Look, he said we could do what we bloody well liked, and I'm hungry.' She stood up. 'Are you coming in with me, or not?'

Sophie would have liked to sit outside for a while longer,

watching the sun sinking; but now that Isobel had mentioned food . . . 'All right.' She followed Isobel indoors again.

Isobel rummaged in the kitchen cupboards, coming up with a tin of tuna, a jar of olives and some dried pasta. The fridge yielded some elderly mushrooms and some butter. Isobel wrinkled her nose. 'It's not exactly going to be *haut cuisine*, but I can do something with this.' She smiled wryly. 'I don't suppose there's any point in banging on his studio door, or yelling up to see if he wants to share this with us.' She shrugged. 'Ah well.'

She put the pasta on to boil, then fried the mushrooms, adding the tuna and olives. While she cooked, Sophie found the cutlery and crockery and a pepper mill, and laid the table.

'It's a shame there isn't any salad – or any bread,' Isobel said. She glanced at the wine rack. 'So we might as well have a bottle to go with this lot, instead.'

'Isn't it taking it too far, raiding his wine rack?' Sophie felt guilty enough about Isobel cooking them a meal, without having actually asked Alex's permission.

Isobel shook her head. 'I'll leave our artist friend some of this. It'll be as good cold as it is hot, so it's up to him when he eats it. But with the sort of day this has been, I could really, really do with some wine.' She rolled her eyes. 'And before you get sniffy about this, Sophie, I'll replace everything I've used. I'll send some wine down with JJ, or something.'

'Right.' Sophie bit her lip. 'I'm sorry. I'm being wet.'

'Yes, you bloody well are,' Isobel said crossly. 'We come all the way here to interview the man; he's rude to me, he won't answer my questions, and then I find that we're stuck in this godforsaken hole until tomorrow.' She shook her head. 'I can't stand it, Soph. The silence. He doesn't even have any music around here!'

'Isobel,' Sophie pointed out quietly, 'number one, you already have the answers for your interview. Number two, a deaf person is hardly going to have a music centre in the house. And number three, it's not his fault that your car's so unreliable.'

'I suppose not.' Isobel paused. 'So are you going to sort that wine, or what?'

Sophie nodded, and chose a bottle of red wine from the rack. The food smelled good, she thought; maybe the aroma wafting through the house would tempt Alex out of his studio to join them. But then, on the other hand, maybe not. A horrible suspicion niggled at her. Just what *was* he doing in his studio? He'd said that he wanted to paint her; she flushed deeply. God, if he had a good memory, and he sketched her, the way she'd been when they'd made love . . .

She shook herself. No. He'd probably just escaped there to avoid any more of Isobel's questions. Her lips quirked. Little Miss Pushy. Deaf people always went for the obvious – even if it was rude – when they had sign names for people. Someone who was fat or pregnant would be signed as a large stomach; someone who was short would be shown as tiny, or tall as very tall. And Isobel . . . Well, her most obvious characteristic was that she was pushy. No wonder Alex had given her that sign name.

Eventually, Isobel finished cooking the pasta; she drained it, and added the mushroom, olive and tuna mixture to it. She spooned a third of the mixture into a bowl, covering it with a plate, and then served up her own and Sophie's meal. She lifted her glass in a mock toast. 'Well, Soph. Here's to a successful interview, and the gem of my series. I hope.'

'Yeah.' Sophie tasted her pasta. 'This is good.'

'Thanks.' Isobel accepted the compliment with ease. She tipped her head on one side, and looked at Sophie. 'So what exactly *did* happen, while I went to the village?'

'Not a lot,' Sophie said shortly.

'Before I left, it was pretty obvious that he was trying to chat you up.'

Sophie rolled her eyes. 'For God's sake, Isobel, do you have to be so bloody inquisitive?'

'It's my journo temperament,' Isobel told her, completely unabashed. 'But okay, if you don't want to talk about it, I won't ask any more.' Sophie had said that she wanted to keep her dream of her idol intact. No doubt he'd made a move, and she'd turned him down. She glanced through Alex's answers to her interview

84

questions while she ate, and her eyes widened in surprise. 'I wouldn't have put him down as a Pre-Raphaelite aficionado.' Her eyes glittered. 'Having said that, that portfolio . . . Soph, I loved them. JJ just *has* to make him exhibit those.'

Sophie shook her head. 'Alex said that he paints just for himself, nowadays. Leave it at that.'

'The public really ought to see them. It's a crime, keeping them locked away like this.'

'Just leave it,' Sophie said. 'And don't think of stealing any, either.'

'I'm not *that* amoral,' Isobel said, nettled.

'I don't mean that you'd take them for yourself – I know you wouldn't do that. I mean that I don't want you taking them to Tony behind Alex's back, for the exhibition.'

'I won't.'

'Promise?'

'All right, I promise.' Isobel was rueful. 'You know, Soph, he's very attractive. When he speaks, and when he smiles, that is. I didn't realise just how gorgeous he was going to be. That mouth, those eyes . . .'

'Isobel,' Sophie said through gritted teeth. 'Please, will you just stop it?'

Isobel grinned. 'Don't worry, I'm not going to vamp him.' She took another mouthful of pasta, savouring the tang of the olives. 'Though, in other circumstances, I'd like to.' She licked her lower lip. 'I can imagine just what he did to his models, to put that sort of look on their faces.'

Sophie flushed to the roots of her hair. She couldn't just guess – she knew from experience exactly what Alex had done. 'Do you mind?' she hissed.

Isobel smiled. 'Keep your hair on, Soph.'

Sophie ate the rest of her meal in silence. Isobel was her best friend but, sometimes, she really wanted to strangle Isobel. The last thing she wanted was to be teased about Alex.

When they'd finished one bottle of wine, Isobel opened another. 'Come on. Let's go and sit in comfort.' Alex's sofa was shabby, but it was surprisingly comfortable; Sophie found herself relaxing. As long as Isobel stayed away from the subject of Alex's paintings, she'd be fine.

Eventually, she yawned; Isobel grinned. 'It's the fresh country air, no doubt.'

'Yes.'

'And you've been working too hard, too.'

'I just need more sleep than you do,' Sophie said ruefully.

'Why don't you go to bed? This place is so small, it won't take you a minute to find the bedroom.'

Sophie already knew where Alex's bedroom was: not that she was going to tell Isobel that. She frowned. 'But – what about Alex?'

'I'll probably still be up when he decides to come out of his studio.' Isobel grinned. 'And he can bloody well sleep on the floor of his studio, to make up for being so awkward, today.'

'Right.' Sophie yawned again. 'Well – see you in the morning, then.'

Isobel smiled at her, and followed her upstairs. 'I need a sheet, or something, to put on the sofa. It's too warm for a blanket or a quilt,' she said. 'There must be an airing cupboard, somewhere – or a linen chest.' Her eyes widened as she peered round the door of Alex's bedroom. 'God, he really believes in living like a monk, doesn't he? No home comforts for Mr Volatile.'

Sophie coloured, but said nothing. It wasn't quite how she viewed things – not after the way Alex had made love to her. There was nothing remotely monk-like about him.

'Well, there's no linen chest in here.' Isobel tried another door; it was locked. 'Obviously his studio, and he wants us to keep out of it,' she said wryly. She tried the last door; in the bathroom, there was indeed an airing cupboard, and there was a pile of neatly folded and crisply pressed white sheets. 'That's me sorted, then.' She smiled at Sophie. 'See you in the morning. Sleep well.'

'You, too,' Sophie murmured.

When Isobel returned to the sitting room, she dropped the sheet over one arm of the sofa, poured herself another glass of wine, and took the portfolio from the coffee table. She leafed through the sketches, marvelling at Alex's eye for detail. He really was incredible, she thought. The way he'd caught his model just on the edge of orgasm, with her mouth open in pleasure and her eyes squeezed tightly shut, as if she couldn't bear light to diffuse the intensity of her inner sparkling.

He hadn't concentrated just on her face, either. The way she was lying, the way her muscles were tensed as her orgasm poured through her... The effect of the wine and the eroticism of the pictures made Isobel's libido stir. She was half lying on the sofa, and it was the easiest thing in the world to undo the button of her trousers, and slide the zip downwards.

She pressed her hand to her belly, her fingers pointing downwards, and slowly moved her hand along her abdomen. She cupped her mons veneris, pressing lightly against her pubic bone and enjoying the beginnings of her arousal. Desire flowed through her; she slid her hand lower. Her middle finger parted her labia, and she began to rub herself, letting her fingers glide along a well-travelled path across her intimate folds and crevices.

The nub of her clitoris was already hard, and she touched it lightly, teasing herself until she could bear it no more and began to press harder, harder, pushing herself to the brink of orgasm. Her internal muscles convulsed sharply but, instead of stopping, she drove herself on, closing her eyes and tipping her head back against the sofa.

She wondered quite what Alex had done to his models, to make them act so lewdly for him? Had he taken them to his bed, first, aroused them to the brink of orgasm, and then led them through to his studio so that he could sketch the results when they climaxed? Or had he taken them into his studio – which was no doubt just as sparsely furnished as the rest of the house? Had he made them strip and lie on a bare wooden floor, feeling the hardness against their bodies rather than sinking into the softness of a rug or a mattress? And then, had he aroused them himself, using his hands and his mouth, or had he made them perform for him?

Isobel shivered at the thought, and wriggled against the sofa. She could imagine performing for Alex – and, my God, would she give him the show of his life! The handsome yet ascetic artist would be working, trying to regard her as coolly as Sophie regarded her arrangements of lilies and irises. They'd start in the studio; he'd expect her to strip for him, coolly and impersonally, but Isobel would do nothing of the kind.

Even though, as he couldn't hear music, there wouldn't be a small stereo in the corner to play sensual jazz – as there was in Sophie's studio – Isobel had an excellent memory. When she'd heard a piece of music once, she could often recall it; in Alex's studio, that talent would come in very useful. She'd gone to an exhibition of belly-dancing, once, and fallen in love with the sensuous wailing music; before Alex, she would replay it in her mind, and dance to it as she undressed, moving her body sinuously and weaving to the music in her head.

Once she'd caught his attention, she'd shed her clothes slowly, so very slowly, giving him tantalising glimpses of an inner thigh, an exposed breast. Then, when she was finally naked in front of him, she'd continue dancing. This time, instead of removing her clothes, she'd run her hands over her body, sliding them over her hips, over the curves of her buttocks, then over her belly, moving up to cup her breasts, and then moving along her shoulders and down again, moving all the time in that sinuous way.

Then she'd let her hands slide down to touch herself more intimately, smoothing the fleshy mound of her mons veneris. She'd tantalise him by moving her hands along her moistening quim, dipping her fingers in the nectar and bringing her hand back up to her face so that she could inhale the aroma of her arousal. Then, slowly, slowly, she'd draw her finger across her lower lip, transferring the musky juice to her skin. All the time, Alex would be pretending to sketch her; he'd be making marks on the paper, but it would bear no resemblance to what was really happening. Because Alex, despite himself, would be aroused. Seeing her breasts swell and breathing in the heavy scent of her arousal, he wouldn't be able to help himself

His eyes would grow dark and luminous with desire, but still he'd keep up the pose of sketching her. Her movements would grow more and more wild, more and more uninhibited, as she pushed him to the same sexual frenzy that engulfed her. While she danced, Isobel would be watching him, and noting the signs of his arousal: his lower lip would redden, becoming full and inviting. The soft faded cloth of his jeans would be no barrier to his erection; she would see his cock growing gratifyingly large as it hardened.

Then, finally, they'd reach the point where Alex could stand it no more. He'd drop the sketch-pad, strip swiftly, and stride over to her, picking her up. He'd balance her weight against the wall, and let her slide oh, so very slowly, onto his cock. They'd stay there locked together for a moment, while her body grew used to the feel of his body filling hers; then, at last, he'd begin to push into her, thrusting hard, until she finally cried out, her body flexing madly round his cock, and his cock throbbing deep inside her . . .

Isobel gave a cry as she came, and slumped back against the sofa. God, if his pictures had this effect on her in a dump like this, then at the exhibition, hung properly in a good light, they would be incredible. Regardless of her promise to Sophie, she had to do something about it. There was no way she could leave these pictures behind. Luckily her briefcase was soft, and would easily accommodate a couple of rolled-up sketches. She smiled, and picked out her three favourites, rolling them up and placing them in her briefcase. Alex would be none the wiser – until it was too late.

Seven

By the time that she heard the door open, and the sound of footsteps on the stairs, Isobel had drunk enough wine to forget her other promise to Sophie, about not vamping Alex. Although she'd masturbated to what she'd thought at the time was satiation point, she suddenly found her sex pooling again, particularly as she remembered the wicked huskiness of his voice, and the sensual curve of his mouth as he'd smiled at her, that once.

She wanted to see him smile like that again but, this time, with his eyes bright with lust. She wanted him to use his mouth on her, to lick her and suck her to a climax. She wanted to hear him whisper all sorts of lascivious things to her, cajoling and wheedling and finally demanding that she perform various acts for him. And she wanted him to fill her, to make her writhe and buck and moan under his clever, sensitive fingers. If, as she suspected, Sophie had turned him down, there was a very good chance that he was feeling sexy and frustrated as hell, so he would welcome her offer. No strings, no emotional demands or baggage – just good, honest sex. And it would be even better in the flesh than it had been in fantasy.

She walked quietly into the kitchen. Alex was making himself another cup of coffee, his back to her. She smiled, and padded over to stand behind him, sliding her hands round his waist. He jumped, and twisted round to face her, scowling. 'What do you want?' he demanded.

Isobel, suddenly remembering his deafness, mimed eating and pointed to the bowl of pasta she'd left for him. 'I cooked for us, earlier. We left some for you,' she said, talking slowly and exaggeratedly so that he could read her lips more easily.

He shook his head. 'I'm not hungry.' He went back to making

coffee, though he didn't offer to make any for her.

Playing hard to get, eh? Isobel thought. She slid her hands down his sides, and pressed herself against his back. His muscles were good; this man would be dynamite in bed, she thought. A man with the imagination to set up those incredible portraits – yes, it would be more than a pleasure to go to bed with him. She was going to enjoy this.

He spun round again, and she smiled up at him, fully expecting him to stoop down to kiss her. She was shocked when he pushed her away. 'Leave me alone, will you?' he hissed roughly.

She frowned. Why was he being so difficult, so unresponsive? She knew that she wasn't unattractive. Men usually reacted well to her petite yet voluptuous figure. Shrugging, she began to undo the buttons of her shirt, revealing her low cut push-up bra. She knew that her breasts looked good: Alex Waters would have to be a very strong man indeed to resist her.

Alex lifted his hands, and grabbed her hands, stilling her movements. 'I said no. Cover yourself up.'

Hot colour flared into Isobel's cheeks. Who the hell did he think he was, talking to her like that? she thought, furious. She glowered at him. 'Bastard,' she hissed. Either he hadn't lip-read what she'd said, or he was deliberately ignoring her, she thought, as his face remained impassive.

'Where's Sophie?' he asked.

Sophie. Yes, she should have guessed. That's why he wasn't interested in her – his taste was obviously more geared to tall blondes with generous breasts, than to pocket-size brunettes. Well. She wasn't *that* bothered. It was only a whim on her part, anyway. Her mouth tightened. But Sophie was vulnerable. If he ever hurt her friend . . . The thought made her decide not to send him up to where Sophie lay sleeping. She simply shrugged, folded her arms and turned her back on him, stalking out of the room.

Alex watched her go, but made no move to follow her. When she slammed the door of his sitting room, he smiled wryly, and sat down at the kitchen table, cupping his hand round his mug of coffee. For the past seven hours, he'd been working on a portrait of Sophie, remembering the way she'd looked when she'd been lying on the soft pillows on his bed, her fair hair spread over the cotton and her lewdly-arranged bra supporting her generous breasts. She was perfect, utterly perfect – the more so because she wasn't a habitual voluptué, like her friend Isobel. Sophie's was an almost unconscious sensuality. It was almost as if someone needed to wake her – to teach her what she was capable of feeling.

And the way she'd reacted to him, when he'd touched her . . . He swallowed hard at the memory. God. If, as he suspected, she was lying asleep in his bed, he'd have to make very sure he stayed downstairs, or in his studio. Otherwise, he'd have a hell of a lot of explaining to do in the morning, when she slept in until midday, tired from spending the night making love with him. Little Miss Pushy would pump her friend for every detail, on the way home; he didn't want to do that to Sophie.

His stomach rumbled; he frowned, and realised that it had been a considerable time since he'd eaten anything. Although he'd told Isobel that he wasn't hungry, it was untrue. He'd never claim to be a *cordon bleu* cook, but he lived well on the simple, plain fare it was his habit to prepare.

She'd said something about cooking food; he moved over to the bowl she'd indicated, and removed the plate which covered it. He raised one eyebrow as he saw the pasta mixture, and sniffed a very tempting aroma indeed. The woman had one mitigating talent, then: she'd made a better meal from the sparse contents of his kitchen than he could have done. Not bothering to heat the pasta, assuming that it would be just as good cold as it had been hot, he took a fork from the cutlery drawer, and began to eat.

Meanwhile, Sophie was lying upstairs, very far from sleep. The night was muggy, and she was hot and sticky; she'd thrown back the thick duvet, and turned the pillows a dozen times, trying to cool the back of her neck. But every time she turned the pillows, pressing her face to the cool cotton, she could smell Alex's clean masculine scent, and it was slowly driving her insane.

Pictures flashed through her mind. Alex, smiling at her and

undressing her. Alex, bending his head to suckle one nipple. Alex, kneeling down and rubbing his face against her thighs. Alex, parting her legs and fitting the tip of his cock to her sex . . .

She groaned, and turned over in the bed. God, what was wrong with her? She was acting like a bitch on heat, waiting for him to come to bed with her. More likely, he'd be working in his studio until he fell asleep, and wouldn't come out again until she and Isobel had gone. This was ridiculous – this stupid, almost teenager-like romance she'd set up in her head. As if Alex would give up ten years of being a recluse for her. And what about Gary? She was practically engaged to him. How could she even *think* about another man, let alone do what she'd done with Alex, that afternoon?

She groaned again, and plumped up the pillows, trying to get comfortable. And if Alex did come upstairs and find her there, in his bed – would he expect her to make love with him again? She'd put up a pretty poor resistance, earlier. Thank God she was on the Pill, and didn't have the added complication of worrying about a potential pregnancy.

Even so, she wasn't sure whether she was more ashamed, angry with herself, or forlorn. She couldn't help wanting him again. Would he come to her room, that night, and introduce her to other delights? Would he let her explore his body with her hands and her mouth, so she could stroke and caress and lick every inch of skin, breathing in the musky scent of his arousal, and bring him to a shattering climax with her mouth?

The thought made her wriggle against the bed, splaying her legs and sliding one hand down her body. God. Alex. She hadn't been prepared for just how desirable she'd find him. Photographs were one thing, but they couldn't reproduce the chemistry of the man himself. It was pheromonal. She knew that. Sheer, unadulterated lust – well, maybe there was a touch of her old hero-worship there, too. And yet she couldn't stop it – she couldn't hold back. She squeezed her eyes tightly shut. She was tired, and yet she couldn't sleep, for thinking about Alex and wanting him.

Supposing they'd been there alone – supposing Isobel had had a last minute meeting, and had asked Sophie to do the interview with him, instead ... Sophie could have spoken to him about his art, about colours and theory and all sorts of things. They would have sat outside in his wild garden, drinking cold white wine and breathing in the scent of summer flowers.

The cottage was incredibly isolated. If they'd made love in the garden, there would have been no-one to see them. They could have made love in the sunset, then lain in each other's arms, watching the dusk settle in the sky, and the first pinpricks of the stars come through.

She smiled wryly. It was a romantic fantasy, but that was it. It would never happen. And neither would the other picture that suddenly flooded her mind: sitting in Alex's studio by candle-light, while he painted her. Then she'd grow bored with sitting still, and she'd stand up. She'd walk over to the small hi-fi in the corner – Alex's concession to her, knowing how much she loved music – and put on a tape. Probably the tape Isobel had done for her, a compilation of all the slushy tracks from her Bon Jovi CDs; and then Sophie would slowly begin to undress, swaying to the music.

Alex would remain by his easel, maybe sitting down on the rough wooden chair he usually leaned on, just watching her. She'd undo her loose blue chiffon shirt, shrugging it off and not caring that it fell in a crumpled heap on the floor. Then she'd reach behind her, undoing the zip of her matching floaty skirt, and let that drift to the floor, too. She'd pull the navy silk scarf from her hair, shaking her hair free so that it fell over her shoulders, and then she'd reach behind again to unclasp her bra, throwing the lacy garment to one side.

Her nipples would be hardening and darkening with anticipation; Alex would be able to see them through her hair, and he'd know that he was the one causing her physical reactions. By the time she'd removed her matching white lacy knickers, he would have stood up again, and come to join her, holding her close and burying his face in her shoulder, breathing in her scent. Even though he couldn't hear the music, he'd move to her rhythm, dancing with her by candle-light.

And then, then he'd let her undress him. He'd let her undo his loose white shirt, and push it from his shoulders. Then he'd help her with the button of his faded denims, helping her remove his boxer shorts at the same time. Every so often, he'd cup her face and kiss her, hard, his tongue pressing against hers and the hardness of his cock pressing against her belly. Then, when they were finally naked, he'd sink to the polished floor with her, pulling her on top of him so that she straddled him, feeling the hardness of his cock against her moist and puffy quim.

She'd shake her hair back, and he'd reach up to cup her breasts, lifting them up and together to deepen her cleavage. He'd rub her areolae with his thumbs, making her gasp, and then – at last – he'd let her raise herself enough to ease one hand between their bodies, curling her fingers round his beautiful cock and fitting its tip to the entrance of her sex. Then she'd sink down on him, moving her hips in small semi-circles to increase the pleasure of his penetration.

She'd close her eyes, then, concentrating only on the way he felt inside her, and the music playing in the softly lit room. Alex would be kneading her buttocks, stroking her face, lifting himself so that he could kiss her breasts; all the time, she'd be moving over him, in perfect rhythm to the music, flexing her muscles as she withdrew from him, and then slamming down hard, grinding her pubis against the root of his cock. And then, finally, she'd feel his cock throb deep inside her, and feel the huge wave of electricity flow through her as they came together . . .

Sophie cried out softly as she came, her hand working feverishly between her legs, and slumped back against the pillows. God, she really had it bad, she thought miserably masturbating in his bed, and fantasising that he was going to join her. She blinked tears from her eyes. The soundtrack in her mind had been all too appropriate: *This ain't a love song.* Because Alex wasn't in love with her, and never would be; he'd merely taken advantage of the situation. This would be the only night she'd ever sleep in his bed, and she knew that she'd be sleeping alone.

Alex, sitting brooding in the kitchen, could stand it no longer. He finished the glass of red wine in one gulp, then walked up the stairs, treading very lightly and avoiding the steps that he knew creaked. His bedroom door wasn't quite shut, and he pushed it open very, very slowly. Thank God he'd oiled the hinges the other week, he thought, so they didn't squeak when he opened the door. The noise hadn't affected him, but the creaky vibrations had annoyed him.

As he'd half hoped, Sophie was lying diagonally across the bed, completely naked, her hair fanned out behind her. She was cuddling one of the pillows; he smiled. In sleep, she looked like a child, though there was still the same hidden sensuality he'd noticed earlier. He couldn't bring himself to wake her; instead, he padded over to his studio, grabbed a soft pencil and a sketchpad, and returned to the bedroom. He had to capture this. He couldn't possibly miss the opportunity.

He stood leaning against the door jamb as he sketched her, an indulgent smile playing around his lips. She moved suddenly, a soft moan escaping her, and his heart missed a beat. Whatever she was dreaming about, it was obviously very erotic, judging by the look on her face. Was she dreaming about him? he wondered. Or was it her committed lover in London, the man who obviously didn't care enough to ask her to marry him?

He wondered whether her lover was married, then dismissed the idea. Sophie wasn't the type to play around with married men – not knowingly, anyway. Unlike Isobel; his face tightened. Isobel pushy Moran. She was so completely self-centred, she wouldn't care about anything else, as long as she got her own way. Still, he had one thing to thank her for: the introduction to Sophie. Sophie, whose other name he didn't even know . . .

God, she was beautiful, he thought. The way her body curved, the hollows and folds . . . He itched to touch her and taste her again. He only just managed to keep himself in check, and continued sketching her. She'd moved so that her hand was resting on the inside of one thigh, and her head was tipped back: exactly as she'd looked when she'd come in his arms, earlier that afternoon.

'Oh God, Sophie,' he said softly. 'I want you so badly . . .' She didn't wake, and he smiled wryly. It would be so easy to go into that room, close the door behind him, and wake her with a kiss. But it would make life too complicated. Best to call it quits, now. He tore the piece of paper quietly from his pad, and went to place it on the pillow next to her, before padding back into his studio and closing the door. He curled up in the armchair, and closed his eyes; but all he could see was Sophie, feel the tiny moans she'd made as he'd thrust into her . . .

He screwed his eyes tightly shut. God, this was crazy. He couldn't afford this to happen. He couldn't allow himself to become obsessed with Sophie – either sexually, or even worse, to fall in love with her. The last time he'd felt like this, it had been with Dee. And that night, when he was supposed to have been driving, but had had a blinding headache and let her have the keys to his car, she'd taken that corner too fast, and they'd crashed . . .

'God, no,' he murmured. He couldn't bear that to happen again. He'd sworn then that he'd never get emotionally involved with another woman. His sex-drive hadn't diminished, and there had been several women who'd been more than willing to model for him – women who'd been equally willing to indulge him with some very earthy love-making, with no strings attached. He'd been living like this for ten years; he wasn't about to change, now.

He grimaced. Why had he had to meet Sophie? He couldn't promise her the emotional security that a woman like her needed. And yet his body reacted so strongly to her . . . He tensed. There was no way he was going to sleep tonight. Not when desire was pulsing through him, and all he wanted to do was to slide his cock into Sophie's warm, sweet, welcoming depths.

He scowled. He'd made love with her once. Once, they could both maybe persuade themselves that it was a one-off, no strings; but twice, and she'd expect more than he was prepared to give. Whereas Isobel – little Miss Pushy, who'd blatantly offered herself to him in the kitchen, and was the type to conduct her relationships with no ties and no fuss – was lying downstairs, on the sofa. Waiting. He'd rejected her, when she'd given him the come-on;

but now – now, his body was tense and quivering. He needed the release of good sex. He didn't know what was on her agenda, but maybe she'd see this as a little extra for her interview.

The decision made, he stood up, and walked quietly downstairs again, avoiding the steps that creaked. He tapped lightly on the sitting-room door, then opened it; Isobel sat upright, her eyes widening, as the overhead light clicked on.

'What the hell—?'

Alex caught the look of surprise on her face, and grinned. He closed the door behind him. 'Hello, Isobel.'

'What do you want?'

'In the kitchen,' he said quietly, 'I believe that you wanted something from me.'

Isobel watched him warily, her eyes narrowed. 'And?'

'Maybe I was a little harsh with you.' He came to sit next to her on the sofa. He noticed with amusement that she'd found herself a sheet, but she wasn't using it to cover her nakedness.

'So what are you saying? That Soph turned you down, and I'll do as a substitute?'

'No.' He lifted one hand, and began stroking her palm, very lightly, with his thumb.

'What, then?'

'Sophie's asleep. I didn't want to wake her.'

'Think you're that good, do you, that you could wake her by screwing her?' Isobel asked nastily.

He grinned. 'Want to find out?'

She glowered at him, then turned her face away. 'You humiliated me.'

Gently, he cupped her chin, and turned her face back towards him. 'Sorry. I missed that. Could you repeat it, please?'

She was embarrassed by his easy and gentle reaction to her deliberate rudeness, and flushed. 'I said, you humiliated me.'

'By turning you down? You asked for it.' He stroked her face. 'Isobel. If you'd like me to go away, all you have to do is say so.' His gaze travelled down to her breasts; the rosy tips were hardening. 'I don't think you want me to go, though. At least, these don't.' He traced one areola, then the other, and Isobel shivered.

'So what's this in aid of?' she asked. 'What made you decide that you wanted me?'

'Women aren't the only ones who can change their minds.' His eyes held hers. 'I like sex, Isobel. I like women with few inhibitions.'

'And you think I'm one of them?'

His lips curved. 'I know what you did to JJ in the restaurant.'

Her eyes widened. 'Pardon?'

'Phoebe told me.'

Her face flamed. JJ had told his *assistant* what had happened between them?

'JJ tells Phoebe everything. And she happened to tell me.' He grinned. 'What's the matter, Isobel? Embarrassed?'

'No – I – oh, bloody hell!'

He chuckled, then. 'Well. So you're not *that* shameless, then.'

Isobel made no answer. She was still digesting the fact that JJ had told the Educated Luvvie about her behaviour in the restaurant. That put a completely different complexion on things; she felt less guilty about her borrowed sketches, now.

'Isobel.' His breath caressed her ear. 'So how about it? Let's make love.'

He was direct, she'd give him that; and yet he hadn't been coarse about it. He could have used a much shorter, much earthier expression; but instead, he'd . . . She shivered, and turned her face to his.

He smiled, and rubbed his nose against hers. Then she felt his lips touch hers, very lightly; she opened her mouth, and the kiss suddenly deepened, with Alex's tongue flickering into her mouth.

Slowly, his mouth tracked down her body; he licked the hollows of her collarbones, and breathed lightly on the dampened skin, making her shiver. Then he moved down lower, taking one nipple into his mouth and sucking gently on it; as he felt her move beneath him, he increased the pressure, and she slid her hands into his thick dark hair, urging him on.

He moved lower, and her stomach kicked in anticipation: he really was going to do it . . . She closed her eyes, tipping her head back against the sofa and widening the gap between her thighs; she felt his breath, warm, against her quim, and shivered in delight. Then she opened her eyes in shock as she felt him move away. 'What?'

He plucked at his shirt. 'I'd rather be skin to skin – wouldn't you?'

She relaxed again. He hadn't been teasing her. Far from it. She locked her hands together, cradling her head, and watched him as he stripped swiftly and methodically. Naked, he was even more beautiful than she'd thought; his muscles were perfectly defined, and his cock was large and very promising.

'Turn round,' she mouthed softly.

He grinned, and indulged her, letting her look at his back. Isobel licked her lips. She'd always had a thing about an old poster of Sophie's, the Raphael line-drawing of the back view of Michelangelo's *David* – the only line-drawing she'd ever really liked. And Alex Waters made that drawing look boring and flimsy. God, he was gorgeous, she thought – and he was hers, for the night.

He turned back to face her. 'Seen enough?'

'Mm.'

'My turn.' He beckoned to her, and she stood up, completely unselfconscious.

'Turn round.'

She did so, and Alex assessed her swiftly. A pocket Venus, all lush curves: not his usual taste, as he preferred his women taller, but she was still very appealing. 'Mm.' He walked over to her, sliding his arms round her waist and burying his head in the curve of her shoulder. She leaned against him, and he let one hand drift upwards to cup one breast, his fingers idly playing with her hardened nipple.

'Isobel.' Gently, he sank to the floor, drawing her down onto her knees; she held on to the front of the sofa for support.

'And you used this on JJ?' He picked up one foot, his fingers

101

feathering across the sensitive arch. 'Tut, tut. In public, too. You like your sex on the dangerous side, do you?'

She didn't bother answering, knowing that there was no point: if he couldn't see her face, he couldn't lip-read.

'And you like being in control, too. I bet you'd like to have me spread-eagled on my kitchen table, my hands and ankles tied, while you did whatever you liked to me: so you could touch me where you liked, and when you liked, and how you liked.' He nuzzled her shoulder-blades, and slowly moved downwards, kissing the curve of her spine. 'Or maybe you'd like to change places with me, now, so I was bent all submissively before you.'

Her head jerked up, at that: she wasn't submissive, at all!

He chuckled softly. 'Easy. I'm playing, Isobel. Just suggesting a few scenarios that I think would appeal to you. You like to dominate your men.'

And how the hell did he know? How did he know what a kick she'd got from spreading Tony over his desk, that time, tying his wrists with her stockings? Or had he been waiting somewhere to see Tony, and seen everything that had happened? No, that was ridiculous. Alex was a recluse; besides, Tony didn't have two-way mirrors or cupboards for people to hide in. It had just been a lucky guess, she thought.

'But do you know, I wonder, what it's like, the other way round? To be tied to a bed, your arms and legs tense, while a man kneels between your thighs and brings you to the edge of orgasm? And then he stops, letting you cool down again, before bringing you to the edge – and repeats it, again and again, until you're scream-ing for him to fuck you?'

Isobel shivered. Christ, the man had an imagination.

'I'd like to paint you like that, Isobel. I'd like to tie you up and arouse you, dip my brush in glycerine and paint your quim with it. I'd like to see you spread your legs, your sex growing moist and puffy every time I touch you. I'd like to paint you when your nipples are so hard that they almost hurt. I'd bring you right to the edge – and then I'd make you watch me make love with another woman, watch me slide my cock between her thighs and do everything to her that you want me to do to you, oh, so badly.'

She felt her sex grow moist. He was barely touching her, just stroking her back and rubbing his cheek against her skin; but what he was saying . . . God, she wanted him. She wanted him now. She wriggled in impatience, and he laughed.

'Isobel. Wouldn't you like me to do that? And then, just when you were crying in frustration – the woman would take my place, crouching between your thighs and touching you, sliding a finger deep into your sex to ease the ache. Maybe even two or three, stretching you a little and making you writhe.'

Isobel felt a pulse hammering between her legs. She could imagine the scenario, oh, so easily; and she was shocked at just how much it excited her. For all her teasing comments to Sophie, Isobel had never actually made love with another woman. Her experiences had been one hundred per cent heterosexual. Although she could appreciate another woman's beauty, she'd never felt sexually attracted to a member of her own sex. But now, with Alex whispering all these lascivious ideas to her . . .

'Or maybe she'd let her finger drift here.' Alex wetted his finger in his mouth, then pressed it against Isobel's anus. 'She'd touch you here, making you writhe and moan and want to be filled. And then – only when you'd come – I'd kneel between your thighs, and take you.'

Isobel couldn't help pushing back towards his finger; Alex grinned, and removed his hand. 'Do you like being touched there, Isobel?' He slid his other hand down from her breast, letting it feather between her thighs. 'Has anyone made you come, touching you there as well as here?' He slid his finger across her swollen clitoris, and she cried out. 'Mm, and you're a noisy lover, too.'

She stilled for a moment. How did he know? Was his deafness only a pose? Then she thought about it again. Sophie had said something, once, about deaf people hearing with their hands, and you could certainly feel the vibrations of a heavy bass track on the stereo, when you were in a car. Maybe it was the same with voices; he could 'hear' noises with his body rather than his ears.

'Mm, you're wet, as well.' Alex inserted a finger into her sex.

'Wet and hot. You want this as much as I do.'

She supported her weight on one arm, and reached behind her to curl her fingers round his cock; he laughed. 'Yes, I believe you do. Well – let's do something about it, then.' Gently, he disentangled her hands, and moved against her; his cock slid over her quim, pressing against her clitoris, and she moaned. He repeated the action again and again; she pushed her bottom back towards him, and he chuckled.

'Impatient, too. All right, then.' At last, she felt the tip of his cock press against the entrance of her sex, and then he was pushing into her, incredibly slowly. She gave a small moan of pleasure, and Alex moved with her, sliding one hand down her arms and lacing his fingers with hers. He began to thrust in earnest, then; Isobel quivered, feeling his balls slap against her quim, and buried her head in the sofa, pushing her bottom upwards so that he could penetrate her more deeply.

Alex's rhythm was slow and regular; she pushed against him, wanting him to speed up and to push deeper, and she was rewarded by a quickening pace. She felt her orgasm build; and then, incredibly, Alex was massaging the puckered rosy opening of her anus.

'Oh God, yes, do it,' she murmured hoarsely, suddenly wanting to feel him there, too.

He pushed gently, and she shuddered, pushing back to meet him.

'Yes, Alex, yes,' she moaned, as he pushed harder: and suddenly, her body was jerking under his, out of control, as she climaxed. The movement of her internal muscles round his cock was enough to push him into his own orgasm; she felt him murmur something against her skin, and then his cheek was pressed against her back, and he held her close.

Some time later, when she'd stopped shaking, he withdrew, and turned her round to face him. He kissed the tip of her nose. 'Coffee?' he asked.

She shook her head, and he smiled. 'Then sweet dreams, Isobel.' He kissed each eyelid in turn, scooped up his clothes, and left the room.

Eight

Sophie stretched, pushing her head back against the pillows – and opened her eyes abruptly. She frowned at the unfamiliar room: where the hell was she? Then memory flooded back, and she flushed. She was in Alex Waters' bed, at his cottage in the middle of the fens – and she was alone.

She sat up; then she noticed the piece of paper lying next to her. She picked it up, and her flush deepened as she saw the picture of herself, asleep. She looked incredibly sensual, her hand sliding down her thigh as though she were about to masturbate, and that smile on her face . . . Alex must have sketched her as she slept, dreaming of him.

Alex. She swallowed, and climbed out of the bed, dressing hastily and heading to the bathroom. Where was he? She showered quickly, leaving the bathroom door unlocked and half hoping that he'd walk in and find her there; she was almost disappointed when she finished towelling herself dry, and there was still no sign of him.

He'd sketched her, the previous night. So why hadn't he woken her and made love to her again? Why had he just crept away and left her lying sleeping in his bed? Still frowning, she went back into the bedroom to put on her watch – and was shocked when she saw the time. It was nearly ten. She hadn't slept that late since she was a child. Perhaps it had been the Fenland air that had made her so sleepy.

God, she was going to be late for work. Very late. She had no idea how long it would take to fix Isobel's car; but even if she walked into the village and caught a taxi to Cambridge, then took the train back to London – no way would she be there in time for her classes. She rolled her eyes, and folded the sketch, hiding it in her handbag before heading downstairs. This was one thing she didn't want to share with Isobel.

Isobel was sitting in the kitchen with her feet up on the table, drinking coffee, when Sophie walked in.

'Morning,' Sophie mumbled.

'Good morning, Mrs Van Winkle,' was the teasing reply. 'I take it you slept well?'

Sophie flushed. 'You should have woken me.'

'I thought you could do with a lie-in. It isn't a problem,' Isobel said. 'Mack's fixing the car.'

'Mack? Who's Mack?'

'The local mechanic. I woke up early, this morning, so I decided to go into the village and get the car sorted. I looked in on you, but you were dead to the world. I left a note on the table, in case you woke while I was gone and luckily, the garage was open early.' She smiled. 'How about a coffee?'

'Thanks.' Sophie bit her lip. 'Where's – where's Alex?'

'I don't know.' At the look on her friend's face, Isobel felt incredibly guilty about making love with Alex, the previous night. She couldn't even use the excuse that it had all been his idea; apart from the fact that she'd come on to him first, in the kitchen, she could also have told him to go, when he'd come down to the sitting room. 'He's probably still sulking in his studio; and we may as well leave him to it. I don't think he'd be too interested in talking to us – do you?'

'I suppose not.' Sophie tried to keep her face impassive, and not wince at Isobel's bald statement of fact. 'Isobel – I'm going to be late. I have a lecture in half an hour.'

'Relax; it's all sorted,' Isobel advised. 'I rang the college from the garage, and told them that you were ill – that you'd come down with one of these twenty-four hour bug things. They were fine about it.'

'But I'm not ill!'

Isobel spread her hands. 'What else could I tell them? The truth – well, it doesn't sound very believable, does it?'

'I suppose not.'

'How about "thanks for covering for me, Isobel"?' Isobel said quietly.

Sophie flushed. 'Mm. Sorry. Thanks for covering for me.' She swallowed. 'So what's wrong with the car?'

Isobel wrinkled her nose. 'I don't know. Well, I don't need to know much about engines, so I've never learned. I'm not interested in fiddling around under the bonnet of a car. As far as I'm concerned, a car is just a thing that gets you from A to B.' She grinned. 'Except for my temperamental rust-bucket, that is! The main thing is, it can be fixed, and it's not going to cost me a fortune. Mack says it'll take about another half hour to finish the job – so do you still fancy having our girly day out in Cambridge, even though it's a day late?'

'I don't know,' Sophie said. 'I really ought to go in to work.'

'For God's sake, Soph, don't be so conscientious! You've gone to work enough times when you've been ill; just play hooky, for once in your life, and relax. They can manage without you for one day.'

Sophie didn't feel like arguing; she felt too mixed up. Where was Alex? Had that picture been his way of saying goodbye? And what had she expected, anyway – protestations of undying love, or something? Alex was a free agent, and he'd made it pretty clear that that was how he wanted things to stay.

Isobel didn't seem to notice that her friend was very quiet throughout breakfast – or that she'd barely touched the slice of toast that Isobel had made for her, crumbling it onto the side of her plate instead of eating it. She merely drank her coffee, and let Sophie brood in silence.

Eventually, a young man with his long hair tied back into a ponytail, no shirt, and a pair of faded denims which didn't have a top button and revealed the dark arrowing of hair down to his groin, walked into the kitchen. 'Right then, Isobel – she's ready to go whenever you are.'

Isobel smiled at him. 'Thanks, Mack. By the way, this is my friend Sophie.'

He turned to Sophie, and smiled at her. 'Hello, Sophie.'

107

Sophie forced a smile to her face; she didn't want to be there, or be polite to him, but there was nothing she could do about it. 'Hello.'

'I might as well pay you now, and you can send me the receipt later,' Isobel said.

Mack named a sum, and Isobel took her cheque book from her handbag, and swiftly wrote a cheque. 'Thanks,' he said.

'Thank *you*. I can get out of this dive and back to the city, now.'

He grinned. 'It's not *that* bad, round here.'

'Oh, yes, it is,' Isobel said feelingly. 'Too much sky, and not enough people.'

'You get used to it.'

Isobel smiled at him, appreciating his unstated offer: but not wishing to take him up on it. 'I'm a city girl, Mack.'

'Have a safe journey, then.' Mack winked at her, and left the room; a few seconds later, they heard his van roaring off down the road.

'Ready to go, Soph?' Isobel asked.

'Yes – no. No, not quite. I've just realised that I've left something upstairs. I'll be down in a minute.' Sophie walked swiftly up the stairs, and tried the door to Alex's studio. To her disappointment, it was locked. If she couldn't say goodbye to him in person, she could at least leave him a note, she thought. She went back into the bedroom, and scrawled him a swift note, including her address at the bottom and a brief message – *get in touch*. There was no point in leaving a phone number. Then she walked slowly downstairs again, to join Isobel.

'What are you doing?' she asked, seeing Isobel scribbling on a piece of paper.

'Leaving Mr Volatile a note – saying thanks for the food, I'll send some wine back with JJ, and I've left him some bread and some milk in the fridge, to keep him going.'

'Right.' Sophie was relieved that Isobel didn't ask what she'd left in the bedroom – or ask her if she wanted to add anything to Isobel's note. Whatever Sophie wanted to say to Alex Waters, she wanted it to be just between the two of them.

Isobel showed unusual tact in leaving Sophie in peace, on the way to Cambridge. She didn't bring up the subject of Alex at all while they wandered round the shops, or when they stopped at a riverside pub for lunch, or when she persuaded Sophie to buy a pair of trousers and a skirt in one of the early summer sales. She waited until they were going back towards London; then she gave Sophie a sidelong look.

Sophie looked terrible. She looked as though she were about to burst into tears; and she was twisting the ends of her hair round and round her little finger as she stared out of the window, which Isobel knew from old was a bad sign. It meant that Sophie was deeply unhappy about something – and that she wasn't going to talk about it, either.

In retrospect, Isobel thought, it had been a stupid idea, asking Sophie to help her with the Alex Waters interview. It looked as though Sophie had fallen in love with her teen idol, and was having an inward tussle about whether she should break off her relationship with Gary and hope that something would happen with Alex, or whether she should stop being adolescent and just chalk it down to experience, staying with Gary. Isobel sighed inwardly. There was no way that anyone as sweet and gentle as Sophie could cope with the darker, sensual side of Alex. The side that would allow him to fantasise with a woman he'd barely met, about having a threesome and maybe tying each other up . . . No, that wasn't Sophie's scene at all.

She coughed. 'Thanks for helping with the interview,' she said quietly.

Sophie shrugged. 'It was nothing.'

'He's a moody bastard,' Isobel continued. 'Attractive, I'll give him that – but not to my taste.' That wasn't strictly true, but she didn't want Sophie to guess what had happened between her and Alex, the previous night. Isobel felt incredibly guilty about it, now – not because of Tony, but because of Sophie. If Sophie found out that her idol did indeed have feet of clay, and would screw any woman he met without compunction . . . Isobel couldn't bear to see her friend's dreams shattered like that.

Sophie didn't reply; she was too busy brooding. How could she have been so stupid as to think that what had happened between them had meant anything to Alex? It had been a one-off, because she was female, he had been in the mood for sex, and she had been there. Stupidly there, ripe for the taking. A gormless cow-eyed woman who had acted like a *gauche* teenager, overawed by meeting the famous Alex Waters – and had let the great artist do whatever he liked with her.

No doubt the reason why he had avoided them, that morning, was because he didn't want to risk her making a scene and embarrassing them both. What made it worse, she thought, was that she should never have done it in the first place. What the hell had she been playing at? Sleeping with someone on a first date was one thing; making love with someone a few minutes after their first meeting, when they knew virtually nothing about each other, was something else entirely. She felt like a tart, a bitch on heat.

And then there was Gary . . .

Gary. Gary, who trusted her, and expected her to remain faithful to him. Which was his right, seeing as he was her boyfriend. Gary, who would never have dreamed of sweeping her off to bed in the middle of the afternoon – let alone making love with the curtains wide open. Gary, who loved her and respected her and . . .

She sighed. In her heart of hearts, Sophie knew that Gary wasn't right for her. Alex was probably too wild and bohemian to want to be tied down with someone like her; but Gary . . . If she was honest with herself, Gary was too far the other way. He didn't really understand the artistic side of her, thinking it just a hobby. He wasn't particularly interested in her career, apart from making politically correct noises of encouragement, and – if she was honest with herself – he saw her more as an accessory. He had a checklist of the things that made up a successful life: the good job, the car, the house, the steady girlfriend, and two holidays abroad each year. He was good on the personal development front, too, taking evening classes in modern languages and law things that would look very good on the CV of a lecturer in economics. And, no doubt, marriage and the two point four kids was the next thing on the list.

Sophie suddenly realised that she didn't want that. She didn't want to go to Greece or Turkey every summer, and the Italian ski slopes every winter. She didn't want to hostess cosy little dinner parties, and make sure that she impressed Gary's head of department with her culinary skills – skills she didn't possess and wasn't interested in possessing, in the first place.

So what do I want? she asked herself I can't have Alex; so what do I want? She wasn't sure of the answer; all she knew was that she wanted someone more exciting than Gary. She wanted to be with someone who could broaden her horizons and make her laugh, both in and out of bed. Someone who would encourage her, who'd give her the space to be herself. Someone who could make her *feel*. Which meant that she had to finish with Gary. It was the right thing to do. But he'd never understand; how the hell could she explain all that to him?

Isobel saw the misery on her friend's face, and decided not to pry. Sophie would talk about it, when she was ready; Isobel would just make sure that she was there to pick up the pieces. In the meantime, Isobel had worries of her own. If Alex realised that the sketches were missing, it wouldn't take him long to work out where they were – or to guess why she'd taken them. What then? Would he threaten to pull the exhibition? Or – and she hoped fervently that this was the case – would Tony think as much of the drawings and she did, and ask JJ to persuade Alex to show more of them?

She smiled to herself. She would enjoy doing the persuading herself, where JJ was concerned. The fact that he'd told his assistant what had happened between them in the restaurant . . . It was too direct a hit for Alex to have been teasing her. He knew exactly what had happened: and maybe that had been part of the reason why he'd agreed to the interview in the first place. And he'd also said that Phoebe had been his source . . . She wondered suddenly whether she'd misjudged Phoebe – whether Phoebe was in fact more than the debby-sounding, Educated Luvvie type. If she was honest about it, she couldn't imagine JJ having an attractive but dim assistant. Firstly, JJ liked mental fencing; and secondly, he was too shrewd a businessman to waste time with an airhead, however pretty she was.

And then there had been the scenario that Alex had described to her. Had he had Phoebe in mind, as the other woman? Had Alex made love to Phoebe? Had Phoebe been one of the models? It was an intriguing idea – but not one, she thought, that she could discuss with Sophie.

When they walked back into the house, the light on the answer-phone was flashing. Sophie's heart missed a beat. Alex? Then she was annoyed with herself for being pathetic. Alex didn't have a telephone, and he didn't have her number, either. How the hell could it be him?

'It's probably for you,' she told Isobel. 'I'll put the kettle on.'

'I could do with a cold beer, rather than a coffee, actually,' Isobel said, crossing her fingers behind her back and hoping that Alex hadn't already noticed the missing sketches, contacted his agent, and that the message was from a very irate JJ.

Sophie nodded. 'I'll get you one. I could do with a cold drink too, to be honest.' When she returned with the bottle of ice-beer, Isobel smiled at her. 'Wrong. It was for you, actually.'

'Oh?' Sophie made an effort to sound uninterested.

'It was Gary. He heard that you weren't well, and wants to know if you're feeling better, now.'

'I'll ring him, later.'

'Okay.' Isobel took the beer. 'Thanks.' She took a swig, then noticed the glass of mineral water in Sophie's hand. 'Going to do some work?'

'A bit.' Sophie shrugged. 'I might as well.'

'Mind if I hog the dining room table, then?' Isobel waved her conference folder at Sophie. 'I want to get this typed up, while it's still fresh.'

'Fine.' Sophie suddenly remembered something. 'You didn't take any pictures, in the end.'

'Pictures?' Isobel's heart began to hammer.

'Photographs. You took your camera,' Sophie reminded her.

'Oh, *that*. Yeah, well – I thought it might not be very tactful to ask, in the circumstances,' Isobel said wryly. 'I'll sort that out with JJ, later.'

'Right.' Sophie turned on her heel. 'See you later, then.'

'Want me to call you, when dinner's ready?'

Sophie shook her head as she left the room. 'Don't bother cooking anything for me. I'm not hungry.'

Isobel regarded her friend's retreating back thoughtfully. Sophie hated cooking, but she was never off food. Alex Waters had a lot to answer for, she thought. Still. Maybe when she cleared the interview with him, via JJ, she could find out what his real intentions were, towards Sophie – and do something about it.

Isobel spent the next couple of hours working up her interview. When she'd finished, she stretched, yawned and leaned back in her chair. She reread the article on the screen of her lap-top; finally, pleased with it, she saved the file. She'd ring JJ in the morning to arrange a meeting, so he could approve the interview; and then, she would be ready to give the editor of *Vivendi* a real coup. Alex Waters' first interview in nearly ten years.

She glanced at her briefcase, then at her watch. Tony would still be at the gallery, just about. On impulse, she picked up the phone and dialled his number. Tony himself answered; it was late enough for the rest of the gallery staff, including Monica, to have gone home.

'Hi, Tony.'

He smiled as he recognised her voice. 'Hello, Isobel. How did the interview go?'

'Not as badly as I expected. He was a bit difficult, at first, but I got what I wanted, in the end.' Isobel shrugged. 'He spoke to Sophie. I'm just finishing writing it up.' She paused. 'Tony, are you busy tonight, or can I tempt you to dinner?'

'Dinner out?'

'No – dinner at your place. I'll cook. Just bring some champagne home; I'll meet you at your place, in an hour.' She smiled. 'There's something I want to show you.'

'Your article?' he guessed.

'No. Something even better.'

'What?'

'You'll have to wait. See you in an hour.' She put the phone down, then wandered upstairs to Sophie's studio, and rapped on the door.

'Come in,' Sophie called.

Isobel leaned against the doorjamb. 'All right, Soph? How's it going?'

Sophie's answer was to tear the piece of paper from her sketchpad, screw it into a ball, and throw it across the other side of the room.

'That good, eh?' Isobel said wryly.

Sophie shrugged. 'I suppose I've just got a few things on my mind.'

'I don't want to pry, but if you want to talk about it, I'm here.'

'Thanks, Isobel – but this is something I need to work out for myself.'

Meaning, Alex Waters. 'Fair enough.' Isobel paused. 'I was thinking about going over to Tony's. Do you mind?'

'Why should I mind?'

'*Not mind,* exactly – just if you'd rather not be on your own this evening . . .' Isobel shrugged. 'Oh, hell. I'm making a mess of this.'

'Yes, you are.' Sophie smiled at her. 'And thanks for thinking about me – but I'm in too bad a mood for company.'

'Hey, everyone's entitled to feel like that, once in a while. You're normally impossibly cheerful.'

'Just go and enjoy yourself,' Sophie directed. 'I'll be fine.'

'Right. I'll see you later. You know Tony's number, if you need me.'

'Yeah. Thanks.'

Isobel went downstairs again, printed out the article, and put it in her briefcase, tucking it behind the rolled-up sketches. Then she left the house, calling in at the deli to buy some smoked salmon, some fresh pasta, a loaf of ciabatta bread and a pot of cream. She caught a taxi to Tony's house in Bayswater; he was already there, to her surprise, and he opened the door, taking her in his arms and kissing her hard.

'I missed you, last night,' he said softly.

'You too,' Isobel said.

'Really?' He tipped his head on one side. 'So – what happened?'

'Hey, come on! Doesn't a girl get a drink, first?' Isobel teased.

'You said you had something to show me.'

'After dinner.'

'Okay.'

'So where's my drink, then?'

He groaned. 'Okay, okay.' He led her into the kitchen, extracted a bottle of champagne from the fridge, and opened it deftly.

Isobel lifted one eyebrow. 'Pink champagne. Wow.'

'It goes with just about everything,' he said. 'And you didn't tell me what you were cooking.'

She waved the carrier bag at him. 'Pasta with smoked salmon sauce and ciabatta bread. I assume you have some salad in the bottom of the fridge?'

'You assume correctly.'

'Good.' She took a sip of champagne, and kissed Tony. 'I suppose I'd better get dinner started.'

He leaned against the worktop, watching her as she prepared the meal. 'I thought you were going to be back, last night.'

'I had a teensy setback.' She winced. 'My car decided to play up, yet again. I'm going to trade the bloody thing in for a newer one, at the weekend, if you want to come with me and do manly things, like poke around in the engine and look at the suspension or whatever.'

He grinned. 'I reckon you know as much about cars as I do! Seriously – couldn't you have called someone to fix it?'

Isobel rolled her eyes. 'You'll never believe this. It was the set of circumstances from hell. Alex Waters lives in this tiny cottage in the middle of nowhere, a good three miles from the nearest village. He's deaf, as you know, so he doesn't have a phone; and, of course, my mobile phone was flat, and I don't carry a spare battery or a charger around with me. He doesn't even have a bike, so I had to walk to the village; and it turned out to be early closing day. I tried a couple of houses – and the people who lived there were either at work, or they didn't have a phone.'

Tony chuckled. 'Ever feel that life's sometimes against you?'

'It certainly was, yesterday!'

'So what was Alex like?'

'Weird,' was Isobel's prompt reply. 'He doesn't like people – and he certainly didn't like me. I'm glad I took Sophie along.'

'So the signing helped, then?'

'Yes and no. He just seemed to take to Sophie more than he did to me. I think he was trying to chat her up, actually.' Isobel bit her lip. 'The only thing is . . .' She sighed. 'Soph's going through a bit of a bad patch, at the moment. He paid her some attention; I don't quite know what happened between them, because she won't tell me and I'm not tactless enough to ask – but I get the feeling that she's fallen head over heels in love with him.'

'How does he feel about her?'

Isobel shook her head. 'I've no idea. I really couldn't tell what went on in that man's head.'

'You didn't pick a fight with him, did you?' Tony asked, thinking of the exhibition and suddenly feeling nervous.

'I shouldn't think he's going to back out of the retro now, if that's what you're worrying about.' Isobel raked a nonchalant hand through her hair. 'And I got my interview, thanks to Sophie. I brought it over for you to have a look at.'

'Oh, so that's what you wanted to show me.'

She shook her head. 'Better than that. And you definitely have to wait until after dinner to see it – because the pasta's almost ready.'

She served up, and they took the plates into the dining room; Tony topped up their glasses. They chatted lightly over dinner; then, finally, Tony pushed his empty plate away. 'If you ever get bored with being a journo, you could always open a pasta bar,' he said.

Isobel shook her head. 'No way. Can you imagine it? I'd be tied to the business, eighteen hours a day. When I wasn't cooking, I'd be sorting out paperwork or preparing menus or shopping. I'd be working, when everyone else was enjoying themselves . . . No, I think I'd rather cook for pleasure.'

'Pleasure being your favourite word,' Tony teased. 'So what was it that you were going to show me?'

'You're not going to let that drop, are you?'

'Not now. You've made me curious.'

She chuckled. 'All right, all right. Wait here, and I'll bring it in to you.'

Nine

Isobel fetched her briefcase, then cleared a space on the table, checking that the surface area was clean and dry. 'I think that you'll like this,' she said. Gently, she extracted one of the sketches from her briefcase and unrolled it, flattening it against the table.

Tony looked at it, then at her, then at the picture again. He touched the edge of it slowly, reverently, as if he couldn't believe what he was seeing. 'Is that what I think it is?' he asked finally. 'A new Alex Waters?'

'It is indeed,' she confirmed.

'And he gave this to you?'

'Ah.' She bit her lip. 'He didn't exactly *give* it to me.'

Tony was shocked. 'You mean, he doesn't know you've got it?'

'Put yourself in my situation,' Isobel said. 'You to go interview an artist. You know he hasn't exhibited any work in years, and the rumour is that he doesn't paint any more. He tells you that he just paints for himself. Now, circumstances mean that you have to sleep on his sofa, that night. He decides to shut himself in his studio in a sulk for the evening, leaving you to fend for yourself, but he just so happens to leave a portfolio lying around. Any psychologist would tell you that he meant you to see the stuff – because he knows that you're a journalist, he knows from talking to you that you're fairly inquisitive, and it's pretty obvious that, true to the stereotype of being a woman *and* a journo, you're going to look in the portfolio.'

Tony said nothing.

Isobel pulled a face. 'Look, Tony, don't be so prissy about it. If he hadn't wanted me to see them, he would have hidden them away in his studio, or something, so there was no chance of my

119

coming across them. But he left them out, so I looked through them.' She spread her hands. 'The minute I saw them, I thought of you. I thought that you really ought to see them.'

Tony picked up on the plural. 'You mean, there's more?' he was shocked.

'Three of them. Well,' Isobel said, 'there were a lot more, but I couldn't put that many in my briefcase, so I picked the ones I liked best.'

'Let's get this straight. You stole three of his pictures.'

'Borrowed,' she corrected.

Tony rolled his eyes. 'Christ, Isobel. He told you that he paints only for himself. If he discovers that you've pinched some of his sketches—'

'Not pinched,' Isobel interrupted. 'I told you, I've merely borrowed them. If you're not interested, then I'll just give them back to JJ, and we'll forget about the whole thing.'

He folded his arms. 'You know damn well I'm interested in a new Alex Waters.'

'Exactly. And these are good.'

'Yeah.' He looked at her. 'So what's the plan?'

'Plan?'

'Come on, Isobel. You always think on your feet. There's no way you'd just take the pictures without having some idea about what you were going to do with them.'

'Well, I thought I'd arrange a meeting between you, JJ and me, to talk it through. We'll get JJ on our side; then he can persuade Alex to let you show them in the retro – and maybe even add some of the others.'

He shook his head. 'I still can't believe that you've done this.'

'Well, what would you have done, in my position?' Isobel demanded. 'Just put them back and thought, "Gosh, what a shame that he's never going to show them to anyone"?'

Tony thought about it. 'I don't know,' he said at last. 'I really don't know.'

Her eyes widened. She'd expected Tony to be as excited about this as she was; his cautious reaction surprised her. Had she misjudged him? Was he really more conventional – and a lot less ambitious – than she thought? 'Tell me this, then,' she said quietly. 'Are you glad you've seen the picture?'

'Well, yes. Of course I am. It's fantastic.' He looked at the sketch again. 'Do you know who the model is?'

Isobel shook her head. 'It wasn't part of the interview. I shouldn't think he told Sophie.'

Tony frowned, not understanding. 'But – I thought you said that you interviewed him?'

'He refused to speak to me,' Isobel said. 'He started whispering to Sophie. She was getting cross with him – you know how well-mannered she is – but he wouldn't talk to me. In the end, I left them to it. I had all the questions written down, so Sophie did the interview, while I walked into the village to find someone to fix my car.'

Tony grinned, then. The annoyance was so obvious in her voice – mingled with hurt pride at the thought that someone had resisted her. 'Alex gave you a hard time, then, did he?'

It wasn't the only hard thing he'd given her, Isobel thought, flushing as she remembered the way he'd slid his cock deep inside her. Tony caught the sudden voluptuous look on her face, and his eyes widened. 'There's something else you're not telling me, isn't there?'

She swallowed. 'Um. Look, Tony, I know that you and I – we're officially an item but . . .' She tailed off, not sure how to say it.

He finished the sentence for her. 'But you still enjoy other men.'

Isobel was surprised at how easily he seemed to have accepted it. He laughed, and leaned over to kiss the tip of her nose. 'I knew that from the first moment I saw you, Isobel – that one man wouldn't be enough for you. So either I can accept you as you are, and enjoy my time with you; or I can make myself miserable about something that I can't change.' He shrugged. 'I like to be happy. So there's only one choice, isn't there?'

'It's nice that you're being grown-up about it,' Isobel said.

'There's no point in being anything but.' Tony's eyes met hers.

121

'So tell me, Isobel – what happened?' His voice grew husky. 'That drawing made you want to touch yourself, didn't it?'

She spread her hands. 'Am I that obvious?'

'That's what it would make me want to do. Touch you – or, if you weren't there, then touch myself.' He paused. 'What happened? Did he catch you with your hands in your knickers?'

'No.' She bit her lip. 'Actually, he turned me down.'

'You what?' Tony was surprised. Part of him wanted to laugh – but the vulnerability in her eyes stopped him. 'He turned you down? How?'

'Well – you're right, I did touch myself. The pictures made me feel horny,' she admitted. 'Then I heard him come downstairs. He'd spent the whole afternoon and evening sulking in his studio; so I went out to see him. I propositioned him – not so much by words, but by actions. And he turned me down.'

'Oh, Isobel.' He stroked her face. 'He's mad. I wouldn't have turned you down.'

'Thanks, but I wasn't fishing.' She smiled at him. 'Anyway, later that evening, just when I was dropping off to sleep, he opened the sitting-room door.'

'I see.'

Isobel smiled to herself. From the look on his face, Tony wanted her to tell him a story. Well – she'd give him exactly what he wanted. 'Tony,' she said softly, 'I prefer telling tales in comfort.'

He thought about it for a moment. 'No. I'm not going to take you to bed, yet.'

'I didn't necessarily mean your bed.' She tipped her head on one side. 'The sofa would do.'

'The sofa. Which is where it all happened – right?'

'Right.' She smiled at him. He was quick enough to pick up what she meant: that she wanted him to help her act out the story as she told it.

He took her hand, and led her into the sitting room; he drew the curtains, switched on a small lamp, and refilled their glasses. Then he sat down on the large squashy sofa, pulling Isobel down beside him. 'So, you were sitting naked on his sofa.'

'Yes.'

He began unbuttoning her shirt. 'Completely naked – not even your knickers?'

'Not even my knickers,' she confirmed.

'Interesting,' Tony said, sliding his fingers under the cup of her bra and forcing the material down so that her breast was revealed, then repeating the action with the other breast. Isobel almost purred with delight. This was exactly the sort of thing she enjoyed most: talking about one lover to another, and being made love to at the same time. 'So what did he say?' Tony asked.

'He sat down next to me, and said that he'd changed his mind – about turning me down, that is. He said that he liked sex, and he liked women who didn't have many inhibitions.'

Tony chuckled. 'He had you sussed out pretty quickly, then.'

'Mm. Then he said he wanted us to make love. And then he kissed me.'

'Like this?' Tony leaned over, touching his lips very lightly to hers.

'Mm.' Isobel closed her eyes. 'A bit.'

'Or like this?' Tony whispered, nibbling at her lower lip until her mouth opened, then pushing his tongue into her mouth.

When he broke the kiss, she sighed. 'Mm. Like that. And then he kissed his way down my body. He sucked my nipples.'

'Like this?' Tony licked her earlobe, then nuzzled her neck. He nipped gently at her skin, making her arch against him in pleasure; then he let his mouth drift downwards, playing over her collarbones. She shivered, and pushed against him; he moved lower, taking one nipple into his mouth and sucking gently on it.

Isobel moaned, and he cupped her other breast, pinching the nipple between his finger and thumb and increasing the pressure of his mouth on the other nipple until she writhed beneath him.

'Mm.' He broke off to look at her. 'What, then?'

'He moved down over my stomach. I thought that he was going to lick me.'

'And you spread your legs for him?'

'Yes.'

Tony nodded, and pushed her skirt up. She put her hands on the sofa, taking her weight on her hands as she lifted her buttocks; he smiled, and removed her knickers. 'You look incredibly wanton, you know,' he said. 'Your shirt open, your skirt rucked up, and your legs spread.' He teased her nipples with the tip of his nose. 'And these are hard, showing me just how turned on you are. You look so . . . lush.' His green eyes had darkened with pleasure; looking at her was one thing, but touching her was something else entirely. Something that made him hard, just to think about it.

She grinned. 'And who made me look like this, in the first place?'

'You have a point.' He licked his lips. 'So, what then? Did he lick you?'

She shook her head. 'He teased me. He made me think that he was going to do it. I felt him breathe against me . . . Then he pulled away.'

'Must have been frustrating for you.'

'It was.' She felt the pulse between her legs begin to beat. The way Tony was looking at her . . . Was he going to do what Alex hadn't?

'So, what then?'

She swallowed. 'He stood up, and stripped for me.'

'I see.' Tony's eyes held hers for a moment; then he stood up, and removed his clothes.

'He turned round so that I could see him.'

Tony did a small pirouette. 'How do I compare?'

'You're about the same size. I think you're probably fitter.'

He grinned. 'So Alex has a pot belly, does he?'

'No, but he's a near-recluse. I shouldn't think he goes to the gym.'

'And his cock?'

'About the same size as yours. Very nice.'

Tony smiled. 'So, when you'd looked at him – what then?'

'He made me stand up and turn round, so he could see me, too.'

'Hm.' Tony tipped his head on one side. 'I kind of like you as you are. Lush and wanton.'

'A sweet disorder in the dress,' Isobel quipped.

'What happened, then?'

'I turned round, and he looked at me. Then he walked over to me, and drew me down to the floor.'

'He took you on the floor? Not very gentlemanly of him.'

Isobel smiled. 'I was kneeling, and holding on to the sofa.'

'Indeed.' Tony looked at her. 'Show me. But don't take your shirt off, or your skirt – I like you as you are.'

Isobel slid off the sofa, then turned round so that she was on her knees, in the same position she'd been in when Alex Waters had made love with her.

'Push your skirt up a bit more,' Tony directed.

She smiled, and did so.

'So, what then?'

'He picked my foot up, and stroked it.' Isobel thought it politic not to tell Tony about what had happened with JJ in the restaurant – or that both Alex and Phoebe knew about it. 'Then he talked to me. He told me that I was a woman who liked being in control.' She couldn't see his face, but she could imagine the amused expression on it. 'He said that I'd probably like to have him spread-eagled on his kitchen table, tied so I could do what I liked to him.'

'Like you had me, on my desk?' Tony asked, stroking her buttocks.

'Something like that.'

'And did you?'

She shook her head.

'But you like the idea,' Tony persisted.

'You already know that.'

'Indeed.'

'Then he suggested having me tied to a bed, while he knelt between my thighs and brought me almost to orgasm – then stopped, letting me cool down, and almost making me come; then stopping again, and bringing me closer and closer each time.'

'Mm. The man has a point.' Tony continued stroking her buttocks, and pulled her shirt completely free from the waistband of her skirt, so that he could stroke her back, too.

'He said he wanted to paint me like that. That he wanted to paint me and arouse me then make me watch him make love with another woman. And then . . . he'd get the woman to make love with me.'

Tony coughed. 'Christ, the man has an imagination!'

'Mm.' Isobel's voice was husky.

'And would you like that, Isobel?'

'It's something I haven't done,' she admitted.

'Maybe we can do something about that – another time,' Tony said. 'In the meantime, it's you and me. What did Alex do with you, then?'

'He touched me.'

'Where?'

'Here.' She reached behind her, taking one of her hands and drawing it round to her breast.

'Just there?'

'And here,' Isobel admitted, moving his hands back to her buttocks and pushing her bottom out towards him.

'You mean, here?' Tony was quick to take the hint, and pushed gently against her anus.

She moaned. 'Yes. And he asked me if anyone had made me come, touching me there as well as my clitoris.'

'And has anyone made you come like that?'

She shook her head.

'I see.'

'And then, he pushed his finger into me.'

'Here?' Tony increased the pressure on her anus, and she shivered.

'No.'

'Here.' He slid his other hand between her thighs, and inserted a finger into her.

'He said I was wet and hot, and I wanted it as much as he did.'

'Mm, that feels about right to me,' Tony agreed.

126

'I reached round to touch him.' She reached behind her, curling her fingers round his cock. 'Like this.'

'Very nice.' Tony licked his lips. 'What then?'

'He moved my hand away, and pushed his cock against my quim. He didn't enter me, at first – he just kept rubbing his cock along my quim, pushing it against my clitoris.'

'And you liked it?'

'I liked it.'

'But you wanted more.'

'Yes.'

'What did you want?' Tony's voice was silky.

'I wanted to feel him inside me.'

Tony chuckled. 'How very staid and quiet you sound.'

Isobel grinned. She didn't use anything stronger than 'bloody', in conversation; but if her lovers liked her to use more earthy phrases, it didn't offend her. 'Okay. I wanted him to fuck me.'

'That's better.' Tony let his cock glide along her quim, teasing her.

She moaned. 'Tony. Don't be mean.'

He smiled, kissing the nape of her neck. 'All right.' He positioned the tip of his cock against the entrance of her sex, and pushed so that his cock slid into her. 'Is this how he felt?'

'Mm. Except he did it a little more slowly, to tease me.'

'Indeed.'

'Until he was completely in me – then he began to thrust, slow and measured.'

'Like this?'

'Yes.'

'And you enjoyed it?'

'Yes.' She began to move with him, pushing back against him as he thrust into her, and moving away as he withdrew. She buried her head in the sofa, pushing her bottom upwards so that he could penetrate her more deeply – just as she had with Alex. Tony began to thrust harder, and Isobel began to pant, feeling her orgasm start at the soles of her feet and coiling up through her legs.

'And he touched me, as well,' she admitted.

'Here?' Tony slid his hand across her belly, and stroked downwards, letting his fingers drift down to her clitoris.

'No.' Her voice was muffled by the sofa. 'But don't stop.'

Tony chuckled. 'Coward.'

'I'm not a coward,' came the fierce retort.

'I know.' He nudged the material of her shirt out of the way, and kissed her shoulder.

'Then we both came,' Isobel said hoarsely. She felt her orgasm splinter through her; and then she felt Tony's cock throb deep inside her, too. He held her close, murmuring how much he adored her, and she relaxed.

Eventually, he withdrew.

'And that's what he did, too,' Isobel said, as Tony turned her round to face him.

Tony grinned. 'Indeed.'

'He offered me a cup of coffee.'

'Which you, as a caffeine addict, accepted.'

'No. Actually, all I wanted was to curl up and go to sleep. So he left me to it, took his clothes, and walked out of the room.'

'Now, that's where he and I will differ,' Tony said. 'Because I'm going to leave my clothes here.' He stood up, drawing her to her feet, and picked her up. 'And I'm going to carry you to my bed.'

Later that evening, Isobel lay curled up in bed next to Tony, sipping champagne. 'So what are we going to do about those sketches, then?'

'We? *You're* the one who took them,' he reminded her.

'Borrowed them.'

'Borrowed them, then. It's your problem.'

'But you're an accessory, because you've seen them – and you haven't phoned JJ to tell him. So you're in it, just as much as I am.'

'Remind me never to get on your wrong side,' Tony teased her. 'Well. I'd like to use them in the exhibition, but that depends entirely upon Alex. If he doesn't want to show them, then I won't show them – because I don't want to risk him pulling the exhibition entirely.'

Isobel thought for a moment. 'How about if he agrees to show the new stuff?'

'And you're going to persuade him to do it, are you?'

Isobel shook her head. 'He doesn't like me very much. He shares my appetite for sex, but that's about all we have in common. I think he only made love with me because he was—' She stopped, not wanting to betray Sophie any more than she'd already done. 'Well – randy, I suppose, and I was there.'

'Right. So what do you suggest we do, then?'

'Like I said earlier, let's meet JJ, and talk it through with him. The worst he can do is say no.'

'The worst he can do,' Tony said slowly, 'is to pull the exhibition.'

'I don't think he will. JJ's a businessman – and he knows what an Alex Waters retro is going to do to his business. Either he's going to make some sales, with some nice fat commission, or he's going to get some good new artists wanting him to represent him. Probably both. To kill that exhibition would be to lose a lot of good publicity.'

'Cynic.'

'No – just stating a few facts.' She sipped the champagne. 'Mm, I do like this stuff. Very summery.'

'Stop changing the subject.'

'I'm not. I've just told you how I think we should deal with it. I'll keep the sketches, for the time being.'

'Don't you trust me?'

Isobel chuckled. 'Of course I do! It's just that I like looking at them. I like having them with me.'

'All right, all right. So do you want me to ring JJ – or will you do it?'

'I will. I have to clear my interview with him, remember; so we might as well tackle him about the new work at the same time.'

'Maybe I should give you a job,' Tony mused. 'Make you my new business executive, or something.'

She chuckled. 'Thanks, but no thanks. I'm unemployable, Tony – I get bored too easily, and I like my own way too much. Being a freelance suits me fine.'

'Even though you have to deal with people you don't like, and be nice to them, to get commissions?'

She grinned. 'After the Alex Waters interview in *Vivendi,* I don't think that will be a problem, somehow . . .'

Sophie pretended to read the paper, but she was concentrating on one sense only: sound. She was waiting for the soft click of the letterbox, the dull thud of envelopes on the doormat. It had been three days. Alex had made love with her, so he found her attractive; and he'd sketched her while she was sleeping, and left her the sketch. It had to be some kind of message. So, the minute he'd seen her note, with her name and address, he would have written to her. Say he'd written her a note on Thursday afternoon, and posted it then; allowing two days for second-class mail, his letter should arrive on Saturday morning. Today.

At last, she heard the post arrive; carefully, she folded the newspaper, pushed her chair back, and went to the front door. There was an assortment of envelopes on the doormat: several pieces of junk mail, promising her the chance to win £25,000 if she had a catalogue delivered, the telephone bill, and three brown envelopes for Isobel.

She swallowed her disappointment. Maybe he'd missed the post on Thursday, and his letter would come on Monday. Tuesday, even. But she knew that she was kidding herself. If Alex was that keen to see her again, he would have written first class – or even come to see her. It was all over. Time for her to go back to her old life – the university, her students, Gary.

The only thing was, she was none too sure that she wanted that, any more.

Ten

'Hello, JJ.'

He recognised her voice immediately. 'Hello, Isobel. How did it go?'

'You know your client,' Isobel said. 'How do you think it went?'

'He had a fit of the sulks, you persisted, and he gave in so he could get rid of you.' It was a statement, not a question.

'Something like that.' Isobel hugged herself with pleasure. Either Alex hadn't discovered that she'd taken the sketches, or he hadn't told JJ. Which meant that she could hang onto them for a little longer. 'Look, I've nearly finished writing up that interview. Perhaps we could meet, later in the week, to discuss it?'

'Fine.'

'How about Friday, at your office?'

There was a rustling of paper as he checked his diary. 'Friday's fine. Some time in the afternoon?'

'That'd be great.' She smiled. 'I'll see you at two o'clock, then.'

'I'll look forward to it.'

She put the phone down, almost hugging herself with glee. This was going to work – she knew it was. The Alex Waters retro exhibition was about to change, for the better. And her career was going to change with it, too . . .

'Sophie. Darling.' Gary nuzzled the skin on her neck, tracking his mouth over the sensitive spots.

Sophie closed her eyes. God, God, God. A month ago, she'd thought herself in love with Gary, enough maybe to marry him. But now – now, she wasn't so sure. Whereas once, she would have been thrilled by the way he caressed her, secure in the knowledge that when Gary behaved like this, he was in the mood for making

131

love, now, she found it irritating, too oblique. She wanted him to kiss her properly, the way Alex had; to touch her, the way Alex had, bring her body to life beneath his hands.

But what was the point of thinking about Alex? He wasn't interested. She should get that into her head, and stop behaving like a teenage groupie – fantasising about a man who was out of reach.

Gary hadn't noticed that his girlfriend wasn't concentrating. 'Mm, Sophie.' He slid his hands under the hem of her loose cotton shirt, stroking her midriff. Sophie shivered and arched against him, the reaction purely physical. He rubbed his nose against hers and kissed her lightly on the lips.

Sophie tensed for a moment. She didn't want this gentle, sweet, kind love-making. She wanted something rougher, something more passionate – something like she'd shared with Alex. Yet Gary . . . Gary wasn't like that. Half of her was tempted to vamp him; but she knew that he'd start asking questions, wondering why she'd suddenly become so passionate, and she wasn't in the mood for explaining. How could she explain to Gary that she'd made love with another man, someone she found far more attractive than him – and someone that she'd probably never see again? Someone she'd only known for a few brief minutes . . .

God, what's wrong with me? she thought. Why can't I just be happy with what I have? And yet Gary's almost perfunctory love-making was no longer enough for her.

'Sophie?'

He pulled away and she opened her eyes. He was looking at her, his blue eyes narrowing with concern. 'Are you still feeling a bit rough? Am I taking it too fast?'

Sophie sighed inwardly. If she said yes, she was still feeling a bit rough, then maybe he'd ascribe her strange mood to that. Then again, he'd probably put her in a taxi and send her straight home, saying that she should have an early night with some hot milk and whisky. She didn't want that. She didn't want to spend yet another night in bed alone, thinking of Alex and bringing herself to a solitary climax. She wanted to feel Alex's body filling hers, she wanted to feel his skin against her, and breathe in his scent. Gary was a poor substitute: but, at the same time, he was a damn sight better than her own right hand.

She slid her hands into his floppy blond hair, bringing his mouth back down to hers. 'Kiss me, Gary,' she murmured.

He did, but it wasn't enough. Sophie was furious with herself. Why was she acting like a bitch on heat? All because of a man whom she'd met for a few brief minutes – a man she'd made love with straight away. Part of her was ashamed of herself, but the other part of her craved for Alex. She tried to push him from her mind; she opened her mouth over Gary's, sliding her tongue between his lips and opening his mouth.

He tensed for a moment, but Sophie continued, pulling his shirt from his jeans and sliding her hands off his back, smoothing his muscles. He relaxed again, but still he didn't do what Sophie wanted. She wanted him to rip her shirt from her, to bare her breasts and suck her nipples. She wanted him to slide one hand between her legs, rub her clitoris and tease her to the point of orgasm, and then use his mouth on her to tip her over the edge. And yet how could she tell him?

He pulled away from her. 'Sophie . . . Not here.'

Not there, in his lounge, in case anyone peered through the net curtains and saw them. He was so boringly conventional, Sophie thought. Had he been Alex, he would have taken her there and then, on the sofa. Had he been Alex, he would have pulled her on top of him, made her ride him and touch her breasts and let herself go wild. Whereas Gary . . . She had a feeling that with Gary, it would be the usual missionary position, in bed, with the lights out. Something she'd been contented with, a few weeks before, but which wasn't enough, now.

She was right. Ten perfunctory minutes later, she was lying on her back, in the dark, hating herself and despising him. She was still unsatisfied. Although Gary was normally considerate, making sure that she came, too, she'd been reduced to faking it. Because after Alex, Gary was too bland, too insipid.

'Sophie?' His hand found hers, and he entangled his fingers

with hers, squeezing them gently. 'Are you all right?'

'I . . .'

'Sophie. There's something wrong, isn't there? Tell me.'

She sighed. 'Oh, God. I don't know, Gary. I just don't know how to say this. This isn't the right place, or the right time.' But then again, when would there be a right place and a right time?

'Sophie?' Gary sounded completely bewildered, and she hated herself. He was a good man, at heart. He was decent – he was safe, he was settled. Why couldn't she just be happy with her lot?

'I'm just in a funny mood,' she said. 'Just ignore me.' Maybe if she gave it time, she would come to love Gary again, be happy with him. She'd wipe Alex Waters from her mind.

'Sophie.' He switched on the bedside light, and sat up.

She turned on her side and blinked, unaccustomed to the light. 'Yes?'

'This probably isn't the right time or the right place. There ought to be violins playing, and a full moon, but – ' he paused. 'Will you marry me?'

Sophie sat upright, shocked. She'd been expecting him to ask her that for months – but his timing couldn't have been any worse. 'I . . .' Marry him? She knew at that moment that she couldn't go through with it. The charade, the pretending . . . It would be too much for her. She shook her head sadly. 'Gary, I'm sorry. I can't.'

'But – why? I mean, we were getting on so well.'

'We were.' She sighed. 'I'm going through a difficult phase, at the moment.'

'What is it – work? Look, when we get married, you don't have to go back to the university. I'm earning enough to keep both of us. You can – oh, I dunno, stay at home and paint all day, if you want.'

She shook her head. 'I really, really can't explain this, Gary. It's just . . . I don't think we're right for each other.'

'But – Sophie, I don't understand.'

She sighed. 'Neither do I, Gary. But if I said that I'd marry you, now, I wouldn't be fair to either of us.'

'Well, look – do you want some time to think about it?'

She shook her head. 'I can't marry you, Gary. In fact, I really don't think we should see each other.'

'What, you mean just have a break for a while?'

'No. I think it's something more than that.'

'Is there someone else? Have you met someone else?' he demanded.

'No.' It wasn't strictly true. She *had* met someone else – but she knew that he wasn't interested in her.

'Sophie, I—'

'I'm sorry, Gary,' she said quietly. 'But believe me, this is the best thing for both of us, in the long run.'

Hurt and bewilderment crossed Gary's handsome face. 'Sophie – look, maybe I'll call you in a week. Maybe then, you'll have worked out what's bothering you.'

It would take more than a week to forget Alex Waters, she thought grimly. A lot more than a week. 'There's no point,' she said. 'It's over, Gary. What we had – well, it was good, while it lasted. But I think, if we carry on, we'll end up hating each other.'

'I could never hate you, Sophie.'

You could, she thought, if you knew what I'd done. 'Could you call me a taxi, please?'

'I'll run you home.'

'No. I'd rather take a taxi.' She didn't want him trying to talk her round, all the way to Pimlico. 'Please, Gary. I'll get dressed.' She swallowed. 'I hope you meet someone who deserves you.'

Shocked, but seeing the determination in her face and deciding that there was no point in arguing with her, Gary slid out of bed, pulled on his boxer shorts, and padded out of the bedroom. When he'd gone, Sophie dressed quickly, and went downstairs.

Gary met her at the bottom of the stairs, unsmiling. 'The taxi will be here in ten minutes.'

'I'm sorry, Gary. I really wish it could have worked out.'

'I don't understand what's gone wrong.'

'No.' She bit her lip. 'I really am sorry.'

They remained in awkward silence until they heard the hoot of a taxi's horn, outside. Without saying another word, Sophie left Gary's house, closing the door behind her.

She felt completely numb all the way home. She didn't bother trying to make conversation with the taxi driver; she sat in silence, wondering what the hell she'd done. She'd either just made the biggest mistake of her life, or made the right choice, and at that precise moment, she wasn't sure which.

To her relief, when they reached Pimlico, the house was in complete darkness. Isobel was obviously out with Tony. There were no messages on the answerphone, no scribbled notes from Isobel; the place was completely silent. Even the cat from three doors down, which often appeared like magic when Sophie arrived, demanding to be fed, was absent.

She locked the front door behind her, took a bottle of mineral water from the fridge, and padded upstairs to her studio. She took a CD of Corelli's violin sonatas from the neat rack beside her mini hi-fi, and put it on at a low volume. The regular smooth music would settle her mood and calm her down, she thought. The thing about Baroque string music was that it was regular, predictable, and you always knew what was going to happen. Unlike life. It was very comforting.

The other sure-fire way of improving her mood, she knew of old, was to start sketching. She closed the heavy navy curtains, then lit the three large church candles which stood on the floor in gothic wrought-iron bases, plus the small tea-light candles in blue glass starfishes which lined the mantelpiece.

The soft lighting and the sombre haunting music suited her mood. She picked up her sketch-pad and began to work, the soft pencil moving over the smooth paper in sure, confident strokes. She worked swiftly and in silence; eventually, she stopped and stared at the finished work. Alex Waters' face stared back at her. His body was as she remembered it: firm, muscular and perfectly toned. And yet there was something about him, something that she hadn't caught. Scowling, she tore the sheet of paper from her pad, screwed it into a ball, and hurled it at the wall.

Alex. God, she had to get over this stupid day-dream. But she couldn't help herself. She couldn't help wanting him. She closed her eyes, sliding her hand underneath her loose shirt, and burrowing under the waistband of her leggings. Alex. When would she be rid of this demon that made her conscious of her body, the whole time? She didn't know, and she no longer cared: as she began to caress her clitoris, the only thing she could concentrate on was pleasure, the pure pleasure that sparkled through her veins as she touched herself . . .

Sophie's bleak mood continued into work, the next day, and the next. She could hardly concentrate in tutorials, and she felt as though the lectures she'd delivered were useless and dry. She sought refuge in her office, closing the door and slumping at her desk, with her elbows resting on the smooth surface of the desk and her hands in front of her face.

She was making such a mess of things. And all over someone who was so obviously not interested in her. Even if, say, her note had somehow escaped his attention – if he'd wanted to see her again, he would have contacted his agent, asked him to talk to Isobel, and found out her address, that way.

'You stupid, stupid cow, Hayward,' she told herself crossly. 'Get yourself a life, and grow up!'

She straightened up, lifting her jaw, and picked up the first of the essays in her in-tray. The first three paragraphs were fine; then she caught his name. Alex Waters. Christ, don't say one of her students had fallen in to the same trap as she had! She groaned. Well, the whole essay had been about art and popular culture – about posters and postcards. She should have guessed that one of her students would pick up on Alex's work. Most of the students she knew – from her time at university, onwards – covered the walls of their rooms with postcards and posters, in an attempt to brighten the place up and establish their identity on the uniform rooms. And it was odds-on that one of Alex's prints or postcards would be up there, blu-tacked to the walls with the rest.

Even the thought of Alex was enough to make her want to touch herself. She closed her eyes, licking her suddenly dry lower lip, and cupped her breasts. She could feel how hard her nipples were, through the thin material of her bra and her shirt, and she couldn't help rubbing them.

She was concentrating so much on thoughts of Alex, and the pleasurable sensation and she rolled her nipples between finger and thumb, that she wasn't aware of the door of her office opening – until she heard a sharp intake of breath, and opened her eyes. She looked straight into the eyes of Lawrence Byfield, one of her second-year students. She flushed deeply, dropping her hands. 'Lawrence.'

'I did knock. You didn't answer.' His eyes widened. 'Sophie . . .'

She rubbed an embarrassed hand over her face. 'Lawrence, you've just caught me on a bad day.'

'I wouldn't say that.' He tipped his head on one side, and closed the door behind him, locking it; then he leaned against the door, smiling at her.

'What do you think you're doing?' she asked sharply.

He smiled at her. 'Sophie. I walked into your office, to find you touching yourself.'

'It's not that big a deal,' she lied.

'Well, I happen to think that it is.' He looked at her. 'If this got out . . .'

She lifted her jaw. 'Are you threatening me, Lawrence? Because if all this is in the hope of getting a better grade for your essay, you're in for a shock. Blackmail doesn't work.'

He grinned. 'Sophie, I wasn't trying to blackmail you. I was just saying that I'm sure you'd rather that I kept this quiet.'

'Yes, I would,' she admitted. 'But if you choose to tell your friends, there's nothing I can do about it, is there?'

'No. That's also true.' He crossed the room to sit on the edge of her desk, and leaned over to stroke her face. 'Oh, Sophie.'

Although Sophie preferred her students to use her first name, rather than the more formal 'Miss Hayward', the way he was saying her name wasn't quite in the way that he usually said it. His voice was richer, more sensual; instead of being slightly deferent, he sounded more confident.

'Sophie. I find you very attractive. I have done, for a long while. I've even sketched you, a few times, in lectures. I've drawn pictures of how I think you'd look, lying on a pile of silk cushions, wearing only a white chiffon wrap, so sheer that I could see your body through it.'

She closed her eyes. 'Lawrence, stop. Stop, right now. You're my student. Nothing can happen between us – it'd be completely unethical.'

'But who's to know about it?' he asked softly. 'I won't tell, if you don't.' He stood up again, and walked over to the window, closing the narrow black venetian blinds.

'What the hell do you think you're doing?' she demanded.

'Well,' he said, 'I'm sure you'd prefer it if no-one could see into your room, at the moment. I certainly would.'

'Lawrence, I've just told you, nothing is going to happen between us.' Though, she admitted to herself, Lawrence Byfield was very attractive indeed. He was twenty, with all the confidence and none of the arrogance of his age, and she found his warm hazel eyes attractive, behind the lenses of his wire-rimmed glasses. Disturbingly so. She'd noticed him, once or twice, in a seminar or tutorial, but she'd always managed to keep the relationship entirely professional – until now.

'Why did you come here today?' She asked, trying to keep some distance between them. 'You're not due for a tutorial.'

'I wanted to talk to you about an essay – I'm having trouble with it. You always said that if any of your students were stuck, they could come and talk to you.'

'True.'

'Like I said, I knocked, but you didn't answer. I assumed you were deep in some marking, or writing an academic paper, and you just hadn't heard me.' He brushed his fringe out of his eyes. 'I thought you were here, so I opened the door . . .' His eyes glittered. 'And then I saw you. God, Sophie, do you have any idea how many of us fantasise about you, in lectures?'

She rolled her eyes. 'Oh, Lawrence, stop being stupid.'

'No, it's true. There's something about you, something that makes me want to – oh, I dunno, awaken you.'

She laughed. 'Now you're being really ridiculous. For God's sake, Lawrence, I'm ten years older than you are.'

'Yeah. I know. But who's to say, Sophie, that I couldn't teach you something?' He walked over to her chair, and reached out to take the silk scarf from her hair. He fanned her fair hair over her shoulders, and smiled. 'Yes. This is exactly how I imagined you to look.' He removed her glasses. 'And your face . . . don't you know how beautiful you are?'

'Lawrence, stop that right now,' she said through gritted teeth. If he carried on like that much longer, she knew what would happen between them and she couldn't afford to let it happen. If she was caught making love with one of her students, it would be the end of her career. Right now, her career was the only stable thing in her life. She couldn't risk it.

'Sophie.' He said her name like a caress. 'You're lovely. There's something . . . untouched about you. We all think so.'

'You're being completely ridiculous, now. I am *not* a lust object for the second years.'

'You are, you know.'

She scoffed. 'What, with Helen Fisher around?' Helen, who had a good figure and legs up to her armpits, and drew attention to them by wearing very short skirts and figure-hugging tops. Helen, who wore more make-up to work than Sophie wore if she was going out for a special evening. Helen, who, rumour had it, had seduced half of her first year students – male *and* female.

'Helen Fisher,' Lawrence told her quietly, 'is a mare. I wouldn't touch her with a barge-pole.'

'That's not a very pleasant thing to say about one of your tutors, Lawrence.'

He grinned. 'Sophie, don't go prissy on me. You're not obvious, like she is; but, the way you react to paintings, you're a sensualist at heart.'

'Lawrence, for God's sake—'

He stopped her effectively by lowering his mouth to hers and kissing her hard. She was taken by surprise; the way he kissed her was so much like the way Alex had, his mouth insistent and demanding, yet not aggressive. She slid her hands into his hair, and he drew her to her feet, sliding his hands down her back to cup her buttocks and pressing her against him so that she could feel his erection throbbing against her pubis.

A detached part of Sophie's mind thought that this couldn't possibly be happening. No way would she be stupid enough to make love with one of her students in her office – even one as attractive as Lawrence Byfield.

'Oh, Sophie,' he said softly. She was wearing a navy patterned chiffon shirt; Lawrence undid the buttons very quietly, pushing the material from her shoulders, and gave a sharp intake of breath as he saw her breasts, the navy lace of her bra contrasting with the creaminess of her skin. 'If any of us had guessed that you were hiding a figure as gorgeous as this . . .' He stooped down to bury his face between her breasts, nuzzling them and breathing in her scent.

Sophie felt a pulse kick between her legs. She gave a small moan of pleasure as Lawrence unclasped her bra, dropping the navy lace garment to the floor, then cupped her breasts, lifting them up and together slightly to deepen her cleavage. He bent his head again, his tongue tracing the outline of her areolae; he blew gently on the skin he'd just wet, and Sophie gasped, her nipple hardening immediately. Then he began to suck, very gently, and she tipped her head back, closing her eyes.

To think that he was so experienced, at such a young age . . . Sophie wasn't sure whether to be shocked, impressed, or excited. A mixture of everything, she thought.

'Sophie.' He murmured her name against her skin, and transferred the attentions of his mouth to her other breast, licking and sucking the nipple, and rolling its twin between his thumb and forefinger, extending it gently but firmly, until she was pushing against him. 'Oh, yes, Sophie,' he said, dropping to his knees before her.

She was wearing a navy silk pleated skirt; he made short work of unzipping it, removing the skirt and her half-slip at the same time, leaving her wearing only a pair of navy lace knickers. He sat back on his heels, looking up at her. 'Christ, Sophie, I don't know whether I want to draw you or fuck you or both.'

Spoken so like Alex. He was, she thought, an Alex Waters in the making. Except maybe Lawrence wouldn't keep himself so far from the rest of the world.

'Sophie.' He stroked her thighs, and she shivered, automatically widening her stance. He smiled. 'You're so responsive. You're adorable, Sophie. I want to touch you . . . May I?'

She closed her eyes, and nodded. He'd gone this far. He couldn't stop, now. Gently, he eased his finger under the leg of her knickers, sliding his finger down to part her labia. She shivered, and he let his finger explore her folds and crevices, finally sliding his finger deep into her vagina. She flexed her internal muscles around his finger, and he smiled. 'Sophie. Look at me.'

She did. He withdrew his hand, then put his finger into his mouth, sucking every last drop of her juices from it. 'I want to look at you,' he said quietly.

She nodded, and let him peel down her knickers, drawing the lacy material over her hips and down to her ankles. She stepped daintily out of her knickers, and widened her stance again. Lawrence crouched between her thighs, parting her labia and sighing happily. 'You look like a perfect rose.'

She smiled. 'That's a very clichéd simile.'

'It's still true,' he protested. 'I wonder . . . do you taste as good as you look?'

She could feel his breath against her quim, and it made her shiver in anticipation. Instead of teasing her, as Alex had done, Lawrence stretched out his tongue, licking from the top to the bottom of her slit in one slow, easy movement which made her stomach kick. 'Oh yes,' she said softly. 'Yes.' She slid her hands down to tangle in his hair, urging him on, and he began to lap at her in earnest, his tongue exploring her and flickering quickly across her clitoris, and then sliding down her quim and pushing deep into her vagina.

Sophie felt her orgasm coil in her gut, and suddenly explode.

She shivered, and Lawrence held her close, continuing to lap her until the aftershocks of her orgasm had died away. He got to his feet, taking her into his arms and kissing her hard; she could taste herself on his mouth, and it both thrilled and shocked her.

'Lawrence.' She swallowed. 'Thank you. That was good.'

'Pleasure.' He smiled. 'At least it's cheered you up a bit. You've been looking pretty upset, all week.'

She flushed. 'Yeah.'

'Well, if you ever want to talk about it . . .'

She grinned. 'Hang on. I'm supposed to be the tutor!'

'You know what I mean.' He kissed the tip of her nose. 'Undress me, Sophie,' he invited huskily. 'And don't say that you can't. We've gone this far; why stop now?'

Far enough that she was completely naked, and he was completely clothed. She smiled wryly, and cupped his face, drawing his mouth down to hers again. Still kissing him, she bunched up the hem of his t-shirt. She broke the kiss and he held up his arms, letting her remove his t-shirt completely.

He had a nice body, she thought, firm and muscular – though not quite as developed as Alex. She drew her hands over his chest, feeling his flat button nipples harden as she touched him, then let her hands drift slowly over his abdomen, down to the button of his jeans. He gave a sharp intake of his breath as she undid the button, then slid the zipper downwards. She eased the soft faded denim over his hips; he kicked off his trainers, and she removed his jeans completely, taking off his socks at the same time. Then she rocked back on her haunches and looked up at him, a question in her eyes.

He shook his head, and sank to the floor beside her. 'Sophie,' he said. 'I want you here.' Somehow, he manoeuvred their positions so that he was lying on the floor of her office, and she was straddling him. He was still wearing his boxer shorts, but she could feel the length and girth of his hard cock pressing against her.

'Oh, Sophie.'

She hooked her thumbs into the waistband of his boxer shorts and slowly drew the garment down. He lifted his bottom, so that she could remove the shorts, then sank back down again. She rested her hands on his shoulders, and slowly rubbed her quim against his cock.

He shivered. 'Sophie. I want to be inside you.'

'I want it too,' she said huskily.

'Then let's do something about it.'

She nodded and sat up straighter, lifting herself slightly and curling her fingers round his shaft, fitting the tip of his cock to the entrance of her sex and slowly sinking down on him. Lawrence licked his lips, tipping his head back and opening his mouth in pleasure as he felt her warm, wet depths encompass his cock. He tilted his hips, and she began to move, lifting and lowering herself and moving her body in tiny circles. He looked at her, then licked his thumb and forefingers and began to tease her nipples again, pinching them slightly.

Sophie moaned, and slid her hands over his, linking their fingers together and helping him rub her nipples. God, this felt so good. It was more or less what she'd wanted from Gary – a wild, animalistic coupling, not caring if anyone around them heard the noises and wondered what was going on.

'Touch yourself,' he urged. She continued massaging her breasts, squeezing them and kneading them and rubbing her nipples. Encouraged, Lawrence eased one hand between their bodies and began to rub her clitoris. She gasped, and quickened the rhythm, still moving over his cock in small circles.

'Tell me, Sophie, does it feel good?' he asked as she gave a low moan.

'Yes.' She tossed her hair back, and shuddered again as his fingertip teased her clitoris, pressing the sensitive nub of flesh.

'Don't stop,' he urged, continuing to massage her clitoris.

She moaned, slamming down harder onto his cock and squeezing her internal muscles round his cock as she lifted herself up again. Then, at last, she felt orgasm wash through her again, her internal muscles convulsing sharply round him. Almost at the same moment, Lawrence gave a groan, and she felt his cock throb deep inside her. She collapsed onto him, and he wrapped his arms round her, holding her close and stroking her hair.

Some time later, when their breathing had slowed, she sat up again. 'Lawrence.'

'Yeah, I know.' He traced her lower lip with his forefinger. 'Firstly, it was a one-off, secondly, you don't want me ever to mention it again; and thirdly, thank you, Sophie.'

She flushed. 'I feel like such a tart.'

He shook his head. 'Tart is the last word I'd use to describe you.' He smiled. 'But at least it'll stop me day-dreaming in your lectures. Instead of dreaming, wondering what it's like to make love with you, I know.'

She swallowed. 'It can't happen again, Lawrence. I've already compromised our student-tutor relationship, and it isn't fair to you.'

He stroked her face. 'You and I are the only ones who know it; and we're the only ones who are going to know it.' He sat up, still inside her, and kissed her lightly on the mouth. 'Sophie, whatever it was that was bothering you – I hope it works out.'

'Thanks.' She smiled ruefully. She didn't see how it could work out; Alex didn't want to know. But at least this experience with Lawrence had confirmed one thing for her: she'd done the right thing in breaking up with Gary.

She climbed off him, and dressed again, feeling slightly self-conscious. Lawrence watched her, a smile on his face, then stood up and dressed, not as shy as she'd been.

'You came here to talk to me about an essay, didn't you?'

'Yes.'

She smiled at him. 'Whatever's happened between us, your essay hasn't gone away.'

'True.'

She nodded her head in the direction of the coffee filter on the window-sill. 'Fix yourself a coffee, then we'll talk about it.'

He grinned. 'Yes, Miss!'

'And enough of your cheek.' She smiled at him, relaxed with him once more. He was once again the cheerful and irrepressible student she liked, not the handsome and intense lover of moments before, and she blessed him for it. At least, now, things could start getting back to normal again.

Eleven

Isobel looked over from her magazine. Sophie was sitting on the sofa, with her legs curled under her and her nose in a book: quite an ordinary sight, because Sophie often spent her evenings reading. The difference was that Sophie hadn't turned a page of the novel she was reading, for the previous twenty minutes, and she was curling the ends of her hair around her little finger and biting her lower lip, looking completely woebegone.

Isobel sighed. She knew that Sophie was upset about breaking up with Gary, but it was really the best thing that she could have done. Gary just hadn't been right for her. The only thing was, Isobel suspected that Sophie was beginning to brood about Alex. Sophie had been acting out of character, ever since they'd gone to the Fens for the interview.

She stood up, and padded out to the kitchen, returning with a bottle of chilled white wine and two glasses. 'Here,' she said, pouring chardonnay into one of the glasses and handing it to Sophie.

'Hm?' Sophie looked up in surprise, then saw the glass of wine. 'Oh. Special occasion, is it?

'No. I just thought that you could do with a glass of wine.'

Sophie shrugged. 'I'm all right.'

'Is that as in that you don't need a glass of wine, or as in that you're feeling perfectly fine?'

'Both.'

'Liar.'

Sophie took the glass. 'Okay. So I'm having a bad week.'

'What is it? Work?'

'Not really.' Though there had been that episode with Lawrence on her office floor. Sophie didn't regret it, exactly – it had felt good, and Lawrence had been a very considerate lover – but she felt guilty about her lapse in professionalism. He was old enough to make his own decisions, but she was his teacher. She shouldn't have let him do it.

'Soph, sitting there bottling it up isn't going to help, you know.'

'And this isn't the answer to everything, either,' Sophie retorted acerbically, nodding at the wine.

'That's best Argy chardy you're talking about, not just any old plonk!' Isobel smiled wryly. 'I admit, drinking doesn't solve problems – but a glass of good wine and a sympathetic friend can often help, especially if you need to talk.'

'Yeah. And I'm an ungrateful bitch.'

'Bitch, never. Ungrateful – well, let's just say that I know what King Lear was on about.'

'What?'

'You know, how sharper than a serpent's tooth – oh, never mind.'

'Stop showing off, Isobel.'

'At least I made you smile.' Isobel removed the book from Sophie's hands, and placed a bookmark between the pages before closing the book and putting it on the floor. She sat down next to Sophie, and filled her own glass. 'Well. Here's to friendship,' she said, lifting her glass in a toast.

'To friendship,' Sophie echoed, chinking her glass against Isobel's and sipping the wine. She smiled wryly. 'And yes, Isobel, you're right – it's very nice.'

'Good.' Isobel paused. 'I'm not particularly good at being tactful, so I might as well ask you straight. What's wrong, Soph? And don't say "nothing" – I've known you for long enough to be able to tell when something's upsetting you.'

Sophie sighed. 'I dunno, Isobel. I just feel that my life's at some kind of a watershed.'

'Well, you've done the right thing in dumping Gary, if that's what you're worrying about. You were wasted on him.'

'We were together for a long time.'

'And you'll find someone better – someone who deserves you,'

Isobel said, squeezing her friend's hand. 'I always thought that Gary was – well, a bit wet.'

'You never said.'

'Because he was your boyfriend, and I didn't want to upset you by criticising him. He was decent enough, but he wasn't really right for you.' Isobel sighed. 'Look, I know you probably thought you'd end up married to him or something – but you'll find someone else pretty soon. Someone who deserves you.'

Alex Waters? Hardly. Sophie shrugged. 'Yeah. Maybe.'

'Look, how do you fancy coming out with me, tomorrow night?'

'Just the two of us?'

Isobel shook her head. 'Tony and I were planning to see a film, and then go out for some pasta, afterwards. Why don't you come with us?'

'Thanks, but I'd rather not be small, round, green and hairy.'

'You won't be, idiot!'

'Thanks for asking, but I'm sure that you and Tony would have a better time on your own.'

Isobel groaned. 'I didn't mean going just with Tony and me.'

Sophie suddenly caught her friend's drift, and frowned. 'Isobel, I'm not in the mood for a blind date.'

'It won't be. You've met Philip before.'

'Philip?'

'I used to work with him at IPC, before I went freelance.'

'Oh.'

Isobel ruffled Sophie's hair. 'Phil's a nice guy, Soph. One of the world's gentlemen. He won't leap on you or make impossible demands. It's just a good evening out with friends, okay?'

It was easier to agree than to let Isobel argue her into it; eventually, Sophie nodded. 'All right.'

When they met up, the following evening, Sophie recognised Philip from a party that she and Isobel had thrown a couple of years before. She'd thought at the time that Isobel was having a fling with him; but then again, Isobel never slept with anyone she worked with, knowing that it would cause too many problems, in the long run.

Philip was nice-looking, with floppy light brown hair, an engaging grin, and brown eyes with gold flecks in them, which were emphasised by his small round wire-rimmed glasses. He had a generous mouth, and he was so unlike Alex that Sophie began to relax and forget her reservations about the evening.

He turned out to be good company, and Sophie found herself laughing at his anecdotes in the pub, despite her bad mood. When they headed for the cinema, Isobel manoeuvred things so that Sophie was sitting next to Philip; Sophie was half-annoyed with her, but resigned herself to the situation. The film was a psychodrama and, during one of the more intense moments, Sophie found herself holding Philip's hand, grateful for the pressure of his fingers against hers.

Something about the way that his thumb rubbed against her palm made her suddenly aware of him in a sexual way; she frowned, cross with herself. She was acting like a bitch on heat. In the past week, she'd slept with three different men – and it was completely out of character. What was happening to her, that she suddenly found all these different men so attractive, and didn't hold back from sharing the deepest intimacies with them?

This was crazy. She'd only just finished with Gary; she really wasn't ready for another relationship. Not yet. But her body seemed to have other ideas; she was uncomfortably aware of the fact that her nipples were hardening. Behave yourself, Hayward, she admonished herself. You are *not* going to sleep with Philip, nice though he is.

She withdrew her hand from Philip's, and was more reserved with him when the four of them went for a meal, afterwards. Philip seemed to sense her mood, and didn't try taking her hand under the tablecloth, or putting his hand on her knee; he simply behaved as though they were just good friends, and addressed as many remarks to Tony and Isobel as he did to Sophie.

When the waiter brought the bill and they'd divided it into four, Isobel yawned, and stretched. 'Time to go home, I think.' She smiled at Tony. 'Home being your place, that is.'

'Right you are,' Tony said.

They left the restaurant, Tony with his arm round Isobel's shoulders, and Philip and Sophie walking together.

'I'll see you tomorrow, then, Isobel,' Sophie said, when they reached the tube station.

'Okay, Take care.' Isobel kissed her friend's cheek. 'See you, Phil.'

'Bye. See you, Tony.' He turned to Sophie. 'I'll see you home.'

She shook her head. 'Thanks, but I can just about manage. I'm over eighteen.'

'Sophie, I'm aware of that; but, at the same time, London's not the safest place in the world. I'd feel happier if I saw you safely home – the same as I would with any of my female friends. No strings,' Philip told her quietly.

As Isobel had said, Philip was a gentleman. She shook her head. 'Phil, it's very sweet of you, but I'm fine.'

'Sophie, I'm not going to leap on you. All I want to do is see that you get home in one piece.'

The words were such an echo of Isobel's that Sophie couldn't help smiling. 'All right, then.'

They travelled back to Pimlico in companionable silence; Philip didn't try to take her hand, or tuck her hand into his arm, as they walked back to the flat. As Sophie unlocked the door, she paused. 'Would you like a coffee?' she asked politely.

'You'd feel happier if I refused, wouldn't you?'

She frowned. 'How do you mean?'

'Because, since the film, you've been jumpy with me.'

Sophie sighed. 'Look, I've just got a lot on my mind, that's all. And the offer of coffee was genuine, not polite.'

'Really?'

'Really.'

'In that case, accepted with pleasure.' He followed her into the house, closing the door behind him. 'This place is more or less how I remembered it from your house-warming party. It's lovely – very light and airy.'

'Mm, that's the main reason why we rented it,' Sophie said. 'At the time, we couldn't afford a mortgage, between us; I'm half-tempted to suggest to Isobel that we ask the landlord to sell it to us, now that house prices have bottomed out.'

'But?'

'But I get the feeling that she and Tony are getting very serious.'

'This is Isobel the Unattachable you're talking about – at least, that's what we used to call her, in the office,' Philip said. 'I like Isobel – I like her a lot – but I can't see her settling down with one man. Ever.'

'Maybe, maybe not.' Sophie switched on the kettle, and took the coffee from the fridge, shaking the grounds into the cafétière. 'How do you take your coffee?'

'Black, two sugars, please.'

'Right.' She bent over to retrieve the sugar bowl from one of the cupboards; Philip watched her, wondering why Isobel's quieter friend still had no idea just how attractive she was. He itched to touch her, and he had felt her response to him in the cinema, when she'd held his hand; then, she'd suddenly backed off. Isobel had primed him to be gentle with Sophie, explaining that she'd just come out of a long-term relationship; whoever the bloke had been, Phil thought, he must have been crazy to let her go.

As she straightened up, she caught his eyes, and flushed. He walked over to her, and stroked her face. 'Sophie.'

She swallowed. 'Yes?'

'I've been itching to do this, all evening.' He dipped his head, and kissed the tip of her nose.

It was very tender, and very sweet; Sophie couldn't help tipping her face up to his, and he kissed her again, touching his mouth to hers and letting her set the pace. She opened her mouth, and kissed him back, letting his tongue slide along her lower lip and then plunge into her mouth.

His hand slid down her back, resting on the curve of her buttocks; Sophie arched against him, and he eased his fingers under the hem of her loose chiffon shirt. She closed her eyes as he stroked her back, his fingertips brushing her skin lightly; he continued kissing her, and let his hands move round to her midriff, sliding upwards until his hands cupped her breasts.

Her nipples were erect, pushing through the lace of her bra; he brushed the hard peaks of flesh with his thumbs, circling her areolae, and pushed one thigh gently between hers. Sophie didn't pull away, and he let one hand move back to the clasp of her bra, undoing it deftly and then cupping her breasts again, pushing her bra out of the way and touching her skin to skin.

She shuddered, and Philip broke the kiss. He took a step backwards, and rubbed his face. 'Sophie, I'm sorry.'

'It's not your fault. I'm as much to blame.'

He swallowed. 'I just wanted to touch you, hold you.' He sighed. 'I'd better go.'

Sophie surprised herself, by taking a step forward and putting a hand on his arm. 'Phil. You don't have to go.'

'Coffee, then. One coffee, and I'll go.'

She nodded, and turned back to making the coffee. She poured water over the grounds, and let the coffee brew for a while, before pouring it into two mugs and adding sugar to Philip's. She handed the mug to him. 'Let's go and sit down, shall we?'

'Yes.'

She hadn't done up her bra, and her nipples were still hard; Philip could see them through the soft material of her top, and it made him want to touch her again. When she kicked her shoes off in the hallway, on the way to the sitting-room, her skirt curved against her, outlining the shape of her legs, and it made him harden. He forced himself to remain calm, and followed her into the sitting-room. He was intending to sit in the chair, but she patted the sofa next to her, smiling at him. 'As friends, we don't have to sit on opposite sides of the room, do we?'

'No.' He paused. 'But I can't really trust myself to sit near you, Sophie. I can smell your perfume, and . . .' He closed his eyes. 'God. I'm trying so hard not to – well, outstay my welcome.'

'And you're doing a pretty good job, so far.' She smiled at him. 'I'll put some music on, shall I?'

'Fine.'

She chose a Beethoven string quartet, putting it into the CD player and then joining Philip on the sofa. 'It was a good film, wasn't it?'

'Mm.' He looked at her. 'We'll have to do it again, some time.'

'I'd like that.'

'Sophie . . .' He set his mug on the floor, and did the same with hers. Then he removed her glasses, putting them on the low coffee table next to the sofa, and did the same with his. 'Sophie.' He took her hands, stroking them and running his thumb and fore-finger along each of her fingers. The gesture reminded her of the way that Alex had touched her, and her stomach lurched; he stroked his face with her other hand. 'I'm making a mess of this, and I know I shouldn't be rushing you, but . . .' He lowered his mouth to hers, kissing her lightly and then deepening the kiss as he felt her response.

He slid one hand between them, unbuttoning her shirt and pushing her unclasped bra up slightly, then pulled back so that he could look at her. 'God, Sophie, you're so beautiful,' he said softly. 'Your breasts are perfect. You're all lush curves.' He pushed her shirt from her shoulders; she didn't resist, and he removed her bra, too, letting it drop to the floor. 'I want to touch you, Sophie. I want to taste you.' He cupped her breasts, pushing them up and together to deepen her cleavage, then stroked her hardened nipples with his thumbs. 'Sophie . . .' He dipped his head, kissing the curve of her throat and licking the soft hollows of her collar-bones.

She arched against him, and he let his mouth drift downward so that he could suckle one breast, drawing fiercely on the erect nub of flesh while rolling its twin between his thumb and fore-finger. Sophie closed her eyes and slid her hands into his hair, urging him on. She could almost forget that it was Philip with her, touching her and kissing her: all she had to do was change his face, in her mind's eye, and it could be Alex again.

He unzipped her skirt, and lifted her slightly so that he could remove it; then he hooked his thumbs into the sides of her knickers, pulling them down, too. Sophie lifted herself so that he could remove them, and he moved her position slightly, so that she was lying down with her right leg hooked over the top of the sofa, and her left foot was flat on the floor. Philip looked at her for a moment, adoring the soft curves of her body, and then bent his head, licking her areolae and breathing on them in turn so that she shivered and arched against him. Then his mouth tracked slowly southwards, nuzzling her belly.

Sophie sighed with pleasure as Philip licked the soft skin of her inner thighs; he smiled against her skin, and blew lightly along her quim. She pushed her hips up to meet him, making a small sigh of impatience, and he drew his tongue along her musky divide, licking from the top to the bottom in one smooth movement. As his tongue flickered across her clitoris, she tipped her head back against the sofa, her lips parting in a silent groan of pleasure. She shivered when his tongue slid down her quim, parting her labia and scooping out her nectar before moving back to her clitoris and working over it rapidly, bringing her to the edge of orgasm.

'Oh God, yes,' she moaned, and she felt her orgasm burst through her, her internal muscles contracting sharply.

He stayed where he was until the aftershocks of her climax had died down, then rubbed his face against her belly. 'Sophie. Lovely Sophie.'

She was suddenly aware who was with her on the sofa – Philip, not Alex. Philip, who'd been generous enough to bring her to a climax without demanding that she return the favour, or pleasure him first. She stroked his hair. 'Thank you, Philip,' she said quietly.

'My pleasure.' He sat up again, his gaze holding hers. 'Sophie. I want to pleasure you properly.'

She swallowed. 'How do you mean?'

'Like this,' he said softly, pulling her to her feet. 'Touch me, Sophie. Undress me. Make love with me.'

It was a command, but given very gently; the real killer, for her, was that he'd asked her to make love with him. Exactly the same words as Alex had used. And as she'd gone this far with him, letting him undress her and use his mouth on her, why balk at this? she thought. Why refuse, when she wanted it as much as he did? When she wanted the pleasure his body could bring her, to wipe away the ache of knowing that what she'd done with Alex was a one-off, never to be repeated?

She nodded, and undid his shirt, smoothing the muscles of his chest and his upper arms as she removed the garment, throwing it onto the pile of her clothes. She undid his belt and the button at the top of his jeans, then slowly pulled the zipper downwards. Philip kicked off his shoes, then helped her slide the denim down his thighs before stepping out of his jeans and pushing his socks off at the same time.

His cock was rigid, clearly outlined by the soft cotton of his underpants; Sophie couldn't resist curling her fingers round it, and rubbing him gently.

'Oh God, Sophie,' he moaned, and guided her hands to help him remove his underpants.

Naked, he was beautiful; the pure clean lines of his body would have made him a good artist's model, Sophie thought. As it was, she knew that her skill lay in other areas. She couldn't sketch him, to capture the moment. But she could touch him, remember him with her hands. She slid her hands down his midriff, over the flat planes of his stomach; then curled her fingers round his cock again, pulling his foreskin back and forth.

He slid his hand over hers. 'Sophie. I want this to be good for you – and if you keep that up, for much longer, it won't!'

She bit her lip. 'Sorry.'

'Hey, it's not a criticism. I like the way you touch me. Your roving hands get licence, any day.'

Sophie suspected that he was semi-quoting something at her; no doubt Isobel would have caught the reference, but Sophie knew more about pictures than about literature. She let the remark pass, and allowed him to draw her gently to the floor. He lay on his back, pulling her on top of him; she rested against him for a moment, delighting in the feel of his hard cock against her quim. Then he lifted her slightly, sliding one hand between their bodies, and positioned his cock so that its tip rubbed against the entrance to her sex. Slowly, very slowly, she slid onto him; he gave a small moan of pleasure as he felt his cock encased in her warm wet depths, and reached up to touch her breasts, teasing her nipples so that she arched her back and tipped her head back.

She began to move over him, lifting herself very slowly, then slamming down onto him again; his hands drifted down to her hips, and he urged her on, steadying her rhythm. God, he felt good inside her, she thought; she loved the way he filled her, almost as Alex had. And had she been riding Alex, no doubt he would have encouraged her to touch herself – so that she had the pleasure of touch, and he had the pleasure of sight, watching her masturbate as she rode him. She closed her eyes, imagining the scene, and cupped her breasts, lifting them up and together and splaying her fingers so that her nipples peeped through them.

He gave a low murmur of appreciation, and she began to touch herself, pulling at her nipples and distending the hard flesh. Then she let one hand slide down over her midriff again, her fingers pointing downwards, until her hand cupped her mons veneris. He linked his fingers with hers, and slowly guided her hand to her clitoris.

She was still aroused from her previous orgasm, and as soon as she touched her clitoris, she gave a sharp intake of breath. She heard him laugh with pleasure, and he urged her on, moving her hand so that she rubbed her clitoris. She found her rhythm quickly, teasing the sensitive nub of flesh with her middle finger, and then rubbing harder as her pleasure grew.

'Oh, yesssss,' she murmured, as she felt the inner sparkling begin again. Her whole body felt fluid and, as pleasure exploded deep inside her, the shudders of orgasm seemed to travel down every nerve-end, making her whole body quiver.

She felt him stiffen slightly, and then his cock twitched deep inside her as he reached his own climax. He wrapped his arms round her, pulling her back against him and cradling her, resting his cheek against her hair.

Neither of them spoke, unwilling to break the spell; finally,

Philip softened and slipped out of her. He stroked her face. 'Oh, Sophie.'

The sound of his voice shocked her; she'd been half expecting to hear Alex's deep voice. Not Philip's. She swallowed. Christ, what had she done?

'Philip.' Guiltily, she kissed the tip of his nose. 'I don't know about you, but I'm getting cold,' she lied, hoping that he wouldn't see her words for the poor excuse that they were. 'We'd better dress.'

'Mm. Or . . . you could let me carry you to your bed, and keep you warm, there.'

She swallowed. 'I—'

'Sorry. I'm pushing you too far.' He stroked her face. 'Just ignore me.'

'It's my fault, too.' She climbed off him, and dressed swiftly; he followed suit.

'Sophie – I'm sorry.'

'Me, too.' She swallowed. 'Look, Phil – I've just split up with someone.'

'I gathered that.'

'You mean, Isobel told you everything?'

He shook his head. 'Only that you'd recently had a pretty bad time, that you needed cheering up, and that I was to be extremely gentle with you.' He smiled wryly. 'Only I ignored her, and pushed you into doing something that you didn't want to do.'

It wasn't quite true. She'd wanted to do it, just as much as he had – but with someone else. She'd even fantasised about Alex while she was making love with another man. Just what sort of bitch had she become? She flushed deeply. 'Phil – I'm sorry. I just think we'd be better off, as friends.'

'Okay.' He fished in the pocket of his jeans, then removed a business card from his wallet. 'But if you change your mind, give me a ring. There's a messaging service on my mobile, if it's switched off.'

'Right.' She smiled. 'Thank you.'

'No strings, and no pressure. If you want to be just good

friends, and you could do with someone to see a film with – ring me anyway,' he said lightly.

'Yes. And Phil – I really am sorry.'

'Me, too.' He stroked her face. 'I'll see myself out, okay?'

She nodded. 'Thanks.'

'Take care. And – whoever he is – I hope he realises what a mistake he's made.'

If he meant Gary, it wasn't a mistake – it had been her decision. But if he meant Alex . . . She sighed as Philip left the room. God. Of course he hadn't meant Alex. Philip didn't know about Alex – or what had happened at the cottage in the Fens. Isobel didn't know, either, though no doubt she'd made a shrewd guess.

'You've really done it this time, Hayward,' she told herself crossly. What the hell did she think she was playing at, sleeping with any man who passed her way, to help her forget Alex? It wasn't going to work.

She could always contact Alex herself – hire a car, or borrow Isobel's, and drive back down to the Fens to see him. But then again, if Alex had been interested in her, he'd have contacted her. She'd left him her address. He obviously just didn't want to know. He'd had sex with her, on a whim, and it was nothing more than that.

Dejectedly, Sophie went upstairs to her bedroom. Alex's sketch of her, asleep, lay face-down on her dressing-table; she turned it over, and stared at it, remembering what had happened – why he'd sketched her like that. He'd used her. She'd been completely gauche and stupid, and he'd used her. 'Well, fuck you, Alex Waters,' she said, in a sudden fit of temper, and tore up the sketch, scattering the pieces on the floor.

Twelve

Isobel sat at the kitchen table, drumming her fingers on the wood and feeling cross and useless. Even a night out with Philip hadn't managed to cheer Sophie up. She still seemed very withdrawn, almost miserable. Isobel's frown deepened. Phil was a genuinely nice guy. He enjoyed life, and had boundless enthusiasm; if anyone could have got Sophie out of her misery, Phil was the one. The fact that he hadn't meant that something was very badly wrong. Something more than breaking up with Gary – which, in Isobel's opinion, was the best thing that Sophie had done, anyway.

Sophie had spent a spent a lot of time in her studio, recently. Isobel wondered whether the room might hold a clue to what was wrong. She glanced at her watch. Eleven a.m. It was highly unlikely that Sophie would come back to Pimlico from the university at lunchtime, so now was the best time to find out. She walked upstairs and tried the door of the studio; it was locked.

'Oh, bugger,' she said, and went to the bathroom to extract a hairpin. An ex-boyfriend had taught her how to pick locks; at the time, she'd thought it a bit of a joke, but now, she was glad that she'd listened to him. It was a skill that was just about to come in very useful. She jiggled the pin in the lock; finally, it gave, and Isobel let herself into the studio.

Her eyes widened as she looked round. Sophie was incredibly neat – almost to anally-retentive standards – and this was way out of character. Shockingly so. Crumpled paper was strewn everywhere, radiating from the corner where Sophie usually sat, as though she'd grown impatient with whatever she'd been drawing, ripped the sheets from her pad, screwed them up and thrown them across the room, her temper making her not bother to use the bin.

Isobel stooped, and uncrumpled one of the sheets of paper. Her surprise deepened as she recognised the face on it: Alex Waters. She unscrewed another one, and another; all the pictures were of Alex. Some were of him in repose; others were studies of his face. Others showed his whole body – Isobel blinked hard, not quite believing what she saw – his *naked* body. She'd seen enough of Alex, that time when they'd made love, to know that the drawings were very good likenesses.

So he *had* made love to Sophie, while Isobel had been away in the village. Christ. She bit her lip. No wonder that poor old Soph had been moping, these past few days. Alex Waters was very good indeed at making love; and no doubt that had been the final straw, to make her break up with Gary. Sophie was obviously head over heels in love with Alex – and, judging by his silence on the letters front, Alex didn't feel the same.

Isobel shook her head. It was so unfair. Why couldn't Sophie have fallen for someone nice, someone kind and gentle and caring, like Phil? Why had she had to fall for a calculating and awkward bastard like Alex Waters? Still, there was one way, Isobel thought, that she could help. She could sound out JJ, when she went to clear the interview. Which would be in – she glanced at her watch – precisely two hours.

Carefully, she crumpled the paper again, and dropped it on the floor in approximately the same place that Sophie had left it. Then she closed the door behind her, and tested it: the lock held firm. Sophie would be none the wiser that Isobel had been in the room – much less that she'd seen the crumpled-up drawings, and had a pretty good idea why Sophie was so unhappy.

JJ's office was in Shepherd's Bush. Isobel caught the tube, and found the place fairly easily, thanks to Phoebe's faxed directions. The office turned out to be a neo-Georgian building: very austere, and very tasteful. Sophie, Isobel thought, would love it on sight. She went up to the front door and pressed the intercom; it buzzed, and she heard Phoebe's voice. 'Hello, JJ Wrenn's office.'

'Isobel Moran. I have an appointment with JJ.'

'Come up. We're on the first floor.' There was another buzz, and the door clicked open.

Isobel walked up the stairs, her feet sinking into the dark blue thick pile runner. The mahogany treads on either side of the runner were perfectly polished, and the ornately-carved banisters were dust-free. Framed paintings hung on the walls; Isobel paused to inspect one, and realised that it was by an artist she'd heard of. It looked like an original, too; obviously he was one of JJ's clients.

There was a navy blue gloss door on the landing; the under-stated brass plate in the middle said *JJ Wrenn Associates*. Isobel knocked. At Phoebe's crisp and cheerful 'come in', she opened the door; she stopped dead as she saw the attractive young woman sitting at the desk in front of her. It was the same woman that Alex Waters had sketched, while she was masturbating . . .

Quickly, Isobel recovered her composure and stretched out her hand. 'Hello. I'm Isobel Moran.'

'Phoebe Montague. Nice to meet you, at last.'

Isobel had to fight hard to stop a betraying flush as she suddenly remembered what Alex had told her: Phoebe knew everything that had happened between her and JJ in the restaurant. 'I'm about five minutes early, I'm afraid. I hope that's not too inconvenient?'

'Ah.' Phoebe winced. 'I'm afraid there's been a slight change of plan. I tried to ring you on the number you'd given JJ, but the phone was switched off.'

Isobel rolled her eyes. 'More like, the battery's run down again. Sorry. I think it's time I bought a new one.'

'JJ's been detained,' Phoebe explained. 'He had a lunch meeting with one of his clients. It's gone off schedule, and I don't think he's going to be back at all, this afternoon.'

'Oh.' Isobel bit her lip. 'I was hoping that he could clear my interview with Alex Waters, so I could take it to *Vivendi* on Monday morning.'

Phoebe shrugged. 'Well, I can do that, if you like.'

'Yes, you must know Alex pretty well.' The words were out before Isobel could stop them.

Phoebe grinned, immediately catching the reference. 'You've seen the sketches, then?'

'Er – yes.'

Phoebe raised one eyebrow. 'I'm surprised that Alex showed them to you. He must have liked you.'

Isobel had the grace to look embarrassed. 'He didn't actually show me them, as such. The portfolio was lying there, in the sitting room.'

Phoebe nodded. 'I would have looked at them, too.' She smiled. 'About the second time I went to see Alex, he talked me into posing for him.'

And what a pose, Isobel thought. 'Do you often – er – pose?'

'Like that?' Phoebe smiled. 'Only for Alex – but then, Alex has this effect on women, don't you think?'

'Yes,' Isobel admitted. Alex Waters was incredibly sensual – when he wasn't being difficult.

'Can I get you a cup of coffee?' Phoebe asked.

'Yes, please. Black, no sugar.'

While Phoebe busied herself making coffee, Isobel glanced round the room. The ceiling was very high, and the walls were painted in a pale aqua colour, contrasting sharply with the white moulded cornices. Framed pictures hung on the walls; they were obviously originals, and Isobel assumed that they were by more of JJ's clients. She wasn't a fan of modern art, but she could see how good they were.

She opened her briefcase to retrieve her conference folder and the typed-up copy of the interview; the carefully rolled-up portraits were still there. Isobel bit her lip. She had been intending to confess to JJ that she'd 'borrowed' them, but she didn't feel that she could tell Phoebe. Clearing the interview with her was one thing, but to explain about the portraits – and the fact that she had a portrait of a naked and masturbating Phoebe in her case – was quite another.

She was surprised that Tony hadn't recognised Phoebe in the picture; but then again, maybe Tony had only ever spoken to Phoebe, not actually met her. Once met, she thought, most definitely not forgotten. Phoebe had dark hair, like Isobel, with very pale skin, piercing blue eyes and an incredible bone structure. She wouldn't have looked out of place in a Merchant-Ivory film, wearing an Edwardian dress and with her curls piled up on top of her head.

At the same time, Isobel knew that Phoebe wasn't the demure woman she seemed and she certainly wasn't the educated luvvie that Isobel had dismissed her as, earlier. Phoebe was a very sensual woman, with a full lower lip and a way of smiling that made you want to see her laugh in pleasure, tipping her head back and revealing her beautiful white throat, just right for kissing . . . Isobel caught her thoughts, and swallowed hard. Christ. She wasn't usually given to fantasising about other women.

Phoebe turned round, having made two mugs of coffee, and nodded to the sofa. 'Shall we sit down in comfort?' It was merely a polite invitation, but Isobel had a funny feeling that Phoebe meant a little more than that. She forced herself to concentrate, and sat down on the sofa next to Phoebe, handing the other woman her neatly typed-up interview.

'This is it,' she said quietly.

'Right.' Phoebe took the paper, and read through it, her brow creased in concentration. Isobel waited in silence, watching her and drinking her coffee. Eventually, Phoebe looked up. 'It's good,' she said. 'It's penetrating, but I don't think there's anything controversial, at all. I'm happy to sign it off. Alex won't have any problem with what you've written.'

'Thank you.'

Phoebe tipped her head on one side. 'He must have liked you,' she said.

'You sound surprised.'

'Mm. Alex is . . . moody, shall we say? One day, he prefers women to be direct with him; the next, he wants them to be oblique. You never know where you stand, with him.'

Isobel smiled. 'Actually, he didn't like me. He gave the interview to my friend Sophie.'

'Sophie?'

'She's learning sign language. I thought that it might make him feel more at ease if I had someone with me who could talk to him in sign.'

'Right.' Phoebe twisted the ring on the fourth finger of her right hand, as if thinking.

Isobel made a spur-of-the-moment decision. 'How well do you know Alex?'

'Do you mean as in the Biblical sense?'

'No, I'd already gathered that, from the sketches. No, I mean do you know how he reacts to things?'

'Why?'

'Because,' Isobel said slowly, 'and this is confidential – I think that he and my friend Sophie . . . Well, let's just say that they rather liked each other.'

Phoebe burst out laughing. 'Are you trying to tell me that you want to matchmake, with your friend and Alex?'

'Not exactly.'

'What, then?'

'I was thinking, maybe if you could talk Alex into coming up to London for the exhibition, I could engineer it so that he bumps into Sophie. Who knows what might happen when they meet again?'

Phoebe still shook her head, laughing. 'Matchmaking and Alex . . . Well, they just don't go together. Even if I could persuade him to come up to London – and that in itself is a big task – I don't know how he'd react to you fixing him up with your friend.'

Isobel coughed. 'Phoebe, can I be honest with you?'

'Sure.'

'Good.' Isobel sighed. 'I'm not very good at being diplomatic, or a hot-shot negotiator. I prefer people to be straight with me, and I'm straight with them in return.'

'That's a good philosophy.'

Isobel nodded. 'Well, I think that something happened between him and Sophie.'

'How do you mean, think?'

'I don't know for sure – she's my best friend, but she wouldn't tell me.' Isobel shrugged, and explained about her car breaking down and her abortive trip to the village. 'They were sitting at the kitchen table when I got back. There was something in the air . . .' She spread her hands. 'I think they'd be good together, Phoebe. She teaches history of art, and she paints a bit – she's very good, but she won't admit it. She's really sweet. Probably too good for him.'

'Ouch. You didn't like him very much, then?'

'He was all right when he wasn't being moody.' Isobel tipped her head on one side. 'So what do you say? Will you help me?'

'I suppose it's worth a try,' Phoebe said thoughtfully. 'I'll give it a go. I could go to the Fens next week, I suppose.'

'Thanks.'

There was a brief silence. 'You're not at all what I'd expected,' Isobel said eventually.

Phoebe grinned. 'One of my ex-boyfriends once told me that I had a voice like cream – thick and rich.'

Isobel winced. 'Sorry. I didn't mean to insult you.'

'It's not a problem. It's half the reason why JJ took me on, in the first place – he wanted someone well-spoken and a bit debby. It was the sort of thing his clients expected.'

'I can see that.'

'Then,' Phoebe said, 'he discovered that I had other talents, not just my voice.'

Isobel couldn't help the question. 'Like the way you posed for Alex, you mean?'

Phoebe nodded. 'That – and a post-grad course in administration, so I could sort out his pit of a filing system and keep his accounts up to date.' She smiled at Isobel. 'To be honest, you're not what I expected, either. What JJ told me about you . . .'

Isobel flushed. 'Yes, Alex said that JJ tells you everything.'

'We're not so unalike, you and I,' Phoebe said. 'We like the same sort of things – good wine, good company . . .' Her voice became caressing. 'And pleasure.'

Isobel licked her suddenly dry lips. Was it her imagination, or was Phoebe giving her a come-on?

'Alex made love to you, didn't he?' Phoebe continued. 'When you were at the cottage.'

'Have you spoken to him?'

Phoebe shook her head. 'I don't have to. I can see it in your face, when you speak his name. And the fact that you've seen the sketches . . . I can imagine the effect they had on you, because I know the effect they would have had on me, had I been in your place.' She grinned, her face lightening. 'He has quite an imagination, hasn't he?'

'How do you mean?'

'Well – he may be deaf, but he likes to talk, in certain circumstances. He likes to fantasise aloud, when he's making love.'

Isobel's flush deepened. She was sure that, somehow, Phoebe knew exactly what Alex had said to her.

'Your friend – do you think she can cope with the wild side of Alex?'

'I don't know, but she's miserable without him. She can't be any more miserable with him.'

Phoebe rubbed her jaw. 'As they say, there's always a first time for everything.' Ostensibly, she was talking about Sophie and Alex; though Isobel knew that Phoebe was talking about something else, too.

'And if I told you,' Isobel said quietly, 'that you're right about me, and I do like pleasure . . .'

Phoebe's eyes glittered. 'I thought as much.' She picked up Isobel's hands, rubbing her thumb against the palm; Isobel shivered, and Phoebe raised Isobel's hand to her lips, sucking each finger in turn, and keeping Isobel's gaze fixed very firmly with her own. Isobel felt a pulse start to beat hard between her legs.

'Phoebe, I—'

'Didn't Alex suggest it to you?' Phoebe asked, her voice husky.

'You mean, you *have* talked to him.'

Phoebe shook her head. 'I just know how his mind works. He's an artist, remember: he'd think that we'd look good together. My hair's almost the same colour as yours, but a different texture; the contrast of that and our skin, the contrast of your eyes and mine . . .'

Isobel swallowed, suddenly feeling out of her depth. 'Phoebe, I've never—'

'Never made love with another woman?' Phoebe shrugged. 'Like I said, there's a first time for everything.' Her eyes met Isobel's. 'The question is, are you brave enough to try it?'

Isobel lifted her chin. 'I'm not a coward.'

'No, I don't think you are.' Phoebe's eyes crinkled at the corners. 'It's unfair of me to challenge you. I don't want you to do this out of a sense of pride, or anything like that. I want you to do this because you want it.'

Isobel flushed. 'When Alex and I . . . He said he'd have me tied up, he'd bring me to the edge of orgasm, and then he'd make me watch him make love with another woman. He suggested you. And then he said that he'd let you touch me.'

Phoebe grinned. 'He actually did that to me, once. It was with one of his other models. I'd gone down with JJ, and, as we left, he pressed a note into my hand. I read it later, and he said that he wanted to paint me. So I went back on my own. He showed me some of his paintings.' She licked her lips. 'I was like you. I'd never made love with another woman. I'd thought myself a hundred per cent heterosexual – but I found myself so turned on by his paintings. I wondered what he'd done to the model, to make her so uninhibited before him. I wondered if he'd used his hands or his mouth on her, or even something else. A dildo, to stretch her, or the handle of one of his paintbrushes. I asked him, and he wouldn't tell me: he just smiled.

'I took my clothes off, and he painted me. And as he worked, he talked to me, telling me what he was going to do with me when he'd finished sketching. He aroused me so much, I ended up masturbating in front of him. I brought myself to a screaming climax, and then, suddenly, he was there next to me, sliding his body into mine. I don't think I've ever been so turned on, before or since. He took me to the edge of another orgasm, and then he withdrew. Then he told me exactly what he wanted to do.' She spread her hands. 'Pretty much the same as he'd told you. But what I hadn't known was that the other model had been there, all the time, sitting behind a screen. I hadn't seen her. She was blonde, and she was wearing just a cornflower blue silk robe; it wasn't properly done up, and I think she'd been touching herself while she was watching me.'

Isobel swallowed. 'And then she made love with you?'

'Yes.' Phoebe paused. 'She did.' Her words hung in the air, a promise and a challenge rolled into one. Then she stood up, taking Isobel's hand and leading her through to JJ's office. The room was large, again with pale aqua walls and hung with beautiful paintings – including one of Phoebe which looked as though it had been done by Alex.

'That's lovely,' Isobel said, nodding to the picture.

'Thank you.' Phoebe's smile broadened to a grin. 'Slightly more demure than the ones you saw at the cottage, no doubt.'

'You could say that,' Isobel admitted, smiling back.

The rest of the room was furnished simply. There were two large brown leather armchairs, a large mahogany desk and, in front of the fireplace, a silk Persian rug.

'JJ didn't have any other meetings booked today,' Phoebe said, 'apart from the one from lunch which ran over. He won't bother coming back to the office, afterwards. So we won't be disturbed.'

A steady pulse quickened between Isobel's legs. If Phoebe was suggesting what she thought she was . . . Then she stopped thinking, as Phoebe cupped her face and kissed her very lightly on the lips. Her mouth was warm and sweet, and Isobel found herself responding, opening her mouth and letting Phoebe's tongue flicker against her own.

Isobel was wearing another business suit, a black one which was more demurely cut than the one she'd worn when she'd last seen JJ. Phoebe unbuttoned the tailored jacket, slipping it from Isobel's shoulders and dropping it on the floor. Then she tugged gently at Isobel's shirt, pulling it free from the waistband of her skirt. Isobel shivered as Phoebe began to undo the buttons, the backs of her fingers brushing against Isobel's breasts.

She stooped slightly to brush Isobel's nose with hers, and finished unbuttoning her shirt, pushing the garment off Isobel's shoulders and dropping it on top of the jacket. 'Mm, nice,' she said, running the tip of her forefinger just under the edge of the cups of Isobel's bra. 'Very nice,' she purred, as Isobel's nipples hardened and began to peep through the lace.

Isobel responded by sliding her hands round Phoebe's neck, and drawing her face down for a kiss. Phoebe opened her mouth under Isobel's, letting Isobel explore her, and allowed Isobel to unbutton her own shirt. She helped Isobel remove the soft cotton garment, then unzipped Isobel's skirt. 'Mm, stockings,' she said, as she pushed the skirt over Isobel's hips. 'JJ said that he thought you wore them. The hold-up type. My favourites, too.'

'JJ told you what happened in the restaurant?'

Phoebe nodded.

'And you told Alex.'

Phoebe smiled. 'JJ wasn't doing very well, talking him into the interview. So I thought we needed something to hook him – some information that would intrigue him enough to agree to it.'

'Right.' Isobel flushed.

'Hey – it's nothing that I wouldn't have done, in your situation,' Phoebe said.

'Are you telling me that you've slept with JJ?' Isobel was shocked.

Phoebe shook her head. 'He's my boss – so he's off limits. Though if I ever switch jobs, I'd be tempted. I'm not sure whether it's his eyes or his voice.'

'I know what you mean,' Isobel admitted, shivering.

'But JJ isn't here. Whereas you are.' Phoebe stroked Isobel's face. 'You have lovely eyes, Isobel. They go green and gold when you're aroused.'

'Whereas yours are cornflower blue.'

'Contrasts of colour and texture. Alex would certainly approve.' Phoebe's lips twitched.

'Pity that he isn't here, now, to see this. I think he'd enjoy it. But he's not.'

'Just you and me.'

'Just you and me,' Phoebe echoed as Isobel removed her skirt. Like Isobel, she was wearing hold-up lace-topped stockings; Isobel suddenly grinned.

'What?' Phoebe asked.

'I was just thinking . . . we're dressed so alike, now, we could almost be twins. Like that film with Schwarzenegger, though – because you're taller than me.'

Phoebe chuckled. 'I think you're a little prettier than Danny de Vito, though.'

'I should hope so, too.'

Phoebe smiled. She hooked her fingers into the straps of Isobel's bra, and drew them down slowly. 'White suits you. I imagine you wear black a lot, but white's so sensual. Like your skin, pale and delicate . . .' She deftly undid the clasp, and let the lacy bra fall to the floor. 'Mm. Perfect. Absolutely perfect.' She cupped Isobel's breasts, lifting them up and together. 'Soft and warm and generous. I want to taste you, Isobel, as well as touch.'

Isobel's mouth was dry. 'I—'

'Shh. Time for talking, later,' Phoebe said, stooping slightly and kissing the soft white globes, her lips cool. She drew her tongue along the undersides of Isobel's breasts, and then finally made her tongue into a hard point and flicked it across the hard buds of her nipples.

Isobel couldn't help a soft moan; Phoebe smiled against her skin, and began to suckle one breast, rolling the other nipple between her thumb and forefinger. Isobel arched her back, closing her eyes and tipping her head back; Phoebe was extremely skilled, and Isobel felt her quim grow hot and liquid as her new lover caressed her.

'Isobel.' Phoebe straightened up, and took Isobel's hand. 'Shall we?'

Isobel nodded, kicked off her shoes, and let herself be led to the Persian carpet. It was pure silk, she discovered, as she sank onto it; Phoebe sank down next to her, and caressed her face. 'Isobel. I think we're both going to enjoy this – don't you?'

'Yes. Though you're wearing more than I am.'

'True. And this is an equal relationship, so . . .' Phoebe stretched, and brought her hands to the clasp of her bra, undoing it and throwing the lacy garment to one side. 'Better?'

'Better,' Isobel confirmed.

Phoebe licked her lower lip. 'Touch me,' she invited.

Isobel stretched out a hand, gently cupping one breast; touching Phoebe felt so much like touching herself. Yet, at the same time, it was different . . . She traced the areola with the tip of her middle finger, watching the nipple harden, then transferred her attention to the other breast. Phoebe made a small purr of pleasure, and took Isobel's hand, kissing her inner wrist and touching the tip of her tongue to the pulse point.

The next thing Isobel knew, she was on her back, and Phoebe was stroking her body, smoothing the lines of her belly and letting her hand drift nearer and nearer to the juncture of her thighs. Isobel shivered, and widened the gap between her thighs; Phoebe eased one finger under the leg of Isobel's knickers, and drew it between her labia, exploring her intimate folds and crevices. Isobel gave a small moan of pleasure, and then at last Phoebe slid one finger deep inside her. Isobel sighed, parting her legs wider and closing her eyes; Phoebe began to move her hand back and forth in a slow and easy rhythm, building Isobel's excitement to fever pitch before pistoning rapidly in and out; meanwhile, she rubbed Isobel's clitoris with her thumb.

Isobel writhed under her new lover's ministrations; Phoebe smiled approvingly. 'Let yourself go, Isobel. Touch yourself. Feel the pleasure,' she commanded huskily.

Isobel was so turned on, that she did exactly what she was told, bringing one hand up to touch her breasts, and sliding the other one beneath her knickers to tangle her fingers with Phoebe's. The pleasure seemed to go on and on and on, and when she came, it was as though she were seeing stars, bright flashes of light. Her whole body seemed to become liquid, and she cried out in bliss.

When her breathing had slowed down, she found herself cradled in Phoebe's arms. 'Okay?' Phoebe asked.

'Mm. Very.' Isobel tipped her head on one side, and looked up at her lover. 'I wasn't expecting it to be – so good.'

'Thanks for the backhander,' was the smiling retort.

'Now – your turn, I think.' Isobel disengaged herself gently from Phoebe's arms, and pushed her onto her back; Phoebe put her hands behind her head and drew her knees up, putting her feet flat on the floor. Isobel crouched between her lover's thighs, and gently lifted her bottom, pulling down Phoebe's knickers at the same time. She tossed the lacy garment to one side, then smoothed Phoebe's thighs apart, looking at her. 'You're very beautiful,' she said softly. 'No wonder Alex wanted to paint you.'

'Not just paint. He touched, as well,' Phoebe said, equally quietly.

'I think I can take a hint,' Isobel quipped, drawing her finger along Phoebe's quim. She was wet with anticipation – and still turned on by what she'd just done with Isobel. Isobel wasn't a hundred per cent sure what to do – she'd never been in this situation before – but she guessed that Phoebe would enjoy the sort of thing that she enjoyed. She smiled, and bent her head, nuzzling Phoebe's midriff. Phoebe moaned, and shifted her position, widening the gap between her thighs; Isobel's mouth tracked southwards, and she paused by Phoebe's quim breathing lightly on her.

Phoebe shivered, and wriggled. 'Isobel,' she murmured, tangling her hands in her lover's hair. 'Don't tease.'

'No.' Isobel breathed in the scent of Phoebe's arousal – a heady mixture of honey and musk – and stretched out her tongue, exploring the delicate folds and crevices. Phoebe's clitoris was already hard, unsheathed from its little hood; Isobel made her tongue into a sharp point and flicked rapidly across it, eliciting another moan of pleasure from Phoebe. She continued lapping, liking the taste and the way that she could make a self-possessed woman like Phoebe shiver and moan, begging for more.

She let one finger dabble in the moisture, then fitted the tip of her finger to Phoebe's sex, pushing gently. Phoebe gave a sigh of bliss, and flexed her internal muscles round Isobel's finger, clutching at her. Isobel added a second finger, and a third, pistoning her hand back and forth while her mouth worked on Phoebe's clitoris.

At last, Phoebe cried out, and her quim rippled round Isobel's finger; Isobel could taste the sweetness of her orgasm, and continued lapping until the aftershocks of Phoebe's climax had died down. Then she shifted up to kiss Phoebe, so that Phoebe could taste her own juices on her mouth.

Phoebe stroked her face. 'Ten out of ten for a first time,' she said softly. 'And I think that you and I are going to be very good friends . . .'

Thirteen

Isobel had made a second appointment to see JJ, on the following Tuesday; by the time she arrived at Shepherd's Bush, she was smiling, eagerly anticipating the meeting. It would be good to see JJ again – and Phoebe. Her stomach turned to water at the thought. JJ and Phoebe . . . She shivered. But today wasn't the day for indulging herself, she knew. Today was the day she was going to confess about the paintings – and persuade JJ to take her side.

To her secret disappointment, JJ himself answered the intercom: Phoebe wasn't there. But then again, Phoebe might have gone to the Fens to sweet-talk Alex into attending the exhibition – the first part of their plan to get Sophie and Alex together properly. Isobel was cheered by the thought.

'Isobel. How nice to see you again.' JJ kissed her lightly on the cheek, and she shivered. She could imagine him using his mouth on other parts of her skin, and it was a delightful thought. The man just exuded sex. 'Phoebe tells me that the interview was a success.'

'Yes.'

'And that she's cleared it, in my stead.'

'Yes.'

He tipped his head on one side. 'So, may I ask why you wanted to see me, today?'

Isobel smiled, recovering her composure. 'At least Phoebe offered me a cup of coffee, before talking business.'

He grinned. 'I'm not Phoebe.' His eyes sparkled as he looked at her. 'I believe the two of you got on rather well.'

Had Phoebe told him what had happened, on his Persian rug? Had she gone into intimate detail of how they'd caressed each other, removed each other's clothes and made love – the way JJ had obviously gone into detail about what had happened between them at the restaurant? Isobel flushed. 'Yes. She was – er – very nice.'

JJ smiled knowingly at her. 'I'll get you that cup of coffee.'

'Black, no sugar, please,' Isobel told him.

He rolled his eyes. 'Don't tell me you're dieting.'

'Good God, no. Diets don't work for me, anyway – I use exercise, to keep my weight under control.'

'Indeed.' The word was loaded: JJ had a pretty good idea what sort of exercise Isobel meant.

'I just like my caffeine unadulterated.' She grinned. 'So where's Phoebe today?'

'She's gone to see Alex.'

Isobel hugged herself inwardly. She'd been right, then. Phoebe really was going to help her get Alex and Sophie together. And once her house-mate was settled, life would start looking very rosy indeed.

JJ made them both a coffee, then handed her a mug. 'Come through.'

She followed him into his office. The last time she'd been in that room, she and Phoebe had . . . She shivered deliciously at the memory. But now was not the time to think of that. She had to win JJ over to her side about the paintings.

She sat down on one of the large leather chairs, putting her briefcase down by her side, and cupped the mug of coffee in both hands, sipping the bitter dark liquid. It was as good as she'd expected. JJ was a true connoisseur of coffee, and he made even better coffee than his assistant did.

'So – to business. What can I do for you, then?'

'Well . . .' Isobel paused. 'I don't know quite how to put this, JJ.'

'That you've stolen three of Alex's paintings?' JJ asked softly.

Isobel's mouth opened in shock. So he knew all about it? But – how? 'I haven't stolen them – just borrowed them.' She frowned. 'How did you know I had them, anyway?' Had Tony spilled the beans?

178

'Alex told me.'

'Alex?' She was surprised. 'When?'

'Last week. The day after you visited him, in fact. He sent me a short and sweet postcard, informing me that three pictures were missing, and where he thought they were.'

'But – you didn't say anything, before. Neither did Phoebe, when she saw me about the interview.'

'No. We were waiting to see what you were up to.'

Isobel digested this. Had Phoebe's seduction been a way of trying to get Isobel to come clean about the paintings? And, if so, why hadn't Phoebe mentioned them then? Especially since Phoebe knew that she'd seen the sketches Alex had made of her? 'Did you really think that I'd stolen them?' she asked quietly.

JJ spread his hands. 'I suppose not. I don't think that being a thief is one of your qualities. But I did wonder quite what you intended to do with them. Did you borrow them because you liked them, or was there more to it than that?'

Isobel flushed. 'I liked them, but you're right, it wasn't just that. They're good, JJ – really good – and you know it. I only took my three favourites, but there were plenty of others, all just as good. Why not make the exhibition half a retro, and half new stuff?'

'And that was your plan?'

'Yes. I didn't think that Alex would miss them.'

'Didn't you?'

'Actually, amateur psychology would say that he wanted me to see them – because he left his portfolio in full view, and left me to it. It's pretty obvious that, as a nosy journo, I'd look at the contents.'

'Perhaps.' JJ paused. 'So, you looked at them, and liked them. What then?'

'I decided to borrow a couple, and show them to Tony; then, if he agreed, I'd talk to you and ask you persuade Alex to make them part of the exhibition.'

'Right. So Tony knew about it?' JJ's voice was soft, but his eyes were very hard.

Isobel winced. 'Yes – but only after I'd borrowed them. He didn't approve – he thought I should have asked.'

'And why didn't you?'

'Because you know as well as I do that Alex would have refused. And leave Tony out of this – none of this was his idea. He wanted to ring you there and then, but I persuaded him to wait.' She frowned. 'JJ, Alex owes it to the world to let them see the paintings.'

'He paints for himself. You know that.'

'God, it's like these rich banks who own Monets and Van Goghs and Modiglianis, and keep them stuck in nice secure vaults. The paintings are stored at the right temperature and humidity, so they're kept well – but no-one ever sees their beauty. It's a waste, JJ. Paintings can bring so much pleasure to people. It's a crime to keep them locked up, out of sight.'

JJ said nothing.

She bit her lip. Suddenly, she felt like a naughty schoolgirl, hauled up to see the headmaster for some misdemeanour or other. Or the way she'd felt before a weekly meeting with her editor, in the days when she worked for a magazine. She'd got on badly with her editor, and every time she went to a meeting, she knew that everything she'd done would be criticised. She had that same sick, nervous feeling, with her stomach churning and the back of her neck growing hot. Just how bad was this going to be? 'What did – ' She cleared her throat, hoping that her voice would drop to its normal pitch again, instead of the betraying squeak. 'What did Alex say, when he told you that the paintings were gone?'

'Just that he was going to pull the exhibition. And I don't blame him – do you?'

Isobel closed her eyes. 'Oh, Christ. Look – I don't want him to do that. There's no need. But . . . Those paintings. They're good, JJ. I want the world to see them. I don't know why he's so set against it – whether he's lost his confidence, or he's worried that people are going to muck-rake about the accident. But whatever happened was years ago, and it wasn't his fault. It doesn't matter any more. It's his painting that matters.'

JJ couldn't help smiling at her. 'Speaks the true campaigner. I bet you'd have been a Suffragette, years ago, chaining yourself to railings and lecturing passionately about a cause you believed in.'

'Probably.' Isobel sighed. 'Well, now you know about them, I suppose I'd better give them back.' She set the coffee on the floor, picked up her briefcase, and opened it. Her colour drained as she realised that the three rolls of paper were no longer in her case. Slowly, she removed her conference folder, her phone and the paperback book she'd been reading on the Tube, but the paintings weren't hidden at the bottom. Her case was empty.

'I thought you said that you had them?'

'I did – I mean, I do.' Isobel closed her eyes. 'I must have taken them out, and left them somewhere safe at home. I thought I'd put them in my case, this morning, but obviously I didn't.' A small trickle of fear ran down her back. She couldn't remember taking them out of her briefcase since she'd put them there, at Tony's. So where the hell were they? And if they weren't safely at home, then who could have taken them? When?

'Tell you what,' JJ said quietly. 'Go home, and get the paintings. When you've given them back to me, we'll discuss what happens next – and, in the meantime, I'll try to persuade Alex not to press charges.'

'Of course,' Isobel said, trying not to betray her mounting panic. 'I'll skip the rest of my coffee, shall I?'

'I think so, in the circumstances.' The hint of steel she'd noticed before was now very much stronger; Isobel decided that trying to flirt with him was not a good idea. JJ Wrenn was not a man to be crossed.

She smiled ruefully. 'JJ. I really am sorry.'

'Just bring me the paintings, Isobel, and we'll take it from there,' he said quietly. The smile had gone from his eyes, and the amusement. He wanted his client's property back, quickly, and that was it. She'd blown it.

She nodded, and picked up her briefcase before leaving the room. Christ, it had gone so differently to what she'd expected. She'd thought that she and JJ would banter over coffee, flirt with

181

each other – even indulge in a little light physicality, touching each other and maybe kissing – and then she'd sweet-talk him over the pictures. The last thing she'd expected was for the paintings to be gone from her briefcase – or for JJ to turn into the forbidding headmaster type.

All the way home, Isobel tried to remember what she'd done with them. Eventually, she came to the conclusion that they had definitely been in her briefcase. Nobody else knew about them, apart from Tony – not even Sophie. Tony wouldn't cheat her . . . So what the hell had happened? Where could they possibly be?

When she let herself into the house, Sophie was already home. She was sitting in silence on the sofa and looking very tense. Isobel forced a smile to her face. 'Hi, Soph. Okay?'

'That depends,' Sophie said.

Isobel stared at her friend in surprise. 'Sorry?'

'There's a message for you on the answerphone.'

'Right.' Isobel bit her lip. Don't say that Phoebe had left her some kind of tactless message about Alex and Sophie. That was all she needed, to make it one of her worst days ever. She walked over to the answerphone, and pressed the play button.

The voice was male, and not one she recognised. 'This is a message for Isobel Moran. If you want the paintings back, you'll have to come and get them. We'll be in touch.'

She frowned, let it rewind, and played it again. Her frown deepened, and she picked up the phone, dialling the number to find out who had called. A smug announcer told her that the caller had withheld the number.

'I've already tried that,' Sophie said. 'So, are you going to tell me what this is about?'

'Nothing much,' Isobel said. 'Just a joke by a friend.'

'Isobel, don't lie to me. I saw your face when you heard the message. It wasn't a joke. So tell me – what's it all about?'

Isobel closed her eyes. Sophie was really going to freak, when she heard this. 'I borrowed some paintings. They've gone missing.'

'Borrowed from where? Tony's gallery?'

Isobel shook her head.

Sophie's eyes widened. 'I hope, Isobel, that you're not going to tell me that you stole them from Alex.'

'I didn't steal them! I borrowed them.'

'Then they were talking about Alex's pictures?'

Isobel nodded. 'Yes.'

'Christ, I don't believe it! How could you do something so *stupid*?' Sophie yelled. No wonder Alex hadn't contacted her. Either he thought that she'd taken the paintings – or he thought that she was in league with Isobel, and had distracted him while Isobel rifled through the portfolio and took what she wanted. How he must hate her.

'Calm down, Soph. It wasn't like that. Look, I just borrowed them. I wanted to show them to Tony.'

'You stupid, stupid bitch. I can't believe you've done this.'

'Soph, will you just shut up and listen to me? Alex hasn't exhibited for years. He agreed to do the retro – and when I saw the new paintings, I thought that they'd make a great show, too. They're brilliant, Soph, and it's a crime to keep them mouldering in the Fens.'

'It's his privilege. He's the artist.'

'Yeah, and he's being selfish, keeping them out of the public eye. All I did was borrow a couple of the pictures to show Tony.'

'How many?'

'Three.'

Three. God, Alex must really hate her, Sophie thought. Invading his privacy, pushing him back into the public eye, putting him in a position where people could muck-rake about his past . . . It was all thanks to Isobel. She'd ruined something really special.

'Does Alex know that you've taken them?'

Isobel winced. 'Yes. But look, he told JJ last week – and JJ didn't say a thing to me, until today.'

'So JJ called you over to see him?'

Isobel shook her head. 'I went to tell him that I had the paintings, and to suggest that Alex exhibited them as part of the show. But when I opened my briefcase, the paintings were gone.

I said that I'd left them at home, by mistake, and he told me to come back when I had them.'

'But you didn't leave them at home, did you?'

'No.'

'So who's got them?'

'I don't know.' Isobel sighed. 'Look, Soph – this won't make any difference to you.'

'Won't it?' Sophie's voice was hard and cold. 'Isobel, you've ruined everything.'

'I haven't.'

'You have. If it wasn't for you, stealing those paintings, Alex would have got in touch with me, by now.'

Isobel closed her eyes. At last, Sophie had admitted what was wrong – that she was pining for Alex. The worst thing was, it was too late. Now that the paintings had gone, Alex had just cause to hate both of them. 'Look, Soph, those paintings have nothing to do with you and Alex.'

'If you hadn't taken them, Alex would have got in touch with me,' Sophie repeated.

Guilt made Isobel sarcastic. 'And how would he have done that? Telepathy?'

'No. I left him my address.'

'And you thought that he'd write to you?'

'Well – yes.'

'Just because he made love with you?'

Sophie's cheeks flamed. 'That's none of your business.'

'Be realistic, Soph. If you broke up with Gary because you were hoping that something would work between you and Alex, you were kidding yourself. Soph, he's a selfish bastard, and he'd eat you for breakfast.'

'Just because he paints explicit pictures, it doesn't mean that he sleeps around.'

'Doesn't it?'

Sophie lifted her chin. 'No. And now you've ruined it.'

Isobel was furious. If Sophie only knew it, Isobel had been trying to matchmake, via Phoebe. And now, Sophie was blaming her for Alex's selfish nature? 'I haven't ruined anything. Christ, that man would sleep with anything in a skirt.'

'Oh, so I'm a whore now, am I? A cheap little tart?'

'No, of course you're not! What I'm trying to say, Soph, is that the man likes sex. He's screwed Phoebe, he's screwed you, he's screwed most of the women who modelled for him – Christ, he's even screwed me. And while he was doing it, he fantasised about having me tied up and watching me with another woman.'

'You *what?*'

Isobel suddenly realised that she'd gone too far. She walked over to Sophie and put a hand over hers. 'Soph—'

Sophie shook her off. 'You're telling me,' she said, her voice icy cold, 'that you made love with Alex? When?'

'It doesn't matter.'

'Yes, it does. You promised not to vamp him.'

'I *didn't.* Well, he turned me down,' Isobel amended.

'So when did you make love with him?'

'That evening, when you were asleep.'

'Even though he turned you down?'

Isobel squirmed. 'Soph, let's just leave this, shall we?'

'No, I want to know what happened.'

'Look, he just came into my room, and propositioned me.'

'You expect me to believe that? He didn't even like you!'

Isobel flushed. 'You don't have to like someone to make love with them.'

'I don't believe I'm hearing this, Isobel. You knew that he was special to me.'

'I knew that you had a teenage crush on him, yes.'

'That day, when you'd gone to the village – you knew that something was going to happen between us.'

'No, I didn't. I just thought that as he'd obviously taken to you, he'd charm you a bit and do the interview.' Isobel sighed. 'Look, I'm sorry, okay?'

'For what?' Sophie's voice was bitter. 'Fucking Alex, or stealing the paintings?'

'Both. And I didn't steal them. I borrowed them. I always intended to give them back.'

'So where are they?'

'I don't know.' Isobel closed her eyes, and flung herself into a chair. 'I don't know, Soph. I kept them in my briefcase. They were definitely there. I only took them out when I showed them to Tony.'

'You didn't tell me that you had them.'

'Because I knew that you wouldn't approve.' Isobel opened her eyes again. 'Don't lecture me, Soph. I was doing what I thought was right.'

'Even though you knew that he paints only for himself, now?'

'Yes, even though.' Isobel grimaced. 'They were definitely in my briefcase, Soph. The only other person who knew about them was Tony – and I know he's not behind this. JJ and Phoebe knew about them, but they were waiting for me to make a move.'

'Phoebe?'

'JJ's assistant.' Isobel shrugged. 'Alex was the only other one who knew, but he wasn't going to do anything, in the Fens. Apart from threaten to pull the exhibition, that is.'

'So start thinking. When did you last have them?'

'Yesterday morning. They were in my briefcase, then.' Isobel frowned. 'I don't know when they went missing. It could have been any time between then and when I got to JJ's.'

'Did you leave the case anywhere?'

Isobel shook her head. 'It's either been here, or by my feet.'

'We know that no-one's broken in, or the alarm would have gone off.'

'If it was set.'

Sophie's jaw lifted. 'I always set the alarm, and you know it.'

'Yeah. Sorry.'

'So someone must have taken them from your case, when you had your nose in a book on the Tube, or when you were in the pub, or whatever.'

'I haven't been to – oh.' Isobel suddenly remembered a lunch meeting in a wine bar, the previous day. 'Surely I'd have noticed if someone had crawled under the table and borrowed my brief-case?'

'Not if it was a professional thief.'

'But nobody knew about them, Soph. Nobody except Tony. He wouldn't steal them and I don't think JJ would have paid someone to do it, to teach me a lesson.'

'So who else could have done it?'

'I don't know.' Isobel rubbed a hand over her face. 'Christ, I don't know what to do, Soph.'

'Wait for these people to contact you, I suppose.' Sophie stood up, and folded her arms. 'I'm going to my room.'

'Do you want me to cook dinner?' Isobel offered.

'No. I'm not hungry. And, right now, I'd prefer it if you left me alone.'

'I'm sorry, Soph.'

'You couldn't even keep your hands off him, for one night. How do I know that you didn't do the same to Gary?'

'Because Gary is a wet fish. Whereas Alex is pure sex – I don't think any woman could have resisted him.' Isobel was so angry that her friend could think that of her, that she didn't stop to think before she spoke. 'You certainly didn't – and you don't make a habit of falling into bed with men you've only just met.'

'That,' Sophie said, 'was the cheapest gibe you've ever made. And I'm going to treat it with the contempt it deserves. Goodnight, Isobel.'

'Soph—'

But it was too late. Sophie had gone.

'Oh, bloody, bloody hell,' Isobel said. She'd managed to hurt her best friend and damage their relationship almost beyond repair, nearly ruin her lover's business, and make a mess of a potentially good business relationship with JJ, all in the space of a couple of hours. All she could do was wait for the unknown man who had the paintings to contact her. And it was going to be a long, painful wait.

Isobel spent the next hour trying to think who else could have known about the paintings. She played the tape over and over again, trying to recognise the voice: a way of phrasing, a slight accent. But there was nothing. Eventually, she decided to go and see Tony. There was a chance that he might have told somebody in confidence, someone who'd betrayed him. Or . . . No, the thought was too horrible. Tony wouldn't have betrayed her, would he?

There was only one way to find out for sure. She went up the stairs, and rapped on Sophie's door. There was no answer. 'Soph, I'm just going to see Tony – in case he has any idea about the paintings.' There was still no answer; Isobel sighed, and turned away.

When she reached Tony's flat, Tony opened the door and beamed at her in delight. 'Isobel! I wasn't expecting to see you, tonight.'

'No, well. I was free, so I thought I'd pop over and see if you fancied spending the evening with me.'

'Of course I would.' He closed the door behind her, and kissed her, his mouth warm and sweet against her own. 'I've been thinking about you all day.'

'Have you?'

He frowned, noticing her leaden tone. 'Isobel, is everything all right?'

'That depends.'

'On what?'

'The paintings.'

'What paintings?'

'The Alex Waters ones I showed you, the other night.'

His face suddenly cleared. 'Oh, yes. You went to see JJ about them today, didn't you?' She nodded. 'How did you get on?'

'Not too well.'

He stroked her face. Never mind. Maybe we can persuade him to show them at some other date in the future. Let's see how the retro goes, first; if it's as good as I hope, then maybe he'll consider doing a new exhibition.'

'I don't know.' She looked at him. 'Tony, where are the paintings?'

'What do you mean?'

'You heard me. I want to know where the paintings are.'

He frowned. 'Isobel, you put them in your briefcase, after you showed them to me.'

'They're not there now. They've gone.'

'Gone?' Tony was shocked. 'But – how?'

'I don't know. I wondered if you might have any ideas.'

'You mean, you think I stole them?' His mouth opened. 'Isobel, I don't believe I'm hearing this. Are you accusing me of stealing them?'

His innocence was obvious; eventually, Isobel shook her head. 'I just had to be sure that it wasn't you. I'm sorry; I should have trusted you.'

'So they really are gone?'

She nodded. 'I opened my briefcase, to give them back to JJ, and they weren't there.'

'Maybe you put them in a safe place.'

'I definitely put them in my briefcase. They were there, yesterday morning. I haven't taken them out, and I haven't told anyone about them – apart from you. Have you discussed them with anyone?'

No. It was just between you and me, until you'd spoken to JJ.'

She bit her lip. 'I think you should know – Alex knows that they're missing.'

Tony was wary. 'And?'

'And – JJ says he's threatening to pull the exhibition.'

'Christ, no.' Tony looked at her. 'We're going to have to get them back. Are you sure you haven't got them at home?'

'I'm sure. And there was an answerphone message. All he said was that if I want the paintings back, I'll have to come and get them – and that he'd be in touch.'

'Did you recognise the voice?'

'No. I have no idea who it is. I've played that tape over and over and over again, and I'm none the wiser.'

'Is there anyone who's likely to have taken it?'

'Not that I can think of. I had lunch yesterday with Ralph, the editor of *Vivendi*, but – ' she shrugged. 'All he knows is that I've done the interview, and it's been cleared. He doesn't know anything about the paintings.'

'Did you give him the interview, yesterday?'

'No. It's not due in until next week; we were discussing the next interview.'

'Right.' Tony looked thoughtfully at her. 'So really, neither of us have any idea.'

'Are you sure you didn't tell anyone about the new paintings? Even in confidence?'

'No.' He paused. 'Though there was another gallery which wanted to hold the Alex Waters retro. I'm not sure who it was, but Alex vetoed it.'

'God, Tony – what am I going to do?' she asked.

'I think all we can do is wait until they contact you – then do whatever they want to get the pictures back.'

'What if they want large sums of cash?' Isobel asked. 'I don't have it.'

'If they want large sums of cash,' Tony said slowly, 'then we'll do it through the gallery. We'll have to involve the police – and we'll trap the bastard who's trying to blackmail you.'

Isobel closed her eyes in relief and sagged against him. 'Tony, what would I do without you?'

'If it wasn't for me showing you the previews, you wouldn't be in this mess in the first place.'

'Even so.' She sighed. 'The worst thing was, I've really hurt Sophie over this.'

'How does Sophie know?'

'She was home before me. She heard the message, and she made me tell her everything. She blames me for the fact that Alex hasn't contacted her.' Isobel bit her lip. 'And I'm afraid I got angry with her, and told her what a callous bastard he really is – and the fact that he'd sleep with any woman, including me.'

'Oh, Isobel.'

'Yeah. She didn't take it very well,' Isobel admitted. 'Mind you, in her shoes, I don't think I would have done, either.'

'Well, then.'

'Tony.' She looked at him, her eyes luminous with misery. 'I feel really bad about this.'

He stroked her face. 'Yeah, I know.' He tipped his head on one side. 'I think I know one way to make you feel a bit better – at least, temporarily.'

'Mm.' She nodded. That was exactly what she needed, the comfort of Tony's body sliding into hers.

'Come on.' He took her hand, and led her upstairs to his bedroom.

Fourteen

The next morning, Isobel was up early, to catch the Tube back to Pimlico. When she walked through the door, she realised that Sophie was either not up, or – as Isobel suspected – was locked in her studio. There was an envelope on the table, with Isobel's name on it. It was a plain white envelope with a press seal, the sort that could have been bought in any high street shop or stationer's. Her name was typed; she frowned, and opened it.

Inside was one folded piece of A4 paper, with a typed message. *See you at Number Seven, tonight, at nine o'clock. Wear your red suit, and no knickers. Come alone.* Isobel's frown deepened. Number Seven was a club in Soho, which had a widespread reputation; her red suit, even worn with no underwear, would seem more than demure to the clientele of Number Seven. It wasn't a sleazy place, as such: rumour had it that the annual subscription was exorbitant. Only those with a penchant for the unusual – and the money to indulge it – were members.

Whoever had written this obviously knew her, otherwise they wouldn't have known about her red suit; and the reference to wearing no knickers. It had to be Tony. There was no-one else it could possibly be. Swiftly, she picked up the extension in the kitchen, and dialled the gallery's number. Tony answered. 'Good morning, Russell Street Gallery.'

'Tony,' she hissed, 'this isn't funny.'

'Isobel?' He sounded surprised. 'What's the matter?'

'Just stop messing me around and give me the paintings, you bastard.'

'Isobel, I don't know what the hell you're talking about.'

'Your letter. It was waiting for me when I got home, this morning. You obviously asked someone to drop it off, last night.'

193

'Isobel, *what* letter?'

She sighed. The confusion in his voice was genuine: he was innocent. 'Oh, hell. I don't know what's going on any more, Tony. I'm sorry. I'm being paranoid, and I'm accusing you of something you haven't done.'

'Look, come over, bring this letter or whatever it is with you, and we'll sort it out.'

'Okay. I'll be with you in the next hour.'

'I'll tell Monica to have some coffee ready.'

Wearily, Isobel replaced the receiver, went upstairs, showered, and changed. She rapped on the door of Sophie's studio, but there was no answer. She tried the handle; it was locked. Hell. Well, she'd have to sort it out with Sophie, later. Her first priority was to get those paintings back. Then, she could start thinking about repairing the rest of the mess – patching things up with Sophie and JJ, and making sure that Alex didn't pull the exhibition.

When she arrived at the gallery, Tony was with a client. She had to wait for twenty minutes – twenty minutes of pure hell, during which she convinced herself alternately that Tony was behind it, and that Tony was innocent. Monica made her a coffee, and Isobel flicked through the glossy magazines on the coffee table, trying to be patient and failing.

At last, Tony's client left, and Monica ushered her into Tony's office. He kissed her lightly. 'So,' he said carefully, 'what is all this about?'

'Does Monica use a typewriter, here?'

He frowned. 'No. Everything's computerised – accounts, letters, the whole lot's logged on the PC. I think I gave our old typewriter to Oxfam or something. Why?'

'Because the letter was typed. Look – you can see that the T is uneven. You wouldn't get that on a word-processor. And the ribbon's faint.'

'Well, it's nothing to do with me – or with Monica, either, in case you're starting to suspect her,' Tony said.

'I trust you. I'm sorry.' She winced. 'God, this business has even got you and me at each other's throats. It's ludicrous. It shouldn't affect us like this.'

'I know.' He stroked her hair. 'Do you mind if I read the letter?'

She handed it to him. 'If you've got any idea who it might be – any idea at all – just tell me.'

Tony read it, and his face darkened. 'Number Seven? Isn't that that place in Soho?'

She nodded. 'I think so.'

'Then I don't think you should go on your own.'

'You can see what the message says. I'm supposed to go alone.'

'No way. Not to Number Seven. I think you should give this to the police. Whoever it is . . . God knows what they're planning to do with you.' His eyes narrowed. 'Why did you think it was me?'

'Because of the red suit and no knickers,' she admitted.

'Isobel.' His eyes held hers. 'I know I've never asked you about your past lovers – they're not important – but have you done that with anyone else? The red suit and no knickers, I mean?'

She shook her head. 'Only with you.'

'But it must be someone who's seen you wear that suit.'

Isobel smiled ruefully. 'Sophie calls it my "get-my-own-way suit". I wear it quite a lot, to meetings – so it could be dozens of people.'

'I can see why she calls it that,' Tony agreed. 'But you're not intending to – well, do what the note says, are you?'

'How else am I going to find out who's behind it? How else am I going to find out where the paintings are, and what they want?'

'I'm not happy about this,' Tony said. 'It's dangerous.'

'Tony, stop fussing. I'll be okay. I'm old enough to look after myself.'

'I think you should tell JJ about it, though.'

'You saw the letter. They said they wanted me to go on my own.'

'But they didn't say that you couldn't tell anyone else – and it's not your fault if the people you tell decide to turn up at Number Seven, themselves.'

'Tony, don't be stupid. Apart from the fact that you're not a member and the fee's a small fortune, whoever's got the paintings obviously knows the connection between us.'

'How do you work that out?'

'Because,' she said sweetly, 'JJ is Alex's agent, and you're staging the retro exhibition. So the fact that I'm the one who had the paintings means that there's a connection between the three of us.'

'Yeah, you're right.' Tony frowned. 'I just wish I knew who was behind all this. And what the hell do they want with you at Number Seven?'

'I don't know,' Isobel said, 'but I'm going to find out.'

'I'd prefer you not to go alone.'

'If I go there with someone, the deal could be off. Tony, I need those paintings. I can't take the risk.'

He thought for a moment. 'Get a taxi back to my place, the minute you leave the club. JJ and I will be waiting for you, there.'

'All right.' She kissed him lightly. 'See you later.'

She spent the rest of the day working on another article. Sophie avoided her, going straight to her room when she came back from the university, then going out again, without saying where she was going or when she'd be back. Isobel sighed inwardly. Once she'd sorted out this mess with the paintings, she'd patch things up properly with Sophie. In the meantime, she certainly wasn't going to let whoever it was intimidate her.

As instructed, she wore the red suit with no knickers. She habitually wore it with no bra; she added a pair of black lace-topped hold-up stockings, and a pair of very high black patent leather shoes. She styled her hair in a more sophisticated manner, and wore dramatic make-up – dark eyes, and bright red lips which matched her suit. She sprayed herself liberally with her favourite *chypre* perfume, then walked downstairs and glanced at herself in the hall mirror. She nodded in satisfaction. Yes, she'd do. If they thought they could intimidate her, they were about to be in for a shock.

She picked up her small black clutch bag, which contained

money, a lipstick and her pocket dictaphone, and left the house. She took a taxi to Number Seven: it was a bit of an extravagance, taking a taxi from Pimlico to Soho, but she wanted to arrive feeling fresh, not hot and flustered after several tube changes. She paid the driver, and sauntered into the club.

It was more or less like she'd expected. The place was very discreet, the decor plain and neo-Georgian. The carpet was lush thick pile; she'd never been into a place where her feet literally sank into the carpet before, and it made her feel out of her depth. There were beautiful paintings on the wall – originals, too, she realised – and everything about the place proclaimed opulence.

There were several tables dotted around the room, covered with white damask cloths which reached to the floor; each table had two or three occupants, wearing evening dress, and all drinking champagne – vintage Bollinger, she guessed. There was a stage at the far end of the room; her eyes widened as she looked at it. This club was a place for people who liked their pleasures very refined, as well as distinctly kinky.

On the stage were two people, dressed identically in a very tight black leather body. Both had shoulder-length blonde hair, and Isobel wasn't sure whether they were women, or men wearing wigs – or even one of each. Both wore very high-heeled shoes and fishnet stockings, and they were dancing very suggestively. One of them turned round, and Isobel realised that the suits were virtually backless, ending in a tiny g-string. She felt profoundly uncomfortable; yet, at the same time, her libido had kicked in. Christ, what *is* this place? she thought.

A waiter came up to her. 'Can I help you?'

'Isobel Moran. I have an appointment at nine o'clock.'

'Ah, yes. With H.'

H? Isobel frowned. Who the hell was H? She was careful to keep a very cool, serene mask; she simply smiled, and followed the waiter to one of the tables.

The man sitting there stood up, and bowed slightly. 'Isobel, how sweet of you to be on time.'

He had a gorgeous voice – low, deep, and very sensual, with a slightly upper-class accent. She favoured him with a tight smile, and sat down. He was in his early to mid-forties, she guessed, with thick dark hair. He was a slightly older version of Tony, except his eyes were harder and there was a cruel line to his mouth. Part of her despised him; but her body couldn't help responding to his sensuality. He was attractive – very attractive. The sort of man she wouldn't forget in a hurry: and she was convinced that she'd never seen him before.

'So you received my message, then?'

She nodded. 'Who are you?'

He ignored her query. 'And you followed my instructions to the letter?'

She looked at him. 'Do you see anyone with me?'

He smiled. 'That's not what I meant.'

She lifted her chin. 'If you want to know the rest of it, there's only one way to find out, isn't there?'

'You're right.' His smile was part-sensual, part-cruel. 'Stand up.'

'What?'

'Stand up,' he repeated quietly.

Her eyes narrowed. 'What are you playing at?'

'Do you want to know about the paintings, or not?'

'That's why I'm here.'

'Then stand up,' he commanded quietly.

Isobel did so, her dislike of him growing by the second. Who the hell did he think he was, ordering her around? But she couldn't afford to argue with him – not until she'd found out what had happened to Alex's paintings.

'Now, pull your skirt up.'

'What?'

'Lift your skirt up,' he commanded. 'I want to see whether you've obeyed my instructions.'

So humiliation was his game, was it? Isobel was furious. 'I'll do no such thing,' she said coldly.

'Look around you,' he said. 'You won't be out of place, if that's what you're worried about.'

She glanced round the room, and realised that although all the men wore dinner jackets and the women, at first glance, were in evening dress, their clothing was far from ordinary. Some of the women wore sheer chiffon, so fine that you could see that they were wearing no underwear beneath their dresses. Others, she realised as one of them stood up and headed in the direction of what Isobel assumed was the Ladies, wore dresses with small lacy panels placed strategically over their genitals – lace through which their shaven pubis was clearly visible.

'As far as these people are concerned,' H said, 'you're over-dressed.'

Defiance lanced through Isobel. Well, if he wanted an exhibition, he'd get one. She stood with her legs wide apart, and pulled her skirt up, baring her delta. 'Satisfied?' she asked.

'By and by. Turn round.'

She gritted her teeth, and did so; when she was facing him again, she lifted her chin haughtily. 'Have you seen enough?'

'For the moment. You can sit down, now.'

Isobel began to pull her skirt down again, and he shook his head. 'No. Leave it as it is.'

'And you'll pay for the cleaning bill, to get the creases out?'

He nodded. 'But of course, fair Isobel.' He took his wallet from his inside pocket, and extracted a twenty-pound note. 'That should cover it,' he said, folding the note and tucking it in the vee of her cleavage.

Isobel was stung, humiliated. He'd given her the money as a kind of tip, and it made her feel like a whore. Furious, but not daring to argue with him, she subsided into silence.

'So, what do you think of the show?' he asked.

She was out of her depth, but she wasn't going to tell him that. 'Different,' she said with a shrug. 'I was trying to work out if they were male or female.'

'Which do you prefer?' he asked quietly.

'It doesn't matter to me.'

'I thought so.' His eyes raked her sensually; Isobel felt suddenly naked. 'I thought you would be our type of person.'

'I'm here,' Isobel reminded him, 'for the paintings. Nothing more.' She paused. 'Who are you?'

'That isn't important.'

'It is, to me.'

'People call me "H".'

'It makes you sound like an extra from a James Bond movie.'

He laughed. 'I believe you mean "Q". Or "M".'

Be careful, she warned herself. Push him too far, and you'll lose the paintings. 'How did you get the paintings, H?'

'Some people can be so careless with their property.' He shrugged. 'As you were.'

Isobel's brain worked like lightning. This was just the opening she'd hoped for. She could pretend to check her bag, switch on the tape recorder, and then find out exactly what he'd done. 'If I'm so careless,' she said, 'then excuse me. I need to check something. After all, I'd hate to find myself stranded here without the taxi fare home.'

'I'm sure we could always provide a taxi.'

Clever, Isobel thought. 'Or my lipstick.' She pouted at him. 'I'm sure I'll need to replenish it, later.'

He smiled. 'Indeed.'

Bastard, she thought. No way was she going to let him lay a finger on her. She forced herself to smile sweetly at him, and opened her bag. Carefully shielding the contents from him, she made a pretence of checking for her money and her lipstick, and switched on the tape recorder, turning it up to full volume. There were fresh batteries in it, too; she hoped that it would be good enough to record their conversation, and incriminate him. She needed evidence, to take to the police. She smiled again, and put the handbag on the table between them. 'Just so that I'm not careless with this – I should keep an eye on it, don't you think?'

'If that's what you wish.' He was amused; she hated him for it.

'So – you were telling me how you got the paintings,' she prompted. 'I've been thinking about that – was it when I had lunch with Ralph?'

'Yes.'

'Are you telling me that Ralph knows about this?'

H shook his head. 'Ralph knows nothing about it.'

'Then how did you get the paintings?'

'A stroke of luck, really. While you were chatting, it was easy to remove your briefcase from by your feet, and look through the contents. We were looking for your interview.'

'My *interview?* But I didn't have it with me – and anyway, it's fairly obvious that I'd have a back-up copy at home.'

'Yes, but it would give us an idea of what Alex is doing with himself, nowadays. That's what we wanted to know.' He paused. 'And then we found these three touching little sketches. Brand new Alex Waters.'

'They're not yours,' Isobel said. 'You've stolen them.'

'But so did you.'

Her eyes narrowed. 'How do you mean?'

'Well, Alex wasn't very pleased when we told him that we had three of his paintings – or where we got them.'

'So Alex knows that you have them.'

H smiled. 'Not knows, exactly. He guesses that we have them – or, at least, that we know who has them.'

'So where are they?'

'Ah-ah. Too early to tell you *that*.'

'I thought the reason you wanted to see me was because you were going to give them back to me.'

'How naive you are, my dear.'

'So what do you want?' Isobel asked.

'Well, you obviously want the paintings back.'

'Yes.'

'And I . . .' He paused, smiling tantalisingly at her.

She waited, refusing to take the bait and ask him again. He smiled, as if acknowledging her tactics. 'I want Alex Waters to exhibit the drawings, and the rest of his new work, at a gallery of my choosing. Not Russell Street.'

Her eyes narrowed. Tony had said that he'd had a rival for the retro exhibition, though he didn't know who it was. From the sound of it, this man was either the gallery owner, or his lackey:

on balance, she decided that it was the former. He didn't look like a lackey. 'Who are you?' she asked again.

'Just call me H.'

'I could go to the police,' she said, 'and tell them that you have the drawings.'

He smiled. 'But we would have disposed of them, by then. You have no evidence at all. Besides,' he added, 'if you did go to the police, I have enough contacts to make sure that you never have another magazine commission again.'

Better and better, Isobel thought. Threats. She could only hope that her dictaphone had picked it up. 'So what do you suggest I do?' she asked.

'Well, we know that you've negotiated with Alex.'

'How do you mean?'

'The interview, in the first place. Plus –' he smiled '– I've seen the pictures.'

'What pictures?'

'Didn't you know? Alex's latest work includes a couple of pictures of you.'

That was one piece of information she hadn't expected. She thought that she'd have been the last person Alex would want to draw. She strove to keep the surprise from her face. 'Indeed.'

'Very pretty, too,' he added. 'Alex has a good eye.'

'So what do you want me to do? Negotiate with Alex to show the new work in your gallery?'

'Yes.'

'And if I refuse?'

'Well.' He spread his hands. 'That's entirely up to you, isn't it?'

A waiter came up with a bottle of champagne, and poured two glasses.

Isobel noted the label: a good vintage Bollinger. She adored champagne. On the other hand, it could be drugged, for all she knew. 'I'm not drinking tonight, thanks.'

'Have a drink with me, Isobel,' H said. 'It's in your best interests.'

Another veiled threat. 'How do I know that you haven't put something in this?'

He smiled, took a sip from one of the glasses, then handed it to her. 'Satisfied, now?' She nodded. He took a sip from the other glass, then held it up in a toast. 'Well, Isobel. To us, and to our new working partnership.'

His eyes held hers; eventually, she picked up her glass.

'Not echoing the toast?'

'It's hardly a willing partnership.'

'Maybe not, but it'll be an effective one.'

'You've told me enough to go to the police.'

'But you won't.'

'How do you know?'

'Because,' he said, 'if you do, you'll lose everything, and you know it.' He smiled sweetly at her. 'So why don't you just relax and enjoy the show?'

The waiter returned with a plate of smoked salmon and quail's egg canapés; H began to eat them with obvious enjoyment. Isobel couldn't bring herself to eat: she was on tenterhooks. If she didn't leave the table soon, the tape would end. If he heard the click as the machine switched off, and made her empty her bag, that would be the end of it. Eventually, she stood up.

'Where are you going?' he asked.

'To–' she shrugged, 'shall I say, powder my nose? Reapply my lipstick?'

'Of course. But leave your skirt where it is.' He snapped his fingers, and a waiter escorted her to the cloakrooms.

The waiter didn't seem at all fazed at the way the woman beside him was dressed; Isobel was hideously embarrassed, but no-one seemed to notice. No-one stared, or acted as if she were dressed in any way out of the usual. And as Isobel passed another woman, who was dressed solely in a white leather corset with a trail of white lacy ribbons protruding from her anus, Isobel realised that, if anything, she still looked very demure.

The cloakrooms turned out to be as luxuriant as the rest of the place, with thick fluffy towels, expensive soap, and marble everywhere. Isobel appraised it briefly, regretting that she wasn't in a position to enjoy Number Seven properly. But the circumstances were beyond her control.

Once safely enclosed in a cubicle, she opened her handbag with trembling fingers, and switched off the dictaphone. There was nowhere to hide the tape; she didn't dare tuck it between her breasts, in case he demanded that she remove her jacket. Her stocking tops were visible, with her skirt pulled so lewdly round her waist, so she couldn't hide the tape there, either. She could only hope that H didn't decide to do something with her handbag.

She reapplied her lipstick, then returned to the table. H nodded his approval at the fact that she hadn't rearranged her skirt, and patted the seat next to him. 'The show gets more interesting, from here,' he said.

Isobel felt a tiny flicker of fear as she sat down. What did he mean? Was he talking about the stage show – or did he mean her to be part of the show?

The two androgynous dancers left the stage. In their place, two others came on. Both of them were dressed in almost identical harnesses, confections of black leather straps and silver chains which highlighted both the shape of their bodies and their genitals. Both had very short, cropped dark hair, which made the woman look gamine and the man look almost like a warrior. His sex was erect, and covered with a black latex condom. Isobel watched, half shocked and half turned on, as the pair's sinuous gyrations turned to the beginnings of lovemaking.

'It's good – very good,' H said softly in her ear. 'Wouldn't you like to be up there, dressed like that, and knowing that everyone was going to watch you as you came?'

Isobel said nothing, shocked: because he'd guessed at her thoughts. Yes, she would like to be one of the pair on stage, moving to that strange hypnotic beat and abandoning herself to pleasure, oblivious of the watchers.

She felt H's hand settle on her knee, stroking upwards and then finally coming to rest with his fingers curved round her inner thigh. Part of her wanted to push him away, but if she did – what would his reaction be? Would he throw her out, without her handbag? She had to keep hold of that, and the tape; if it meant keeping him sweet, and letting him do as he liked, then so be it.

She made no movement; he smiled his approval, and continued stroking her thigh, letting his fingers brush tantalisingly across her quim. To Isobel's horror, she found that she was already wet, from watching the dancers on the stage; her nipples, too, were hard and easily visible through her red jacket.

H made a small pleased noise in the back of his throat. 'I can see your nipples,' he whispered. 'Undo your jacket.'

Isobel couldn't move; he tipped his head on one side. 'Stubborn, hm? Well. There are other ways.' For a moment, she thought that he was going to rip her jacket open, regardless of the buttons, but he undid it gently, carefully. 'Mm, very pretty,' he said, pushing the jacket from her shoulders and down, so that it pinioned her arms. 'Very pretty,' he said again, tracing her areola with the tip of his finger, then rolling the hard peak of flesh between his finger and thumb. He did the same with the other nipple, and Isobel had to bite back a small cry of pleasure.

'Don't fight me, Isobel,' he said, his voice smooth and threatening at the same time. 'We're dedicated to pleasure, at Number Seven.'

'I'm not one of you,' she said, through gritted teeth.

'Oh, but you are. I can see it in your eyes. Pleasure – pure pleasure,' H said. For one heart-stopping moment, Isobel thought that he was going to tell her to stand up again, but he relented, and let his hand slide over her midriff, over her bunched skirt, and back down to her inner thighs again.

At least the table cloth was long, Isobel thought, and hid what he was doing to her. Though she suspected that a similar scene was taking place at each of the other tables. His long, tapered fingers explored the folds and crevices of her quim; he probed her wetness, and she forced herself to stay still as his finger slid inside her. Even when his thumb settled on her clitoris and began rubbing it, she didn't move; but he could tell that he'd brought her to a climax, by the rosy mottling on her bared breasts and the way that her internal muscles clutched his fingers.

When he'd finished, he removed his hand, then licked every scrap of juice from his fingers. Isobel flushed, embarrassed. 'I think,' she said quietly, 'that I need to go, now.'

He grinned. 'Yes. But the skirt doesn't come down.'

'I want you to button up my jacket.'

'If you wish.' He straightened her jacket again, doing it up. 'Think about what I said. You've got until Friday morning to give me your answer. Either you work with me, or you work against me – and I'm not a good enemy, Isobel.'

She nodded.

'And if you bring in the police, you won't work in this town again – especially for *Vivendi*. Magazines fold so often nowadays, don't they?'

'You'll close *Vivendi*? How?'

'Very easily.' He smiled. 'Because I own it.'

So that was how he'd known about the Alex Waters interview – and about her lunch with Ralph. She nodded, and left the table, clutching her bag to her. When she left the room, she pulled her skirt back down to its normal state, then, shaking, walked outside and hailed a taxi, giving Tony's address.

Fifteen

Isobel was virtually silent during the taxi ride. She usually enjoyed chatting to the drivers but, this time, she was too shaken to do anything other than huddle in the back seat and wish that Tony was there. She was annoyed with herself for being weak, and wanting a man's protection: but H had unnerved her.

At last, the taxi pulled up outside Tony's house; Tony opened the front door before she'd even walked through the gate. He'd obviously been waiting for her, she thought.

His face registered shock at the state of her clothes, and the pallor on her face; he pulled her into his arms. 'Isobel. Darling, are you all right?'

'Yeah, I'm fine.' She grimaced. 'I just want a bath.

'If that bastard's laid so much as a finger on you—'

'Tony, just leave it,' she cut in.

'Did you get the paintings back?' he asked, as he closed the front door behind them.

She shook her head. 'He's given me until Friday to make up my mind.'

'About what?'

'In a minute, Tony. I just want a bath, okay?'

'Okay.' He stroked her hair. 'But did you recognise him, at all?'

'No, but I think I know who he is. I need to check that with JJ.'

'I'm here,' JJ said, walking out of the sitting room. His eyes narrowed as he looked at her. 'My God, what's happened to you?'

'It doesn't matter, and I don't want to talk about it. I'm all right.' She pulled a face. 'I just want a bath. Then, maybe, we can listen to the tape and see if it picked up.'

'What tape?' JJ asked.

'I recorded most of the conversation. I used my dictaphone;

the thing is, it was in my handbag, so I'm not sure how good the quality is. I did it at full volume, though, so I hope it's good enough.'

'I don't know,' JJ said, 'whether you're extremely brave, or extremely foolhardy. From what Tony tells me, we're dealing with professionals, here. If you'd been caught—'

'Well, I wasn't,' she cut in, not wanting to think about that.

'Look, you go and have your bath, and help yourself to my dressing gown. I'll have a cup of coffee waiting for you, okay?' Tony said.

'Thanks.' Isobel smiled gratefully at him. 'Keep hold of that. It's important.' She handed him her bag, and went upstairs to the bathroom. She'd left some make-up remover there, before, when she'd stayed at Tony's overnight; she cleaned her face thoroughly, then stepped into the shower. She scrubbed at her skin until she felt clean again, then washed her hair. Then, finally, with her wet hair wrapped in a small towel and the rest of her wrapped in Tony's large navy towelling robe, she went downstairs again.

'I'm never going to wear that red suit again,' she said. 'I'm going to throw it in the bin. And as for the money he gave me for the cleaning bill –' she grimaced '– it's going to charity, first thing in the morning.'

'Was Number Seven really that bad?' JJ asked.

'Yes and no.' Isobel shrugged. 'I think if I'd been there for a different reason, I probably would have enjoyed myself. It's very . . . decadent, in a classy way. But I felt out of my depth, tonight.' She pulled a face. 'Look, I want to see if that tape worked.'

'Here.' Tony gave her the bag.

She rummaged inside, and took out the dictaphone. It used standard cassette tapes; she handed it to Tony. 'It needs rewinding, but everything's on there. I think it'd sound better on your stereo than on this little machine.'

'Sure.' Tony switched on his stereo, turned up the volume, and slotted the tape into the cassette holder.

They listened to it in silence; it was very muffled, but the words were distinctive enough.

'You do know,' JJ said, 'that it's illegal to tape conversations without the other party knowing about it?'

'What he was doing was illegal, full stop,' Isobel defended herself 'It's good evidence – just what we need. Even if he destroys the paintings, we can nail him.'

'She's right.' Tony agreed. 'All we need to do now is play this tape to the police, and tell them who it is.'

'That's the problem,' Isobel said. 'I only know him as "H". But the bit on the tape when he was saying that he wanted Alex's new pictures exhibited at another gallery . . . You said to me earlier, Tony, that someone else wanted to do the retro.'

'That's right,' JJ said. 'Howard Langton-Smith. I've never heard him refer to himself as "H", before, but there's always a first time.' He paused. 'Can you describe him, Isobel?'

Isobel nodded. 'I'd say he's in his early to mid-forties. He's about the same height as Tony, with dark hair and very piercing blue eyes. He's nice-looking, but he has a cruel mouth.'

'That sounds very much like him.' JJ rubbed his jaw. 'I've thought for years that he's been mixed up with dodgy business. Most of my associates think the same way. No-one's ever been able to prove it, though. I'm surprised that he was so indiscreet with you, Isobel. Are you sure that this isn't some kind of trap?'

'I don't think so. He looked pretty serious to me,' Isobel said. 'He's very influential. If he owns *Vivendi,* God knows what else he's involved with.'

'Mm, he has a finger in quite a few pies,' JJ agreed. 'The gallery at Bloomsbury and a couple of restaurants, plus this magazine: they're his public and acceptable face. He probably owns at least part of Number Seven, and rumour has it that he has a collection of erotic drawings that makes Alex's work look like a timid nun's.' JJ shrugged. 'And then there's the other side: no-one has any proof, but in the industry, everyone thinks that he's been involved in some forgery rings.'

'He said that he'd finish my career. He really could do it. And he'll close down *Vivendi.*' She bit her lip. 'I know a lot of people who work for that magazine – people I've worked with. They're really nice, and they're a hundred per cent honest. I'd hate to see them lose their jobs because of me.'

'Hey, if any of them knew what a scumbag Langton-Smith is, they wouldn't want to work for him anyway,' Tony said. 'And there's always a chance they could set up a management buy-out at *Vivendi*.'

'I suppose so.' She paused. 'I think we should call the police, and get them to come out here now. Let them hear the tape and make a transcription of it – before he has a chance to guess at what I've done, and destroy the evidence. If we leave it until tomorrow, and he gets any idea that I might have taped the conversation, he might burgle you, Tony – or even set fire to the house, with us inside it.'

'That's a bit dramatic, isn't it?' Tony asked.

Isobel's voice was calm, and very quiet. 'I think he's capable of doing it, Tony. I think he's capable of a lot of things.'

'All right, we'll play it your way,' he soothed.

Isobel winced. 'The only thing is – I don't think we'll get Alex's paintings back.'

'Are you suggesting that we wait until you can talk Langton-Smith into giving them back?' JJ asked.

'Well – no.' Isobel grimaced. 'I don't want to wait before telling the police. But Alex won't be too happy when he finds out about the paintings.'

'We can ask him, if you like,' JJ said.

Isobel frowned. 'Don't tell me that he's here, too?'

'No, but I can give him a ring.'

'He doesn't have a phone.'

JJ smiled. 'Phoebe does – she always carries a mobile. She's with him at the moment.' He looked at her. 'As you probably know, because you put the idea into her head in the first place.'

'What idea?' Tony asked.

'Getting Alex to come to the opening.'

Tony whistled. 'She'll have to be persuasive in the extreme.'

'She is,' Isobel said, without thinking.

JJ grinned. 'I rather gathered that.'

She flushed. 'Why don't you ring him, JJ?'

'All right. Mind you, I have a pretty good idea about how he'll react, anyway. He hates Howard Langton-Smith.'

'Why?' Isobel asked. 'Was it an exhibition that went wrong, or something?'

JJ shook his head. 'It was his party that Alex went to, the night of the accident. Langton-Smith had given people a little unexpected extra in their drinks. That's why Alex had a headache; and that's why he let Dee drive home, because she'd been on orange juice all night.'

'And her drink had been spiked?' Isobel asked, shocked.

'No-one can say for sure. Alex thinks so, though.'

'Christ.' Isobel bit her lip. 'I'm surprised he didn't flip when he found out who had the paintings.'

'That may have been a bluff,' JJ said, 'because Alex certainly didn't tell me – and I doubt if he would even let Langton-Smith into his cottage, even if he knew where Alex lived.' He shrugged. 'I'll ring him, then, if that's all right with you, Tony?'

'Sure. The phone's in the corner, by the bookcase.'

JJ walked over to the phone and dialled swiftly. It seemed to take a long time, before Phoebe answered; then, at last, Tony and Isobel heard him chuckle. 'Phoebe. Sweetie. Yes . . . I'm with Tony and Isobel. Look, can you ask Alex a question for me? . . . Yes, it's about the missing paintings . . . Yes, we know who's got them. Howard Langton-Smith. Yes, I know he's going to go mad when you tell him. I'm sure you'll manage to calm him down.' There was a pause, then JJ chuckled again. 'Yes, I'll tell them . . . Yes, we've got the evidence, on tape. We want to call the police, but he might not get the paintings back. Is he happy with that? . . . Oh, *right!*' He sounded surprised. 'Yes, I'll tell them. See you, then.'

Tony and Isobel waited expectantly; JJ smiled at them. 'Alex says we can go ahead – nail the bastard, and do anything we can to stop him doing this to anyone else. He doesn't mind about the paintings not being recovered.'

'That's great,' Isobel said, relieved.

'I should add,' JJ continued, 'that he's pulled the retro.'

'He's *what?*' Tony closed his eyes. 'Oh, God.'

JJ grinned. 'Perhaps I worded it wrongly. He wants to change the exhibition, so it's half retro, and half his new stuff.'

'He *what?*' Tony opened his eyes again, and looked at JJ in utter shock. 'Are you serious?'

'Yes, but he says that he wants to choose which pictures go in, okay?'

'Okay,' Tony said, relieved and delighted at the same time.

Isobel suddenly flushed. 'Do we – er – have a chance to veto any of them?'

'Why's that?' JJ asked, tipping his head on one side. 'Is there something you want to tell us, Isobel?'

'It's just something that Langton-Smith said to me. He said that he'd seen a picture of me, which Alex had drawn.'

'It was probably a bluff. Like I said, no way would Alex let him into the house.' JJ grinned. 'But I wouldn't be too surprised if Alex has sketched you. It's his equivalent, shall we say, of carving notches on the bed-post.' He looked at her. 'Do you want to go home and change, before we call the police?'

Isobel shook her head. 'I already told you, I want them here as soon as possible.'

'If you're sure.' Tony went over to the phone, and dialled the number. He spoke rapidly into the receiver, then replaced it and walked back over to Isobel and JJ. 'They'll be here shortly. Do you want some more coffee?'

'I can wait until the police arrive,' Isobel said.

'Same here,' JJ agreed.

They waited in near-silence; when the police arrived, Tony answered the door, then ushered them into the sitting room. He introduced everyone, then Isobel made some more coffee, while the police listened to the tape. She knew the thing virtually off by heart, and didn't particularly want to listen to it again.

To her relief, the police agreed that the tape would be good enough evidence to arrest Langton-Smith. She agreed that she was happy to be a witness in court; in exchange, the police would try to keep Alex's name out of the papers, and minimise publicity on the case.

When the police had left, Tony poured them all a stiff gin. 'I think we need this,' he said. He tipped his head on one side. 'Isobel – those remarks about keeping your skirt where it was. What happened?'

She flushed. 'Ritual humiliation, I think. Not something that turns me on, particularly.'

'Humiliation?' JJ probed.

She sighed. 'You want the whole story, do you? Well, I dressed as he'd said – in my red suit, with no underwear. He wanted to check that I'd obeyed his instructions, so he made me pull my skirt up round my waist.'

Tony's eyes widened. 'And you did it?'

'I didn't have much choice.' She shrugged. 'Anyway, I wasn't the most lewdly-dressed there, by a long way. If anything, I was a bit over-dressed.'

'Indeed,' JJ said softly.

'Anyway, he said I'd been careless with the paintings, which was my cue to check my bag – and switch on the dictaphone. I was paranoid that the tape was going to run out, before he'd given me the evidence I needed, or that he'd hear the click at the end of the tape; so I made an excuse that I wanted to go to the loo. That's when he told me to leave my skirt in place.'

'Right.' Tony looked at his lover. 'And you obeyed?'

'Like I said, I didn't have much choice!' Her eyes sparked angrily. 'What are you trying to say, Tony? That I'm an exhibitionist?'

He thought of the way she'd made love to him on his desk, and raised an eyebrow. 'Sometimes.'

'Thanks a lot.'

'So what happened then?' JJ asked. 'Once you'd switched off the machine?'

'I went back to the table. Then he told me that that was when the show started to get interesting; for a moment, I thought he

213

was going to have me up on the stage.' She shrugged. 'But he didn't. He just made me watch.'

'What were they doing on the stage?' Tony asked softly.

Isobel swallowed. 'They were making love. They were dressed just in black leather and chain harnesses – and they were dancing, touching each other.'

'And it turned you on?' Tony guessed.

She nodded. 'He stroked my thighs, then he touched me – and he could tell that I was wet, straight away. He said he could see my nipples.' She was aware that her nipples were hardening again at the memory.

'What then?' JJ asked.

'He told me to undo my jacket. I didn't – I couldn't move – so he undid it, then pushed it down so that my arms were pinioned.' Her voice became deeper, huskier. 'Then he began to touch me. He said I was one of them – dedicated to pleasure – and he drew his hand over my body. He began to rub my clitoris – and he made me come.' She swallowed. 'Then I told him that I had to leave. He said that I had to keep my skirt where it was, but he did my jacket up again. Then he said that I had until Friday to decide.'

'Well, you've made your decision, now,' Tony said softly.

'Yes.' Isobel's face was a picture of misery. 'I just hope it was the right one.'

'It was,' JJ said. 'You've done the right thing.' He paused, and met Tony's eyes; then he stroked Isobel's face. 'Isobel – what Langton-Smith did to you . . .'

'Mm?'

'Well – we could take the taste of him from you, if you like,' he said softly.

Isobel swallowed. 'You mean . . . ?'

'Yes,' Tony said. 'We could make you feel better. But only if you want to.'

'I . . .' Her throat dried. She'd imagined making love with JJ – but not at the same time as making love with Tony. The thought of it thrilled her; and yet she was suddenly nervous, shy.

'Isobel.' JJ kissed her forehead. 'You're lovely. Truly lovely.'

She said nothing, merely lifted her face for a kiss. JJ lowered his mouth onto hers, his kiss gentle at first, and then becoming harder. Isobel opened her mouth, and he kissed her properly, sliding his tongue into her mouth and exploring it.

She heard the rustle of cotton and the sound of a zip, as Tony undressed swiftly; then JJ pulled back, and Tony took his place, while JJ undressed.

The next thing Isobel knew, Tony had pulled her onto the floor, and had undone the robe, baring her body. He took a sharp intake of breath as he looked at her. 'Christ, Isobel. You're so lovely. I can imagine what you looked like, with your skirt round your waist and your jacket pulled down.'

Isobel flushed. 'I told you, I'm throwing that suit away.'

'We'll buy you another one. Navy, I think,' JJ said, moving to sit beside her, on the opposite side to Tony. 'The colour suits your skin.' He looked at Tony, who nodded; then, almost in unison, they bent their heads, cupping a breast each and sucking gently on her nipples.

Isobel closed her eyes, and tipped her head back; she didn't notice how hard the floor was. All she was aware of was the fact that she had two extremely sensual men beside her, kissing and caressing her.

She felt a hand slide over her abdomen to cup her mons veneris; she wasn't sure whether it was Tony or JJ, but she shivered as he slid one finger between her labia, exploring her aroused flesh and then began to rub her clitoris. The other one let his hand glide along her inner thigh, then slid first one finger and then a second into her already well-lubricated channel. Under their combined ministrations, she came within seconds, crying out and clenching her fists in an agony of pleasure.

Tony kissed her lightly on the lips. 'Well. You look better, already.'

'I don't think we've finished, yet,' JJ said.

'No. But the floor's a bit hard; I think this might be nicer in comfort, don't you?'

'Indeed,' JJ agreed.

With a smile, Tony drew Isobel to her feet, stripping the robe from her and letting it fall on the carpet; then he scooped her up into his arms. Isobel slid her hands round his neck. 'Now, you're being macho,' she teased.

'Yeah?' Tony rubbed his nose against hers.

'Yeah.'

He grinned. 'Let's see what you say, in an hour's time.' He nodded to JJ, who smiled, and followed him up the stairs to the bedroom. Gently, Tony lowered Isobel onto the bed, then sat on the mattress next to her. He leaned down to kiss her, nibbling at her lower lip until she sighed with pleasure, slid her hands around his neck and kissed him back, her mouth opening under his and her tongue exploring his mouth.

As his hands smoothed over her skin, cupping her breasts, she felt another pair of hands caressing the soft arches of her feet, feathering their way up her calves in tiny spiral motions. JJ. His hands were followed by his lips and tongue, little cat-licks on her skin which made her shiver and want more.

JJ's breath fanned her thighs; almost on auto-pilot, she parted her legs, and he settled between them with a sigh of contentment, his hands wrapped round her thighs and his mouth teasing her labia. At the same time, Tony's mouth tracked over her throat, nibbling at the sensitive spots at the side of her neck in a way that made her quiver with pleasure. His mouth moved southwards, oh, so very slowly; then, at last, he began to suckle one nipple, while his finger and thumb pulled gently at the other, arousing her even more.

Isobel wasn't sure which she loved most: the idea of all her erogenous zones being pleasured at the same time by her two good-looking lovers, or the fact. She was on the point of coming when they both stopped; she opened her eyes in surprise. 'What's the matter?'

'We were thinking,' Tony said. 'We want this to be mutual pleasure.'

'Agreed,' JJ said.

'And when you're lying on your back . . . well.' He shrugged. 'We can't.'

'You put me here, in the first place,' Isobel reminded him with a grin. 'If you're not happy – then do something about it.'

'I was hoping you'd say that,' Tony breathed. He pulled away from her slightly; he and JJ flipped her onto her stomach, then guided her to a kneeling position. Tony stroked her arms, and she lowered her hands to the bed. He stooped to kiss the tip of her nose, then knelt in front of her so that his cock was on a level with her face. Meanwhile, JJ knelt behind her.

'Beautiful,' he said softly, stroking her buttocks. Isobel pushed back, wanting to feel him inside her; to her surprise, he didn't fit his cock to the entrance of her sex. Instead, he bent down, kissing her buttocks and encouraging her to spread her legs wider. Then, she felt his tongue pressing against the puckered rosy hole of her anus.

She moaned, pushing back again, and he began to tease her, licking her and sliding one finger into her sex. Her muscles flexed hard beneath the dual onslaught; JJ's hand began to move faster and faster, pistoning in and out of her. It was too much for her; she gave a low hoarse cry as her orgasm rippled through her.

'Better?' Tony asked softly, stroking her face.

'For starters.' She looked up at him, her eyes glowing.

JJ straightened up, and slid his cock into her by now well-lubricated quim. Isobel almost purred as he entered her, his cock thick and firm. 'Yes,' she said. 'Yes. This is what I want.' And it was the best way of wiping out the memory of the way Langton-Smith had touched her, wanting her humiliation and his own pleasure. Tony and JJ were both concerned about her pleasure, as well as their own.

Her lips curved sensually as she looked at Tony and realised just how aroused he was. She stretched forward, curling her fingers round his shaft and lowering her head so that she could lick the droplet of clear fluid from the tip of his cock. It was salt-sweet, and she probed the eye of his cock with the tip of her tongue.

Tony groaned, and cupped her face as she massaged his balls with her other hand, then lowered her mouth over his glans, sucking gently. He arched back, his body a taut bow as he thrust his cock towards her.

As her mouth moved over Tony's cock, so JJ's cock plunged in and out of her quim. When she moved forward to take more of Tony in her mouth, working as far down the shaft as she could, JJ pulled out of her, and as she moved back from Tony, JJ pushed back in hard, his balls slapping against her quim and arousing her even more.

Isobel felt pleasure fizzing through her veins: nothing mattered except this, the way they made her feel. She loved it, the feeling of being filled; JJ's finger pressed lightly against her anus again, and she sighed, letting her muscles relax so that he could penetrate her there. It felt good, so good; she flexed her internal muscles round his cock, in almost the same rhythm that she used while sucking Tony.

She felt JJ's balls lift and tighten against her, and as her own orgasm exploded, she felt him come, his cock throbbing deep inside her. At exactly the same time, Tony gave a groan, and his seed spilled into her mouth.

They remained locked together for a while longer, Tony's cock deep in her mouth and JJ's cock deep in her quim, his finger in her up to the second joint. When their pulses had slowed down, JJ removed his finger and leaned over her, resting his cheek tenderly against her back and cupping her breasts in his hands, while Tony moved his fingertips gently over her scalp, massaging her affectionately.

Eventually, JJ withdrew from her. 'You're irresistible, Isobel,' he said softly.

Tony, too, withdrew from her, bending down to kiss her and tasting his seed on her lips. 'Mm, I agree. You're fantastic.'

She grinned, amused and pleased at the same time. 'You two weren't so bad, yourselves.'

'But we haven't finished, yet.' JJ turned her round gently so that she faced him, then kissed her lingeringly, his tongue exploring the soft contours of her mouth. He could taste Tony's semen on her tongue, and he couldn't help wondering what it would feel like, to have Isobel's mouth working on his cock and bringing him to a climax.

Meanwhile, Tony was caressing her buttocks, the flat of his palms curving over her skin. Gently, he parted her thighs, and bent to draw his tongue along her satiny cleft. She tasted of seashore and honey – and also of JJ. He'd never made love to a woman almost immediately after another man had ejaculated inside her. He had a feeling that it wasn't the first time that Isobel had enjoyed the attention of two men: as he'd known, right from the start, one man wasn't enough for her. But he hadn't expected to be so turned on by the idea . . .

He worked at her with his mouth, liking the way her flesh became warm and puffy under his tongue; then he dropped a kiss on each buttock, straightened up, and slid his cock into her. Like JJ, he wetted his finger, and began to massage her anus; having seen Isobel's reaction to it, he knew how much she liked it.

JJ, too, straightened up and let Isobel set the pace as she lowered her mouth over his hardened cock. It felt as good as he'd expected; he shivered, and licked his lips. She was extremely talented – not just as a journalist. She was the sort of woman who'd be a sultan's favourite concubine. 'Cleopatra,' he said softly. 'Nor custom stale her infinite variety.'

Tony looked at him, surprised; JJ smiled wryly, and raked a hand through his hair. The rocking motion of Isobel's mouth along his cock echoed the motion of Tony's cock inside her quim, and the sheer symmetry of it appealed to him. No wonder Langton-Smith had reacted so strongly to her, too. Had JJ been in his place, and watched her pull her skirt up defiantly, baring her delta, he wouldn't have been able to keep his hands off her.

He slid his hands into her hair, urging her on; then, at last, he felt his balls lifting and tightening, pleasure rushing through him. At the same time, he felt Isobel quiver; he opened his eyes, and saw that Tony, too, had just reached a climax.

'You're one hell of a woman,' JJ said, stroking her face and removing his cock from her mouth.

'You're telling me,' Tony said huskily, withdrawing from her.

Isobel smiled, and rolled over onto her back, patting the sheet. 'Come on. I could do with a cuddle. And a drink.'

'Cuddle, first,' Tony said. 'And yes, there's a bottle of Chardonnay in the fridge.'

She grinned. 'I like a man who can read my mind, and anticipate my needs.'

'One man?' JJ teased, cupping one breast.

Tony followed suit, playing with her nipple and teasing it into erection. 'One man couldn't be enough. Not for Isobel.'

'Hey, I'm not a tart,' she protested.

'Just a sensualist. Langton-Smith was right about you, in that respect,' Tony mused. 'You could easily dedicate your life to pleasure.'

'But it has to be mutual pleasure,' Isobel said. 'Not selfish.'

'Very true.' JJ kissed her forehead. 'And, thanks to you, I think he's about to find that out.'

Sixteen

When Isobel went home, the next morning, dressed in the skirt from her now-hated red suit and a large cream sweater belonging to Tony, Sophie was sitting in the kitchen, reading the paper. Isobel looked warily at her friend. 'Hello.'

'Are you all right?' Sophie asked, her face filled with concern. Isobel decided to play it cool. 'Yes. Why?'

'Tony rang me.' Sophie's eyes darkened. 'He told me what happened last night, at Number Seven.'

'Oh.'

'Isobel, you idiot, why did you go on your own? Why didn't you ask me to go with you, if you didn't want Tony there?'

'I don't think it would have been your sort of place, Soph. It was a bit – well, even I felt a bit gauche and innocent, there.'

'*You* felt gauche?' Sophie was thoughtful. 'It must have been quite some place.'

'That's one way of putting it,' Isobel agreed wryly.

'The main thing is, are you all right? I mean, really?'

Isobel nodded. 'I'm fine. He didn't hurt me; he just made a few threats, that's all.'

'Look, Isobel . . .' Sophie winced. 'The other day – I over-reacted.'

Isobel shook her head. 'No. You're right, I was a complete bitch, and I should never have touched Alex. But I swear that I never laid a finger on Gary.'

'I know. He wasn't your type. Whereas Alex . . .' Sophie shrugged.

'He's quite something, isn't he?' Isobel said. 'I've never met anyone who exudes pure sex, like that.'

'Yeah, well.' Sophie really didn't want to talk about that. 'Do you want a coffee?'

Isobel nodded. 'If you've got time, then yes, please. That'd be nice.'

'Of course I've got time. It's Thursday – I don't have any students until twelve.' Sophie made some fresh coffee, pouring them both a mug. 'I've been marking essays from home.'

'Don't you mean reading the paper?' Isobel nodded at the newspaper spread over the table.

'Mm.' Sophie grinned. 'I've marked a huge pile of essays, though.'

'You don't normally work from home.'

'I wanted to wait for you – to see if you were okay.'

'Oh, Soph. I'm fine, honestly.'

'I'm not sure if you're incredibly brave, or completely mad.'

'Probably a bit of both,' Isobel said with a grin. 'Soph, I'm glad we're on speaking terms again. I really have been feeling bad about it.'

'That makes two of us.' Sophie bit her lip. 'I've been going through a bit of a bad time, lately. I don't know what's been happening to me; I feel like I've been going off the rails.'

'Well, you didn't do it when you were at university, like nearly everyone else did. Maybe it's your turn to do it now,' Isobel suggested.

'When you're eighteen, and you've left home for the first time, you go a bit crazy. It's expected. But at thirty, you don't start acting out of character.' Sophie rubbed her jaw. 'I still can't believe that I actually went to bed with Alex, the first time I met him.'

'I don't think you're alone there,' Isobel said quietly. 'And I'm not just talking about me, either. It's the way he is, Soph.'

'Yeah, I suppose so.' Sophie tipped her head on one side. 'Isobel, can I ask you a personal question?'

Isobel was slightly wary. 'Ye-es.'

'Did Alex *really* suggest watching you make love with another woman?'

Isobel nodded. 'But before you start getting ideas, he didn't mean you and me.'

'Who, then?'

'Phoebe, the model from his sketches. She's actually a very nice woman.'

'You mean, you've met her?' Sophie was surprised. 'Where?'

'She's JJ's assistant – as I discovered, the other day.'

Sophie chuckled. 'I wish I'd been a fly on the wall.'

'Mm. I didn't know quite what to say, at first; luckily, she was the one who brought up the subject of the paintings. I think she guessed, from the look on my face.' Isobel shrugged. 'She wasn't at all like I'd expected. I'd spoken to her, a couple of times, on the phone; she sounded like some debby type, an educated luvvie. She's not like that, at all; you'd really like her.' She smiled. 'Maybe you'll meet her at the exhibition.'

'So it's still on, then?'

Isobel nodded. 'Phoebe managed to calm him down about the missing paintings. Actually, it's a bit more complicated than that. The man who's got them . . . Well, it was his party Alex had been to, the night of the accident.'

Sophie winced. 'Ouch.'

'Anyway, Alex is on our side. He says as long as the guy is caught, and made to pay for it, he doesn't care about the paintings.'

'That's good.' Sophie took a sip of coffee.

Isobel looked at her. 'You still feel a lot for him, don't you?'

Sophie sighed. 'If you mean, do I still have the hots for him – then yes, but I'm trying to block it out. Though I don't know if I've been doing it the right way, these past few days.'

'Want to talk about it?'

'Yes and no. I feel such a tart, Isobel.'

Isobel chuckled. 'Soph, that's the last thing that anyone could say about you.'

'That's what the men involved said.' The words were out before Sophie could stop them.

'Men?' Isobel picked up on the plural.

'Well . . .' Sophie bit her lip. 'After I made love with Alex . . . I suppose I realised what I'd been missing.'

'With Mr Wet Blanket, you mean?'

223

'Don't be cruel. Gary's a nice guy.'

'But he wasn't right for you, Soph.'

'I know.'

Isobel licked her lower lip. 'I have to admit, Alex was pretty good. I'm not surprised he bowled you over.'

'Yeah, well. I just kept wishing that I was with Alex, instead of Gary. I even fantasised that it was Alex inside me, when he was making love to me. Then he asked me to marry him.'

'He *what?* You didn't tell me that!'

'I didn't want to talk about it.' Sophie shrugged. 'It's not important now, anyway. I said no, and I know it was the right thing to say. I'd have been miserable, being Mrs Gary and being what he wanted me to be.' She looked at Isobel. 'I spent the next couple of days brooding. I thought that Alex was bound to contact me, and I kept waiting . . . but then I realised that he wasn't going to. I suppose, at the time, I didn't handle it too well.' She sipped her coffee. 'I was marking some essays, and one of my students had used Alex's work to illustrate her essay.' She closed her eyes. 'Oh, God. Isobel, have you ever had days when you've just had to touch yourself, to ease the ache?'

'Yes. I think most women have,' Isobel said gently.

'Well, that's what the thought of Alex made me do, right in the middle of my office and I was caught.'

'Who was it? Not your head of department, or anything like that?'

Sophie shook her head. 'One of my second years, actually – Lawrence Byfield.' Her smile was rueful. 'You'd probably like him, Isobel. He's very attractive. Anyway, he locked the door behind him, and we ended up making love. I felt such a bitch, Isobel – it's a really unprofessional thing to do, bedding your students.'

'Sometimes, you can't help circumstances,' Isobel said softly. 'And if you both enjoyed it. Where's the harm?'

'He's my student. I'm supposed to be guiding him and looking after him, not leaping on him!'

'But you enjoyed it?'

'Yes – but I felt too guilty about it, afterwards.' Sophie sighed. 'And he wasn't as good as Alex.'

'Not many men are.'

Sophie rolled her eyes. 'Then you dragged me out with Philip.'

'And he saw you home. I hope he didn't leap on you. I told him to be nice to you, keep it slow and gentle.'

'That's what he said to me, too,' Sophie said wryly. 'But we ended up in bed together. I think we both needed it. He was good, kind and considerate – but it didn't feel right with him, either.' She bit her lip. 'I don't want to go to bed with every man I meet.'

'Like me, you mean?'

Sophie smiled. 'You're a bit of a man-eater, yes – but you're choosy.'

'Thanks for the compliment.'

Sophie's smile broadened. 'You asked for it.'

'Yeah.' Isobel patted her hand. 'You're just trying to get Alex out of your system. If you've told the men concerned that there are no strings, no-one's going to get hurt.' She paused. 'Except maybe you. You're in love with Alex, aren't you?'

Sophie thought about it. 'Yes. I am,' she admitted quietly.

Isobel hoped fervently that Phoebe had managed to persuade Alex into coming up to London. If Sophie was feeling this bad about it . . . then Isobel had to get them together again. She smiled at her friend. 'Look, I'm sure it'll work out.'

'Yes, but Alex hasn't contacted me. It's obvious that he's not interested, otherwise he would have written to me, or even maybe come to see me.'

'Alex avoids London,' Isobel said. 'But you're right, he could have written.' Her eyes narrowed. 'But then again – how would he know your address?'

'I left a note for him.'

'Maybe he didn't see it.'

'I put it in the middle of his pillow.'

'Ah.' Isobel sipped her coffee. 'Look, I'm sorry, Soph, I really am. But I suppose at least you do know what you want out of life, now.'

'Yes.'

'Soph . . . The exhibition isn't going to be a retro, any more. Alex is going to show some of his new work – you know, the stuff we saw in the cottage.'

Sophie was surprised into silence.

'That's JJ's influence, I think,' Isobel said. 'I was wondering . . . would you like to see them?'

Sophie shook her head. 'Thanks, but I really don't think I can handle it.'

'He's not going to be there, and there won't be that many people you know – apart from Tony and me, that is. It'll give you a chance to meet JJ and Phoebe – you'd like them both, you really would.'

'Thanks, but no.'

'Soph, don't torture yourself over him. Don't deny yourself the treat of seeing his new work, just because the man himself is a callous bastard who treats people like dirt.'

'I'll think about it.'

'Oh, Soph.' Isobel stood up and walked round to the other side of the table, putting her arms round her friend. 'I really wish I could just wave a magic wand and make it all right. Look, why don't I drive you down to the Fens, so you can talk to him? I'll make myself scarce – I'll chat up Mack at the garage, or something like that.'

Sophie shook her head. 'There's no point. He's not interested, so I might as well just get him out of my system.'

'But you will come to the exhibition?'

'I said I'd think about it.'

'Please? It's important to Tony that it goes well.'

'You're going to bully me until I give in, aren't you?' Sophie asked.

Isobel grinned. 'Whatever gives you that idea?'

'Okay, okay, I'll come.'

'Good.' Isobel hugged her again. 'I'm so glad we're back on speaking terms. You're my best friend, and no man's worth this kind of hassle.' She decided not to tell Sophie that she'd been driven to breaking into her studio, to find out what was going on.

226

'Yeah, you're probably right.' Sophie smiled ruefully. 'I'm glad that, for the most part, we don't have the same taste in men. I couldn't handle this again.'

'It wouldn't feel right, sharing a man with you, anyway.'

'So, you and Alex ... it really was just the heat of the moment?'

'Yes. Like I said, when I tried to vamp him, he pushed me away and told me to cover myself up.'

Sophie chuckled. 'I can't see Alex being that prissy.'

'Believe me, he was!' Isobel shrugged. 'I suppose I sank a fair bit of wine, afterwards. Then, for some reason, he changed his mind.'

'I think he was watching me, when I was sleeping,' Sophie said. 'He left me a sketch.'

'He sketched you?'

'Yes. I tore it up in a fit of pique.' She wrinkled her nose. 'I half regret it, now. It was a good drawing, and it was his. But – oh, I hated him for it. I felt he'd been leading me on, and he'd dropped me.'

'Maybe he's just scared of having another relationship,' Isobel suggested. 'Keeping things purely on a physical level means that he won't get hurt again.'

'Maybe.' Sophie pulled a face. 'Anyway, enough of him.'

'But you will come to the exhibition?'

'Yes.'

Isobel beamed at her. 'Good. I'll cook dinner, tonight. In fact, I'll cook, for the next week!'

Sophie chuckled. 'You really are feeling guilty, then!'

'Yeah.' Isobel drained her coffee. 'Anyway, you ought to be going off to work. Want a lift?'

'Will the rust-bucket make it?'

'Yes. And I swear, I'm getting rid of it, this weekend.'

Sophie grinned. 'I've heard that one before. Okay, I'll get my stuff, I'll be ready in about five minutes.'

'Okay.' Isobel smiled as her friend left the room. Now she and Sophie had sorted out the mess, she felt a lot better; the atmosphere in the house would improve, too. And in the meantime, she and Phoebe needed a couple of clandestine meetings to work out their strategy for making Alex come to his senses over Sophie. Isobel's smile broadened: she was going to enjoy playing fairy godmother.

The phone rang; Isobel picked up the receiver. 'Hello?'

'Hello, Isobel.'

She froze, recognising the voice. Langton-Smith. She'd expected that the police would have picked him up, by then – not left him free to bother her. 'Hello,' she said, keeping her voice carefully neutral, and trying to remember whether she'd left the front door unlocked.

'I take it you know who this is.'

'Yes.'

'And you remember our little conversation at Number Seven.'

'Yes.'

'It's Friday morning.'

'Yes.' Isobel's pulse was beating erratically. The line was echoing slightly, so he was using a mobile phone – a digital one, which was untappable. Where was he phoning from? Was he parked outside her house?

'I gave you until this morning to make your decision.'

'Yes.' She swallowed hard. Christ. She hadn't been expecting this.

'Did I tell you that I had photographs taken, at Number Seven?' he asked silkily. 'They're quite clear. You, standing up and pulling up your skirt to reveal your pretty little quim. You, with your jacket pulled down and your breasts bared, your nipples standing proud and hard, your skirt round your waist and my hand between your legs. Quite an interesting addition to your portfolio, don't you think?'

'You're bluffing.'

'Am I?' She could imagine the cruel smile on his face. 'Well, Isobel. I have the prints in front of me. I'm sure some of your contacts would be very interested in seeing them.'

'Are you trying to blackmail me?'

'I just want to make sure that you make the right decision.'

'I've made my decision.'

'Good girl.'

His assumption that she would go along with his bully-boy tactics made her furious; but she couldn't afford the luxury of giving vent to her anger. She had to play this cool. Sophie was at work, Tony was at the gallery, and JJ and Phoebe were the other side of London. She had to work out what to do – and fast.

'So when are you going to talk to Alex?'

'When do I get the paintings back?'

'After the show.'

She calculated that even if he was outside, she had time enough to lock the front door, and then call the police. 'So it looks like never, then.'

'Don't you think you can sweet-talk Alex?'

'It's not a case of can't.'

'I beg your pardon?'

'I've made my decision, H. No deal.'

'I could publish those photos of you.'

'Publish and be damned.' She dropped the receiver without waiting for his reply or hanging up, ran to the front door, and slid the bolt across. Then she went back to the phone; the line was dead. She cleared the line, and dialled 999.

A couple of weeks later saw the opening night of the exhibition. Isobel's interview hadn't been published in *Vivendi*; Langton-Smith had carried out his threat and closed the magazine. But Ralph and some of the other staff were setting up their own magazine, based on their redundancy money from Langton-Smith. Langton-Smith himself had left the country, and was believed to be in Amsterdam; there was a warrant out for his arrest. The pictures of Isobel, and Alex's paintings, were nowhere to be found; Isobel was assured that she could sue for very large damages if Langton-Smith published the photographs.

She still kept the door locked, and was trying to persuade

Sophie to move from the house in Pimlico; she didn't trust Langton-Smith. Now that she'd crossed him, she knew that she'd made a difficult enemy.

At the exhibition, she pushed her fears to the back of her mind. Tony needed her more. He was walking about nervously, wondering if he should have hung the pictures differently, and fretting about whether people would turn up, or whether the whole thing would be a flop.

In the end, Sophie took him under her wing. 'For goodness' sake, Tony, you know it's going to be a success. His name alone is enough to attract a lot of people; and Isobel says that the stuff is good. I'm sure that tonight is going to be brilliant. Just have a glass of champagne, a few canapés, and stop worrying.'

'Yeah. I suppose so.'

'Really.' Sophie handed him a glass, and he took a sip.

Isobel smiled at her friend. 'You're a genius, Soph. He won't listen to me.'

When the gallery began to fill up, Tony started to relax, and Sophie decided to look round the exhibition properly. Although she was trying to suppress her feelings for Alex, she still wanted to see his work.

She recognised the pictures in the retrospective half of the exhibition from her old textbooks; but seeing them 'in the flesh' was completely different to looking at reproductions. The textures and colours of the paintings were much clearer, and she felt the hairs stand up on her arms as she saw one of her favourites: Alex's rendition of Morgana as a siren.

She walked into the next room, to look at the newer work, and her eyes widened in shock. The centrepiece of the exhibition was a charcoal sketch of a woman in orgasm. That was nothing unusual, for an Alex Waters piece – but it was a portrait of Sophie.

'Christ,' she said under her breath. Both Tony and Isobel must have known about this. Why hadn't they warned her? Slowly, half dreading what she might see next, she moved to the next picture. Again, it was of her, abandoned to pleasure with her mouth open and a rosy mottling over her breasts. Another picture was similar to the one he'd left on her pillow: Sophie lying asleep, a dreamy smile on her face and her hand snaking down her thigh, as though she were dreaming of her lover and about to touch herself

'Oh, my God,' she said. 'The bastard. I don't believe he's done this. He's been using me for his bloody career!' She turned on her heel and stormed out of the room, colliding with Isobel, who just about managed to save the contents of the glass she'd been holding.

'Soph, what's the matter?'

'Did you know about those pictures?' Sophie demanded.

'What, the new ones?'

'Yes.'

'Well, you were there when I looked through the portfolio.'

'Not *those* ones,' Sophie said. 'The ones through there.'

'Well, aren't they the ones we saw?'

'No.' Sophie ground her teeth. 'You must have known about them – and if you didn't, then Tony bloody well did.'

Isobel took Sophie's arm. 'Soph, instead of growling at me, can you just explain what the hell is the matter?'

'This.' Sophie marched her friend over to the centrepiece, and pointed at it. 'This is what's the matter.'

Isobel's face whitened. 'Oh, my God. Soph, I swear I didn't know about this.' She bit her lip. 'Tony didn't say a word about this to me.'

'Tony didn't say a word about—' a male voice began by her ear, and then stopped. 'Oh.' Tony looked at Sophie, and then at the sketch. 'Sophie, I'm so sorry.'

'You knew about this?'

'Yes and no.' Tony winced. 'Alex didn't want anyone to see the new work until he was ready. JJ and Phoebe hung them; I was banned from these rooms.'

'You're the gallery manager. You're telling me that you went along with it?' Sophie demanded, furious.

He nodded. 'I wanted the exhibition; I thought they were just like the ones Isobel showed me, so I let Alex have his way. If I'd had any idea that they were of you, I would never have agreed to this.'

'I can't believe that I'm seeing this.' Sophie shook her head. 'You'll have to cancel the exhibition, Tony. I can't let people see these.'

'Sophie, I have to. It's all booked.'

'In that case, I'm leaving. Now.'

'Sophie . . .' Isobel put her arm round her friend's shoulders. 'Calm down. I know it looks bad, and I'd be really furious, if I were in your shoes. But no-one's going to connect you with the paintings, if we go and change your hair and your make-up, and you stay out of these rooms. Please don't go.'

'They go, or I do.'

'Sophie . . .' Isobel drew Sophie to one side, dropping the tone of her voice to a whisper. 'If this exhibition bombs, the gallery will be in a lot of financial trouble.'

'I didn't know things were that bad.'

'It's the recession.' Isobel bit her lip. 'Well – that, and a bit of bad luck, last year.'

'Tony told you? Or did you just so happen to come across a file?'

Isobel was unabashed. 'Look, if I'm going to spend a serious part of my life with this man, I need to know whether he's solvent. I can't afford to keep both of us. Actually, he showed me the file.'

Sophie swallowed. 'Oh.'

'I don't want to put any pressure on you, Soph, but this is almost like the night when I met Langton-Smith. It was a case of telling the police and knowing that he was going to close the magazine and put some of my friends out of work, or letting the bastard get away with it.' She shrugged. 'I had to do what was right. It meant that my friends would be hurt, but it's turned out for the best, because they're setting up on their own. Soph, if you feel it's the right thing, then I'll ask Tony to pull it.'

Sophie closed her eyes. 'Now I feel like a complete bitch.' She sighed. 'Hell. Better leave it. I'm going home, though.'

'Look, nobody's going to recognise you. Come to the Ladies with me, and I'll change your hair and your make-up. You're wearing your glasses, you're fully clothed – no-one will recognise you,' Isobel soothed.

Sophie wasn't quite so sure, but she allowed herself to be persuaded. 'Okay, but I'm staying with the old pictures. I'm not going anywhere near the other room.'

'Attagirl.' Isobel smiled at her. 'Thanks, Soph. I know you feel bad about this, but Tony and I will make it up to you.'

'That's what friends are for, right?' Sophie said wryly.

'Something like that.' Isobel eyed the pictures. 'Though on the plus side, Soph, he's captured the sensual side of you. If I were a man, I'd want to—'

'Well, you're not, are you?'

Isobel grinned as Sophie coloured. 'Sorry. I didn't mean that as it sounded!'

'No.'

'I have to admit, Langton-Smith said that Alex had drawn a picture of me. If that had been here, I would have thrown a fit on Tony,' She smiled. 'But I think that Langton-Smith was bluffing. At least, I hope he was.'

'So you haven't seen the other pictures?' Sophie eyed her. 'Well, if the ones of me are there . . . There could be some of you, too.'

'I don't think so.' Isobel looked at the pictures. 'And there's something different about these, Soph – they're not like the ones he did of Phoebe. It's almost . . .' She didn't finish the sentence, but it was almost as though Alex were in love with his model. It showed in every line; but she was none too sure whether Alex was going to turn up or not. If he did turn up, she wasn't sure what sort of mood he'd be in; she didn't want to raise Sophie's hopes, only to dash them down even further.

'Isobel, sweetie!'

Isobel turned round to face JJ. 'Hi! How are you?'

'Fine, fine.'

'There's someone I want you to meet. JJ, this is my best friend, Sophie. Sophie, this is JJ, Alex's agent.'

JJ smiled at her. 'Well, well. It's the mystery girl from the paintings. I asked Alex who she was, and he wouldn't say a word. All he'd do was tap his nose and say "wisdom".'

Sophie looked at Isobel. 'So much for people not recognising me,' she said. She turned to JJ. 'And as for you – you can go to hell.' She turned on her heel, and was about to storm from the room, when she saw who was leaning in the doorway. Alex.

Seventeen

Her heart missed a beat. God, he was as attractive as ever: dressed in a white shirt and a pair of olive-green chinos, he looked almost edible.

'Hello, Sophie.' He smiled at her.

She stared at him, stony-faced. This was the man who'd betrayed her – the man who'd made love to her, ignored her, and then drawn intimate pictures of her to show the world at his first exhibition in ten years. 'Leave me alone, Alex. I'm going.'

He switched to sign, bending his elbows so that his flat hands were at ninety degrees to his body, and pushing them down slightly but emphatically. *Wait.*

She shook her head, and tried to push past him. She could smell his scent, and it made her shiver. Her body yearned for him, but she forced herself not to weaken. Alex used people for his own ends; he'd be nice to her when it suited him, and bed all her friends at the first opportunity. She couldn't trust him.

He barred her way, and continued to sign to her, placing the tip of his right thumb on his forehead, then making a circle of his fingers and thumbs, moving his hands in small circles, then pointing to her. *I knew nothing about you.*

She stared at him disbelievingly. Apart from the fact that she'd left him the note, he could have talked to JJ and Phoebe. They would have put him in touch with Isobel, and Isobel could have told him all about her. Her lip curled, and she extended her right index finger, putting it flat against her chin so that it pointed towards her nose, and sliding her finger to the right. *Liar.*

Alex stared at her in surprise, and she pushed past him, ignoring his attempt to hold her arm. She left the gallery at a run, flagging down a taxi and giving the driver her address. As far as

235

she was concerned, she never wanted to see Alex again.

The driver dropped her off outside the house, and waited while she opened the door. She slammed the door hard behind her, the violent action easing her frustration slightly, then kicked off her shoes, and went into the sitting room to pour herself a stiff gin. The answerphone was flashing; she pressed the play button, more from habit than a desire to know who had called.

'Soph, it's Isobel. If you're home, ring me at the gallery. I just need to know that you're all right.'

Tough, she thought. She didn't particularly want to talk to anyone – and she wasn't giving Isobel the chance to persuade her into talking to Alex. 'Forget it,' she said aloud, and took a large swig of the gin. She padded upstairs to her studio, put some chamber music on at high volume, and began to sketch.

Sketching usually calmed her down, but she found herself drawing Alex's face over and over again. She screwed the piece of paper into a ball, hurling it savagely across the room, swore, and began another sketch. Again, she found that she was drawing Alex.

A hand settled on her shoulder, and she shrieked, dropping her pad, and looked up. It was Alex.

'How the hell did you get in?' she demanded.

He dangled a bunch of keys. 'Isobel gave me these. She thought you might come here.'

'I don't want you here,' she said. 'Go away.'

'Sophie, Sophie. Don't fight me.' He took her hand. 'Don't be angry with me.'

'Angry with you? You bastard! You used me. You sketched me in the most intimate way and showed the whole of London!'

He stroked her face. 'Slow down, Sophie. I can't read you.'

She repeated her words, this time more slowly.

He looked ruefully at her, his dark eyes filled with concern and pain. 'Sophie, I never wanted to hurt you. Yes, I admit that I was hoping you'd see the pictures – so you could see what I felt about you, and maybe then you'd get in touch with me again.'

'Get in touch with you? But I left you a note, with my address!'

'A note?' He shook his head. 'I didn't see any note.'

'I left it on your pillow.'

'There was nothing there, Sophie, honestly. I've been trying to find out about you. All I knew was that your name was Sophie, and you came down with Isobel to interview me. I knew nothing else about you.'

'You could have asked your agent.'

'JJ didn't know anything about you. All he knew was that you were a friend of Isobel's.'

'He could have passed a message through her.'

'Yes – but JJ's very focused on business. He probably thought it was a whim on my part, and forgot it.'

'You're used to bedding women, then.'

He held her gaze. 'I've had relationships with my models, if that's what you're asking. Purely physical.'

'And with Isobel. You slept with Isobel – the same day you slept with me.'

'There's no comparison.'

'I don't trust you, Alex. I don't want anything to do with you. So just get out of my life.'

'Do you mean that?'

'Yes, I do.'

He regarded her thoughtfully. 'That's not what Isobel says. Or Phoebe.'

'I've never even met Phoebe; and Isobel's just stirring.'

'Is she? I wonder.' Without warning, he bent his head, touching his lips to hers. His mouth was warm and sweet, coaxing rather than demanding; Sophie couldn't help opening her mouth under his and kissing him back.

He broke the kiss, and rubbed his nose against hers. 'Sophie. I've been dreaming about that, since the moment you walked out of my door.'

'You weren't there, when I left.'

'Figure of speech. I've been thinking about you, every night since we made love. Remembering the softness of your skin, the way you tasted, your scent.' He stroked her face. 'I've been working like a demon on those sketches. All I wanted to do was

237

paint you, relive what happened between us on paper – until I could find you again.'

'I don't believe you.' Her voice was shaky; although he couldn't hear her tone, he could see the tears glittering in her eyes.

'Sophie.' His hand slid round to the nape of her neck; he frowned. 'You're tense.'

'What do you expect?'

'I can do something about it.'

'I don't want you touching me.'

'Non-sexual, I promise. Turn round.'

She frowned. 'What?'

'Turn round,' he repeated softly. 'This is something a good friend of mine taught me, years ago – after the accident. It helps.'

She looked suspiciously at him. 'What?'

'Turn round,' he said, 'and you'll find out.'

Eventually, she did so; his hands settled on her shoulders, and he began to massage her through her thin shirt. His fingers dug into the knots of tension in her shoulders, loosening them.

'Relax,' he whispered against her ear; she shivered as his breath fanned her skin. Christ. She knew he couldn't be trusted – and yet even when he touched her in a non-sexual way, it turned her on. She could imagine him touching her more intimately, undoing her shirt and then letting his hands slide round to her front, curving over her ribcage and touching her breasts.

'Sophie.' He brushed the hair from the nape of her neck, and kissed the sensitive skin; she couldn't help arching her back, and she heard him give a small sigh of pleasure. 'Sophie. I know I said this would be non-sexual, but I want to touch you properly. I want to feel your skin, not a piece of paper. I want to hear you with my hands.'

'That's not fair,' she murmured, knowing that he couldn't hear her.

'Sophie.' He licked her earlobe. 'If you want me to stop, just move my hands away.' He continued massaging her shoulders with one hand, and reached round with the other to undo her shirt. He gently removed the garment, then she felt him undo her bra and slide that off her shoulders, too.

Alex paused, waiting for her to protest; when she said nothing, he continued rubbing her skin, his hands working gently down her spine, his fingertips moving in tiny spirals. Eventually, he let one hand curve over her ribcage to touch the underside of her breasts, and then cupped the warm soft globe. The nipple was erect, her areola puckered; he made a small sound of pleasure. 'Mm, Sophie, you're so responsive. I want to touch you.' He kissed the curve between her neck and shoulders, and let his other hand slide round to cup her other breast; he pushed them up and together slightly. 'Mm. You feel so good.'

He stopped, then, and walked round to face her. 'Sophie.'

'I—'

'Take me to your bed, Sophie. Make love with me.'

She swallowed. 'That's today. Tomorrow, you'll be with another woman. Maybe even tonight.'

He shook his head. 'Since the day you left my house, I haven't slept with anyone. Even Phoebe.'

'Phoebe?' Sophie was shocked to feel a surge of jealousy.

'It's past. Phoebe and I . . . we're just friends, now.'

'Isobel said you wanted to watch her making love with Phoebe.'

He grinned. 'Did she, now? Well. That was with Isobel. I don't want to share you with anyone else.'

Her eyes narrowed. 'I'm not in the market for a one-night stand.'

'Neither am I.' He looked serious for a moment. 'Your almost-fiancé—'

She shook her head. 'We're not together, any more.'

'Because of what happened between us?'

She didn't answer; Alex smiled, and kissed the tip of her nose. 'Sophie. Let's talk, later. Right now, I want you to take me to your bed. I want you to let me pleasure you. I want to feel your body all fluid against mine.'

'Alex . . . you're being unfair.'

'I know. True to the proverb.'

'What?'

'All's fair in love and war.' He stroked her face. 'And you can tell me which it is.'

She flushed. 'Alex . . .'

'Let's stop talking, Sophie. For now.' He held her gaze, and clenched his fist, drawing it down over his breastbone.

She shivered. *Desire*. That was what she felt for Alex, and what he obviously felt for her. But was it enough?

As if he guessed her thoughts, he drew her to her feet. 'Take me to your bed, Sophie,' he invited. 'Skin to skin . . . let's be kind to each other. Then, we talk.'

Making love with Alex. She'd fantasised about it; she'd even made love with other men and pretended that they were him. And now, he was here, in her studio, wanting her to take him to her bed. She knew that she was going to do it; even if she ended up despising herself in the morning, she was going to do it.

She nodded, and Alex smiled at her. He picked up her shirt, helping her put it on – but not letting her button it up again. She walked out of the room, and Alex followed her across the landing to her bedroom. He nodded approvingly at her double bed; she suppressed a smile, and walked over to close the curtains, switching on the bedside lamp.

'Sophie.' He pulled her into his arms again, sliding one hand beneath her hair and drawing her mouth to his. He eased his other hand down her back, cupping her buttocks and pulling her closer to him; she could feel his erection pressing against her, and it was enough to wipe out her last doubts.

'Oh, Sophie. Sweet, sweet Sophie.' He pushed the shirt from her shoulders, then helped her to unbutton his, and push the garment from his shoulders. Then he dropped to his knees, undoing her skirt and removing her half-slip at the same time. He rubbed his face against her midriff, breathing in her scent, then tipped his head back so that he could lick the undersides of her breasts.

Sophie gasped, and he smiled against her skin, taking one

nipple into his mouth. He sucked gently, at first; when Sophie pushed her hands into his hair, he drew more fiercely on her nipple, using his teeth but keeping it the right side of the line between pain and pleasure. He slid one hand between her thighs, his finger curving under the edge of her knickers, and she shivered as she felt his finger part her labia. She widened her stance, allowing him easier access, and felt him sigh with pleasure against her skin.

She was already wet; Alex continued sucking her breast, and pressed his finger to the entrance of her sex. He added a second finger, and a third; his thumb concentrated on her clitoris, rubbing it rapidly and very effectively. Sophie's climax reached boiling point, and she cried out, her internal muscles contracting sharply round his fingers.

He waited until the aftershocks of her orgasm had died down, and then gently removed her knickers and stockings. Then he stood up again, removing his olive-green chinos, and kicking his shoes and socks off at the same time. Sophie's shyness had vanished with her climax, and she looked hungrily at him, seeing the bulge of his erection through the soft cotton of his underpants, and wanting him.

Alex gave her an inviting smile. 'All yours,' he said softly.

Sophie licked her suddenly dry lips, and dropped to her knees in front of him. She hooked her thumbs into the waistband of his underpants, drawing them down; Alex stepped out of them. She sat back on her haunches, looking at him; he was as beautiful as she remembered. Her sketches just hadn't done him justice.

She let her hands drift up his thighs; Alex tensed, and she saw his mouth open slightly with pleasure as she curled her fingers round his cock. 'Sophie – you don't have to do this.'

She looked up at him, smiled, and clenched her other hand, drawing it down her sternum.

He grinned. 'It's mutual, Sophie. Very mutual.'

'Then let me do this,' she said. 'I want to touch you, to taste you.'

She felt his cock twitch as he read her lips; and then, she

241

lowered her mouth onto his cock, taking just the tip into her mouth, and then working him properly.

He groaned, sliding his fingers into her hair and urging her on; she continued to fellate him, until finally he cried out her name, and his cock throbbed, filling her mouth with warm salt-sweet fluid. Sophie swallowed every last drop, then stood up and kissed him hard, so that he could taste himself on her mouth.

'Thank you,' he said softly, when she broke the kiss.

She smiled at him. 'Talk later, you said.'

He smiled back. 'Not another word.' He took her hand, kissing it and drawing each finger in turn into his mouth; then he drew her over to the bed, pushed off the duvet, and lifted her up, settling her gently in the middle of the bed.

'Macho,' she teased.

He grinned. 'Shut up and kiss me.' He climbed onto the bed beside her, and lowered his face to hers; Sophie slid her hands round his neck, drawing his mouth to hers, and kissed him hard.

Alex ran his palms lightly across her midriff, then stroked down towards her thighs. Sophie arched her back, parting her legs, and he smiled at her, shifting to kneel between her thighs. He fitted the tip of his cock to the entrance of her sex; she pushed up, welcoming him, and he slid deep inside her, thrusting with long, slow, deep strokes.

Sophie moaned, and wrapped her legs round his waist, her heels pushing into his buttocks and her back arched so that he could penetrate her more deeply. His rhythm changed, becoming harder and deeper; Sophie cried out as she felt the first wave of her climax, her flesh convulsing sharply.

Without missing a stroke, Alex rolled over onto his back, gently guiding her legs so that she was straddling him. He blew her a kiss, and mouthed, 'Your turn.'

She nodded and sat up straighter, arching back to change the angle of his penetration. She began to move, lifting and lowering herself and moving her body in tiny circles. This was what she'd done with Lawrence, the day he'd caught her masturbating in her office over Alex: and this was what she'd imagined doing with Alex.

'Yes, Sophie, yes,' she heard him whisper; she lifted her hands to her breasts, cupping them and pushing them up and together, the way he had, and then pulled at her nipples, massaging the taut peaks of flesh.

Alex lifted his upper body from the bed, and bent his mouth to one nipple, sucking hard on it; at the same time, he eased one hand between their bodies, his fingers seeking and finding her clitoris.

She gasped, sliding her hands into his hair and increasing her movements, rocking over his penis and pulling up until he was almost out of her, before slamming down hard again. He continued rubbing her clitoris, bringing her to a higher peak of pleasure; she cried out as her orgasm swept through her.

Alex murmured something into her breast, then flipped her over onto her back again, driving hard into her, the long slow strokes lengthening her orgasm. Sophie was almost sobbing, it was so good; Alex continued pushing into her until they both felt another climax surge through her. She cried out, her internal muscles clutching sharply at him; then she felt his cock throb deep inside her.

Alex couldn't bear to withdraw; he kept his weight on his elbows and knees, and buried his head in her shoulder. Sophie slid her hands up to caress his back, stroking his hair and holding him close. They lay there in silence for a while; at last, Alex withdrew from her, rolling onto his back and tucking her into the curve of his body, keeping his arms protectively round her.

She tapped him lightly on the midriff, he looked at her. 'What?'

'Alex. We need to talk.'

'Okay.' He shifted so that they were lying facing each other, and he could see her lips. 'Now, we'll talk.'

'Why didn't you contact me?'

'I told you, I didn't ever see your note.'

'I left it on your pillow.'

He shrugged. 'Well, it wasn't there, later. My cleaning lady probably threw it away.'

'You have a cleaning lady?' She was surprised.

He grinned. 'I hate housework. I can cook, though, to a reasonable standard. Not as good as Isobel, but it's edible.'

'Right.'

He stroked her face. 'I'm sorry, Sophie. All I knew was that your name was Sophie, you taught history of art, and you lived in London with Miss Pushy.'

'Isobel's all right.'

'Yeah. She gave me her keys.'

'I thought you'd only wanted sex with me.' She bit her lip. 'I destroyed your sketch of me.'

'You can have whatever you want, from the exhibition. Or I'll do another one of you.'

'Maybe.' She looked levelly at him. 'I had a bad row with Isobel, when she told me that you'd slept together.'

'*That* was just sex. You looked so tired, so beautiful, when you were asleep. I didn't want to wake you; but it turned me on, watching you. You were smiling in your sleep, looking like you were dreaming of your lover.'

'You could have masturbated.'

He grinned. 'I have, ever since. When I wasn't sketching you.'

She flushed. 'Oh.'

'Did you?' he asked softly.

She nodded. 'I was caught, in my office.'

His eyes widened. 'But you haven't lost your job?'

'No. It was one of my students.'

'Embarrassing.'

She lifted her chin. 'Yes. We made love.'

'To ease the ache?' He looked hurt.

'Alex, we don't know each other. We can't make demands on each other.'

'Why not? I want to make all sorts of demands on you – and I want to pleasure you, in return.'

She flushed. 'Alex, this won't work. My life is in London, not in the Fens.'

He smiled. 'I know that. I don't expect you to move in with me.' He paused, and Sophie winced inside. What the hell had she expected from him? A declaration of love, a proposal of marriage?

'Yet,' he said softly.

'What?'

'I don't expect you to move in with me, yet. Not until you're ready.'

'You want me to move in with you? Like I said, my life's here.'

'I know.'

'And you hate London.'

'Hated,' he corrected. 'I've been thinking, a lot. And talking to Phoebe.'

Her eyes narrowed. 'She modelled for you.'

'Yes, and we made love. But it wasn't the way it is with you.' He stroked her face. 'Phoebe's a good friend. We talked. I showed her the pictures, and she guessed that you were the one Isobel told her about.'

'Isobel told her what, precisely?'

The frostiness in her tone was obviously evident in her face, because he grinned. 'Isobel and Phoebe decided to play match-maker. Isobel worked on you, persuading you to go to the exhibition; and Phoebe worked on me, telling me that it would be worth my while to go to London. In the end, I agreed.' His face grew serious. 'And then I saw you. I wanted to sweep you off your feet and carry you off somewhere – but you wanted nothing to do with me.'

'I thought you'd just used me, to further your career.'

He shook his head. 'Like I said earlier, I wanted you to see the paintings, so you could see how I felt about you.'

'Which is?'

'Don't you know?'

'I want to hear you say it.'

He sighed. 'After the accident, I felt so guilty about Dee; and I was in love with her. I blamed myself. If I hadn't taken her to that party, if I hadn't had a headache and let her drive—'

'Hey, it wasn't your fault.'

'Maybe. But I swore, then, that I'd never get involved with anyone again. Keep it simple: sex or friendship, nothing deeper.'

'So which is it, with me? Sex or friendship?'

He stroked her face. 'It's more than that. I'm in love with you, Sophie. I can't stop thinking about you.' He looked at her. 'So now you know. But I don't know how you feel about me.'

'Haven't Isobel and Phoebe told you?'

'Yes – but I want to hear you say it.' He echoed her words.

She sighed. 'I love you, Alex.'

'So maybe we can make it work between us.'

'Long distance?'

He shook her heard. 'I'm coming back to London.'

'For me?'

'Mm. Plus it's about time I resumed my career. I'm going to teach, part-time; but I have a small problem.'

'Oh?'

'I need someone who can help me with my students. Act as my ears.'

'You mean – me? I'm not good enough.'

'You are. I can help you with your homework, for your signing classes. Besides, you understand art – that's more important. You paint, yourself.'

She wrinkled her nose. 'Flowers and stuff. Nothing brilliant.'

'The stuff that Isobel gave JJ was pretty good.'

'What stuff?'

He grinned. 'She likes borrowing paintings, doesn't she?'

'That's one way of putting it.'

'So come and work with me. Part-time will do.'

She shook her head. 'I'm not an artist, like you. My tutor told me when I was seventeen that I was just perfunctory – that I'd never make a great artist.'

'Prove him wrong.' He stroked her face. 'You were sketching me, earlier.'

She flushed. 'Yeah, well. Anatomy gives me problems.'

He grinned. 'Work with me. I'll give you private lessons in anatomy – and I mean teaching you to draw.'

'Indeed.'

His grin broadened. 'Well, to understand how muscles work,

you have to feel them. I think we'll both enjoy that side of it . . . don't you?'

She smiled back. 'Alex. Supposing it doesn't work?'

'We won't know unless we try.' He kissed the tip of her nose. 'Anyway, I think you're going to have to look for a new place to live, in the next couple of weeks. Isobel and Tony were on the point of announcing their engagement, according to Phoebe.'

'They *what*?' Sophie's eyes widened. 'You're kidding!'

'No, seriously.' His lips twitched. 'I thought about making an announcement myself, but I thought I'd better ask you, first.'

'To get engaged to you?'

'Or live with me, if that's what you'd prefer. As long as you're with me.' He paused. 'I'm not the world's most even-tempered guy.'

'Artistic temperament, eh?'

'Something like that. But making up makes most rows worthwhile.' He kissed her eyelids. 'Come live with me, and be my love.'

She groaned. 'Isobel quotes like that, too.'

'Well, I wouldn't want you to miss that, too much. So how about it?'

She thought about it. 'Well, I can always be persuaded.'

He smiled, sliding his hand down her body and stroking her buttocks. 'I was hoping you were going to say that . . .'

More Erotic Fiction from Headline Liaison

SEVEN DAYS

Adult Fiction for Lovers

J J Duke

Erica's arms were spread apart and she pulled against the silk bonds – not because she wanted to escape but to savour the experience. As the silk bit into her wrists, a surge of pure pleasure shot through her, so intense that the darkness behind the blindfold turned crimson . . .

Erica is not exactly an innocent abroad. On the other hand, she's never been in New York before. This trip could make or break her career in the fashion business. It could also free her from the inhibitions that prevent her exploring her sensual needs.

She has a week for her work commitments – and a week to take her pleasure in the world's wildest city. Now's her chance to make her most daring dreams come true. She's on a voyage of erotic discovery and she doesn't care if things get a little crazy. After all, it can only last seven days . . .

0 7472 5094 4

Adult Fiction for Lovers from Headline LIAISON